"Natasha!" McGuire said. "What happened?"

"Somebody died in that elevator, Mac. Died horribly."

"Yes, two Bureau agents," said McGuire, nodding.

"No . . . there was only one."

McGuire shook his head. "There were two. Agents Silver and Whelen. And one police officer. He survived, but he's in the hospital, in critical condition."

Natasha shook her head. "No . . . that can't be right," she said. "There was only one who died in that elevator . . . and he died extremely st——————————— ———————ind screaming.

"Magic," she continued as she started to circle around the apartment, walking slowly with her arms slightly spread out from her sides, her eyes wide and alert, glancing all around, her breathing shallow. "Magic happened. There were several extremely powerful adepts here. I'm talking about the people who were living here. And the one who came for them."

"It was a raid, Natasha," McGuire said. "Silver and Whelen came here to make an arrest."

She shook her head. "No . . . he came here to kill."

Also by Simon Hawke

The Wizard of 4th Street
The Wizard of Whitechapel
The Wizard of Sunset Strip
The Wizard of Rue Morgue
Samurai Wizard
The Reluctant Sorcerer
The Nine Lives of Catseye Gomez
The Wizard of Camelot

Published by
WARNER BOOKS

THE WIZARD OF LOVECRAFT'S CAFE

SIMON HAWKE

WARNER BOOKS

A Time Warner Company

WARNER BOOKS EDITION

Questar® is a registered trademark of Warner Books, Inc.

Cover design by Don Puckey
Cover illustration by David Mattingly
Hand lettering by Ron Zinn

Warner Books, Inc.
1271 Avenue of the Americas
New York, NY 10020

 A Time Warner Company

Printed in the United States of America

First Printing: December, 1993

10 9 8 7 6 5 4 3 2 1

For John Silbersack
Fifteen years later and we're at it again.
Just goes to show you, be nice to the people
you meet on the way up, they're the same
people you're gonna meet on the way down.

With grateful acknowledgments to Robert M. Powers, consultant and confidant; Peggy Wiley, a man who's trying to do about a hundred things at once couldn't ask for a better "gal friday"; Bruce Wiley, for lending me his wife to bring order to the chaos; Marge and James Kosky, the Black Nag will never be the same; Tina Morin, Emily Tuzson, Eve Jackson, and Michel Leckband, for calling every now and then to see if I'd self-destructed yet; Adele Leone and her staff, for helping to keep all the balls in the air; and all my fans, who help keep the madness going.

PROLOGUE

DETECTIVE LIEUTENANT JOHN Angelo had never busted a sorcerer before and he wasn't crazy about the idea of starting now. In fact, he was furious about the whole thing. Fresh out of the academy, he had started out in vice, which meant working undercover, something that appealed to Angelo. He enjoyed the thrill, the edgework. He had stayed there, turning down a transfer to the more glamorous homicide division and piling up an enviable record of arrests until he was assigned to the D.A.'s special Organized Crime Task Force. He had never worn a uniform and didn't look anything like a cop. What he looked like was a gangster, or a cheap hood, or a pimp. Angelo could look like almost any sort of lowlife, but he had trouble looking like a cop. Still, when the B.O.T. agents had arrived at headquarters, it had been his bad luck to be there, pulling files on a case he was working on, and he had been swept up for the Bureau's raid.

"You don't understand," he had protested, "I work for the D.A. . . . ."

"Not today," the agent had replied. "Today you're working for the Bureau."

"No way, Jack," Angelo said. "I'm undercover."

"Perfect. We can use you."

"Listen, jerkoff, I'm *undercover*, you know what that means? Organized Crime Task Force. I get spotted on your raid, my fucking cover's blown. Forget about it."

"What's your name, Detective?"

"Angelo. Lieutenant John Angelo. And if you've got a problem, you can take it up with the D.A. I don't have time for—"

"I'm not the one who's got a problem, Lt. Angelo," the B.O.T. agent had said. "What I've got is a warrant signed by Superior Court Judge Chambliss and a carte blanche from Chief Morgan to requisition any personnel I need. You just got requisitioned."

"Yeah? Well, requisition this," said Angelo, grabbing his crotch. "I work for D.A. Mathews."

"If I want your balls, Detective Angelo, I'll have them on a plate," the agent replied dryly. "It so happens the D.A. is very interested in this case. She's liable to ride into the mayor's office on this one, so I don't really think she's going to give a shit about one undercover cop's cover being blown. Now you can either come with me right now or you can hand over your shield. I don't have time to argue. What's it going to be?"

There had been nothing more to say. He knew the Bureau man could take his badge, just like that, and getting it back would be damn near impossible. All he could do was go along on the damn raid, try to keep his head down, and hope like hell he wasn't spotted by anybody who could blow his cover. The Bureau didn't care.

He had never worked with the Bureau of Thaumaturgy before, but he had seen how they could throw their weight around. When the Bureau snapped their fingers, the entire department jumped. And they snapped their fingers pretty much anytime they felt like it. Crime involving magic use was a very big deal and the B.O.T. had sole jurisdiction in that area. Angelo did not begrudge them that. Not being an adept himself, he had no desire to go chasing criminal adepts. Chasing ordinary criminals was challenging enough. What he resented was the Bureau's lording it over the department, as if the cops were just a bunch of flunkies they could call on anytime they needed some warm bodies. Like this time.

They were in a hurry. They hadn't even bothered with a full briefing. It was a sensitive case, they said, and the department personnel were on a strict "need-to-know" basis. What that meant was there were some minor details they didn't want the rank and file to know about. The sort of minor details that could get somebody killed, thought Angelo. He hadn't wanted to go on this damn raid in the first place, and as things developed, he felt less and less enthused about it.

Why had they swept him up in it? Because they had also swept up about half the cops in the entire city, or so it seemed, at least. When they got to Sutton Place, enough unmarked cars had converged on the block to start a used car lot, and even more black-and-whites had taken up position in the surrounding six-block area. He noticed snipers stationed on the rooftops and several choppers cruising over the East River. Whatever the hell was going down, Angelo thought uneasily, it had to be pretty damn big. The reason he felt uneasy about it was that he would be one of the first to go in.

"This isn't a raid, it's a fuckin' invasion," Angelo said to the Bureau man seated next to him in the back of the unmarked unit. "Just what is it this guy Cornwall is supposed to have done?"

"He's a cop killer," Agent Silver replied. "And he's taken out several of our top Bureau agents."

"No shit. So how come I've never seen a sheet on him?"

"Because you weren't cleared to," Silver said curtly. "This is a top priority I.T.C. case."

"The Commission wants this guy?" said Angelo. He whistled softly. If the International Thaumaturgical Commission had jurisdiction in this case, then it was major magic crime and international in scope and that would explain why the Bureau was so hot and bothered. The Bureau answered to nobody . . . except the I.T.C. "Who the hell *is* he?"

"A renegade adept," said Silver's partner, Whelen, from the front seat. "That's all you need to know."

"Wrong, Gandalf," Angelo said. "If you expect me to go

in there and put my sweet alabaster ass on the line, I'm gonna have to know a lot more.''

"All we expect you to do is provide a brief distraction," Agent Whelen said. "We'll take care of the rest. We know what we're doing."

"Yeah, right. That's why you assembled a goddamn army to take this guy down," said Angelo. "What is he, a fuckin' necromancer, for Christ's sake?''

The B.O.T. men simply stared at him in stony silence.

"Aw, fuck me," said Angelo, slumping back against the seat. "It's him, isn't it, the guy who wasted all those people in L.A. and New Mexico?''

"You seem rather well informed," said Silver.

"What do you think, I live in a closet? If this is the same guy, he's the biggest serial killer since Count Dracula. And you expect me to go in there and *distract* him while you blow the whistle?''

"We'll be right behind you," Silver said.

"That's a real comforting thought," Angelo replied wryly. "Why me? Why do I get this dubious honor? I'm not an adept.''

"That's precisely why," said Silver. "He might well be able to detect it if you were. Also, you don't look like a cop. You may be able to take him off guard."

"May?"

"There are no guarantees in life, Lieutenant. But if you pull this off, you'll be able to write your own ticket. There may even be a captaincy in it for you."

"And if I don't pull it off, I'll be a dead man. And to think I was only worried about my cover being blown." Angelo snorted. "What exactly is it I'm supposed to do to distract this guy?''

"It's simple enough," said Agent Silver. "You will deliver pizza to him."

"Pizza?"

"Pizza."

"You gotta be kiddin' me. He'd have to be a moron to fall for that.''

"Which is precisely why it's going to work," said Silver. "He would never suspect something so obvious. You're young and you don't look like a cop. And you dress like a slob, which helps. He will simply think it's an honest mistake and you got the wrong address. You will be insistent, and—"

"Yeah, yeah, I know the dodge, it's one of the oldest tricks in the book," said Angelo, shaking his head. "A two-bit dope dealer wouldn't even go for it."

"Well, if he doesn't go for it, then you've got nothing to worry about," said Silver. "He simply won't let you up and we shall have to try a more direct approach."

"And meanwhile he's been warned that something's going down," said Angelo.

"Perhaps," said Whelen. "That depends on how convincing you are."

"Swell," said Angelo.

An unmarked unit pulled up beside their car. "I got your pies," the driver said.

"Okay, Angelo, you're on," said Agent Silver.

"Shit," said Angelo.

The man in the unit with the pies gave him a jacket and a hat from the pizza delivery service, then handed him two steaming pizza boxes.

"All units, stand by," said Silver into his handset. He turned to Angelo. "We'll be coming in right behind you," he said. "Just act like a delivery boy, that's all. Don't try any heroics. This man's a skilled adept and he's a killer. What's more, he's probably got at least two or three confederates in there with him. Just get them to open the door and keep them talking, then when we make our move, get the hell out of the way. Shoot only if you absolutely have to, but try not to hit any of us."

"Very funny," Angelo said wryly. "What do I do if the bastard throws a spell at me?"

"Duck," said Whelen.

"You guys are a couple of real comedians," said Angelo, zipping up the red, white, and blue jacket and adjusting his cap. "How do I look?"

"Like a guinea delivery boy from Brooklyn," Whelen replied.

"Up yours," said Angelo. "Okay, we goin'?"

"We're going," Silver said, getting out of the car. He spoke into his handheld. "This is Silver. All units, stand by to move on my word. All backup uniform units, start sealing off the area right now. I want the roadblocks up, nobody in or out. That means *nobody*, no exceptions. Sharpshooters, stand by for targets of opportunity. First team, move into position now. Silver out." He glanced up at the darkening sky. "Looks like it's going to rain."

"Yeah, there's a big storm front coming in," said Whelen. "It's going to ground the choppers. And the sharpshooters won't be able to see a damn thing when it hits."

"Then we'd better not waste any more time," said Silver. He turned to Angelo. "Okay, let's get this show on the road."

They crossed the street to the building entrance, Angelo carrying the pizza boxes in an insulating warmer. They went through the front door into the alcove. Angelo glanced at the rows of buttons on the buzzer panel.

"Wait," said Silver. He pointed at the camera mounted over the panel. He made a slight gesture at the inner door and the locking mechanism quietly clicked open.

"What the hell do you need me for?" Angelo asked as the door silently swung open by itself.

"I told you, a distraction," Silver said. He spoke into his handheld. "First team, repeat, first team . . . move in now. All other units stand by."

They waited a moment or two, then heard the sound of running footsteps as the S.W.A.T. team came around the side of the building and up the steps to the front entrance, weapons held ready. Silver held the door for them as they moved quickly inside. "Stairs," he said. "Move it."

The S.W.A.T. team members fanned out across the lobby and headed for the stairway doors. Whelen and Silver followed them inside, while Angelo waited in the alcove. Whelen went to get the elevator. When the door slid open, he quickly checked inside, then waved to Silver. Silver motioned Angelo to hit the buzzer.

Angelo pressed the button for the penthouse. A moment later a young female voice responded, "Yes?"

"Pizza man," said Angelo in a monotone.

"We didn't order any pizza."

Angelo made a pretense of checking the address, then glanced up toward the camera. "It says here two large pies, one plain, one pepperoni, deliver to penthouse, this address."

"There must be a mistake."

"Your name ain't Bellamy?"

"There's no one here by that name. I'm afraid you've got the wrong address."

"Fricken' Christ," said Angelo. "They screwed up on me again. What the hell am I supposed to do with these pies?"

"I'm sorry."

"Shit. Hey, lady, look, how's about I give 'em to you half price? Keep 'em from goin' to waste. Help me out, whaddya say?"

"Half price?"

"Yeah, two large pies, ten bucks, includin' tip. Such a deal. Nice and hot. How's about it? Whaddya say?"

"What kind are they again?"

"One plain, one pepperoni. Come on, lady, gimme a break. These are good pies. Be a shame to waste 'em."

"Oh, all right. Come on up."

The buzzer sounded. The door was already open, however. Whelen had wedged it when he went through.

"Okay, all units, count down thirty seconds and move in!" Silver said into his handheld. "Repeat, count down thirty seconds and move in!" He grabbed Angelo's arm and hurried him toward the elevator. "Well done," he said with a nod at the panel. The floor button was keyed, so they would have to bring him up.

Angelo pressed the intercom button. "Hey, lady? It's me. The pizza guy."

"All right," said the female voice over the speaker. "Hold on."

The door slid shut and the elevator started to ascend.

"Okay, we're in," said Angelo, turning around. "Jesus, I can't believe they fell for . . ." His voice trailed off as he saw Whelen's body slump to the floor of the elevator. "What the . . ."

Silver turned to face him. His eyes were glowing with a bright blue fire. Angelo tried to drop the pies and go for his gun, but not a single muscle in his body would respond. He felt himself suddenly go cold all over as icy tentacles squirmed into his mind. Inwardly, he screamed, but outwardly, he couldn't make a sound. He felt a curious, numbing, vertiginous sensation, and then he could no longer see or hear or smell or feel a thing.

CHAPTER
ONE

"WHO WAS THAT?" asked Wyrdrune, coming out of the kitchen with a cup of coffee.

"Pizza man," said Kira.

Billy looked up from the computer screen. "You ordered pizza?"

"Well, no," Kira explained, "he delivered to our address by mistake, but said he'd give me half off on two large pies if I took them anyway, so I figured what the hell. We haven't eaten yet and I was getting kind of hungry."

Wyrdrune stopped in the center of the room. "He delivered to our address by mistake? To the penthouse?"

Kira shrugged. "That's what he said. I checked him out. He looked okay, so I buzzed him in."

"That was rather careless, wasn't it?" Billy said, swiveling his chair around.

"He's on his way up right now," said Kira. "Why, you don't suppose—"

The lights suddenly started strobing rapidly.

"Somebody's just set off the spell wards in the stairway," Wyrdrune said.

Billy quickly turned back to the computer. "Archimedes, security check!"

"Working," said the little sentient computer, speaking in a voice that sounded like a chipmunk on helium. The monitor screen flashed quickly from one remote security camera to another. "Intruders present on the stairs and in the front lobby," the computer said.

"Shit," said Billy, looking at the screen. "We've got an entire S.W.A.T. team on the stairs, coming up fast, and the whole lobby's crawling with cops!"

The sound of sirens drifted up from the street.

"I'm sorry," Kira said, looking chagrined. "I thought—"

The elevator door slid open behind her. As she turned, Wyrdrune leapt toward her, shapechanging into his Modred aspect in the blink of an eye.

"Look out!" Modred shouted, shoving her aside.

The energy blast that came out of the elevator struck him squarely in the chest. It lifted him right off his feet and threw him back clear across the room.

"*No!*" screamed Kira.

As Silver came out of the elevator, he suddenly found himself face-to-face with Billy Slade. He raised his arm to hurl a bolt of thaumaturgic force at him, but Billy's eyes strobed with a blaze of bright blue fire and twin bolts of energy lanced out from his pupils, striking Silver in the chest and knocking him backward. Billy followed with another burst of force, but then Angelo came out of the elevator, arm raised, a vacant look on his face, a 9-mm semiautomatic in his fist. His first two shots missed, but the third struck Billy in the shoulder. Before he could fire a fourth time, Kira was on top of him. She leapt and brought him down, wrestling with him for the gun, and then the heavy stairway door exploded off its hinges and the S.W.A.T. team came pouring through into the penthouse suite.

They were exhausted from fighting their way up the final flight of stairs. They had double-timed it all the way to the top floor and broken through the stairwell doorway leading to the penthouse only to hit the spell ward at the final flight of steps. Suddenly it was as if they had run into a solid wall of invisible molasses. They piled up against each other, trying to force their way through, but it was like trying to run underwater. Knowing that officers had already gone in and were in need of backup, they had bulled their way through by sheer weight of numbers, but it had taken almost every ounce of energy they had left, and when they blew the door and forced their way into the penthouse, they were completely unprepared for what awaited them. They suddenly found themselves faced with a knight in full armor, complete with shield and broadsword.

The first two S.W.A.T. men through the door were involuntarily brought up short by the amazing sight, and their fellow officers behind them ran right into them. It caused a pileup, and as the disoriented officers scrambled to their feet, the armored knight hit them full tilt, shield first. Like a bulldozer, he plowed them back through the open doorway, forcing them back into their fellow officers and pushing them back down the stairs. They went down like dominoes. Nobody had time to get a shot off, nor was there an opportunity to do so without hitting their own men. They tumbled backward down the stairs, going down much faster than they had come up, and when they realized the knight had retreated, they attempted to regroup, but found the stairs beneath them suddenly coated with a thick layer of ice. As they struggled to find their footing, they kept falling back into each other and going down in a jumble once again.

Billy came back into the penthouse. Kira was lying on the floor, trying to get up. There was no sign of the other two men. The elevator doors were closed. He rushed over to Kira and helped her to her feet.

"Are you all right?"

"I think so . . . . I got his gun, but he nailed me with a shot to the jaw and . . . oh, God! Modred!"

They hurried to where Modred lay on his back . . . only it wasn't Modred anymore. He was Wyrdrune once again, younger, unbearded, with longer hair . . . and badly hurt. His chest was burned and blackened, the shirt cooked right into the flesh. He was unconscious and his breathing was ragged and shallow.

Kira stared at him, aghast. "Is he . . . ?"

"He's still alive," said Billy, crouching by him, "but just barely. We've got to get him out of here. Those S.W.A.T. cops won't be held back for long."

"What are we going to do?"

"We'll have to teleport. Quick, get Broom and Archimedes."

Several shots shattered the sliding-glass door as Kira went across the room. She dove onto the floor and rolled.

"Christ! They've got sharpshooters on the roof across the street!"

"Kiii-raaaah . . . ."

There was a clunking sound as the little computer fell over on its side, its monitor screen and casing smashed by the rifle slugs.

"Archimedes!" she cried.

"Forget it, it's too late!" shouted Billy. "*Broom!* Where the hell are you?"

Kira crawled back across the floor toward Billy. "Can you teleport all of us?" she asked.

"Merlin could have," Billy said. "No reason why I shouldn't be able to."

"You mean you're not sure?"

He shook his head. "No, but we don't have any other choice. Wyrdrune needs help and we're caught right in the middle of a hornet's nest. We've got to get out of here right now. *Broom!* Where the hell *is* that bloody stick?"

"Probably hiding," Kira said. "I'll go look—"

"There's no time," said Billy. "We've got to go now."

"Wait! Shadow!"

"Forget the bloody cat! There's no damn time!"

"I'm not leaving without—"

Machine-gun fire stitched the wall behind them as the S.W.A.T. cops managed to struggle back up the icy stairs. They burst into the penthouse suite, firing as they came, then stopped abruptly, looking all around them. There was no one left inside.

* * *

Deputy Police Commissioner Steve McGuire stood in the center of the penthouse living room, looking around at all the damage. All around him, the lab boys were bustling about with their equipment, dusting for prints, bagging evidence, and taking photographs. "What the hell happened here?" McGuire said, turning back toward Ron Gavorachek, captain of the S.W.A.T. team.

"It was a B.O.T. operation, sir," Gavorachek replied, looking at McGuire uneasily. He knew that tone, and it did not bode well.

"Bullshit," said McGuire. "It was an N.Y.P.D. operation, complete with S.W.A.T. team, choppers, sharpshooters, and a whole goddamn division. Why the hell didn't my office know anything about it?"

"Sir, I was told that Chief Morgan gave his authority—"

"Where *is* Chief Morgan?"

"I'm told he's on his way, sir," Gavorachek replied. "He's supposed to be coming with a Bureau representative—"

"Right," said McGuire, impatiently interrupting him. "Meanwhile, you still haven't answered my question, Captain. What happened here?"

"Bureau Agents Silver and Whelen were in charge of the operation, sir," Gavorachek replied. "They had reason to believe a fugitive adept named Michael Cornwall and several of his confederates were holed up in this penthouse—"

"Nobody 'holes up' in a penthouse," McGuire said wryly.

"Uh . . . yeah, well . . ."

"Go on."

"The building was surrounded and sharpshooters were stationed on the nearby rooftops," Gavorachek continued. "My team was to go in first and take the stairs. Agents Silver and Whelen went up in the elevator with a plainclothes officer disguised as a pizza delivery guy—"

"What plainclothes officer?"

"Detective Angelo, sir. He was an undercover guy the Bureau agents brought in. The whole operation was put together very quickly. They requisitioned units left and right. Chief Morgan gave them—"

"Gave them his authority, yes, I know," McGuire said impatiently. He waved him on. "Get on with it."

"Right. Well, my men took the stairs, but we ran into a spell on the last flight up, just before we reached the penthouse."

"What sort of spell?"

"I don't know, exactly," Gavorachek replied. "There was something slowing them down, making them struggle for every step they took, but it was nothing they could see. And then there was the knight—"

"The *what*?"

"The knight," Gavorachek said. "Guy all dressed in armor, with a shield and a sword—"

"You're kidding."

"No, sir. He charged my men and pushed them back down the stairs—"

"*One man* did this? Armed only with a sword?"

"Well, he had the advantage of surprise, sir. And the stairs had turned to ice—"

"Ice."

"Yes, sir. My men had a hard time getting their footing. And by the time they got back up here, well, they were gone."

"*Who* was gone?"

"The knight, the girl—"

"What girl?"

"There was a girl, sir, and at least one other male, both young, my men didn't really get a good look at them. There may have been others present, I'm not sure. I figure they must have teleported. There was no other way out. When the elevator came back down, both Agents Silver and Whelen were on it, dead. Detective Angelo was still alive, but he was unconscious. He was taken to the hospital. I haven't heard any word on his condition." Gavorachek looked past him. "Oh, there's Chief Morgan, sir."

McGuire turned around to greet the chief. "Ed," he said.

"Hello, Steve," said Morgan. He indicated the man beside him. "This is Agent Case, he's the new head of the Bureau office in the city."

"We've met," McGuire said with a curt nod at the Bureau man. "We've got a problem here," he continued. "The media's all over us about this, and we don't know what the hell to tell them. The commissioner wants me to give him something yesterday, so he can make a statement, but so far, all I've got is a massive police raid, six city blocks cordoned off, shots fired, two dead Bureau agents, and a goddamn knight in shining armor, right out of King Arthur. If you think I'm going to the press with that, you're nuts."

"Why don't you let us worry about a statement to the press?" said Case. "Tell the commissioner to refer them to me and I'll take care of it. It's nothing you need to concern yourself about."

McGuire stared at him. "That's it?" he said. "That's all you're going to give me?"

Case stared at him steadily. "For the moment."

"Well, I'm afraid that's not good enough, Agent Case. Who's this guy, Cornwall?"

"A renegade adept the Bureau has been after for a long time. The I.T.C. has a special interest in this matter. This case is international in scope, but it's somewhat sensitive. We don't need a lot of publicity."

"Well, your people should have thought of that before they staged one of the largest police raids in the city's history," McGuire said. "That sort of thing tends to attract attention. Especially when it fails so spectacularly."

Case nodded. "Yes, well, it seems that Agents Silver and Whelen somewhat exceeded their authority in this instance."

"Is that so?" said McGuire.

"Apparently, Agent Silver took it on his own authority to obtain the warrant from Judge Chambliss, and he went directly to Chief Morgan without checking with his superiors, first."

"Meaning you," McGuire said.

"Meaning me."

"So you're saying you didn't know anything about it," said McGuire.

"That's correct."

"And now both Silver and Whelen are dead," McGuire said. "Makes things rather convenient for you, doesn't it?"

"Take it easy, Steve," Chief Morgan cautioned him.

"That's all right, Chief," said Case.

"Like hell it's all right," McGuire said. "It stinks."

"Steve . . ." said Morgan uneasily. "You're out of line here."

"It's quite all right, Chief," said Agent Case in an even tone. "The deputy commissioner is right. It does stink, and I fully appreciate his position. Unfortunately, there's not very much I can do about it now. Fortunately, on the other hand, we do not have to effect a great deal of damage control. A raid took place, it failed; two Bureau agents are dead and one police officer is in the hospital. Some people in the area were inconvenienced. It could have been much worse. My office will take care of any statements to the media. If the commissioner feels it necessary to make his own statement to the press, he can merely say the department was extending its cooperation to the Bureau, at our request, in an attempt to apprehend some fugitives wanted for felony magic crime. And he can then refer them to me for any details."

"Which you will fudge," McGuire said.

"Of course. But the department will be off the hook."

"Yeah? Tell that to the guy in the hospital."

"Regrettable," said Case. "But at least he's still alive. I've got two men who are dead." He glanced around at the activity in the penthouse. "When your people are finished here, I would appreciate a copy of the full report."

"You don't want to have your own people in here?"

"I'm sure your lab people are quite competent," said Case. "I'll be satisfied to see their report. And I would appreciate it if you would forward whatever evidence you may collect to my office. There's no need for you to burden yourself with an additional investigation."

"There's a lot you're not telling me, Case," McGuire said.

"I don't like it. I don't like when the Bureau comes along and tells the department to look the other way and mind our own business. If it impacts on our city, it *is* our business."

"Duly noted," Case replied. "I'm sorry about your man. I hope he recovers. Chief . . ." The Bureau man nodded to Morgan, then turned and left the premises.

"That's it, huh?" said McGuire. "Thank you very much, turn over everything you find and stay the hell out of it. Just like that."

"Steve, don't rock the boat," Chief Morgan said. "It's the Bureau, for chrissake."

"Fuck the lousy Bureau," said McGuire with a scowl.

"We're dealing with adepts here, Steve," said Morgan. "We don't want the headache. We're not qualified. Leave the adepts to the adepts."

McGuire sighed heavily. "I suppose you're right," he said. "I guess I just don't like being pushed around."

"They're not the bad guys, Steve," said Morgan. "They're just worried about the public perception. Magic crime can be a nasty business, especially when the media gets hold of it. That's why the Bureau plays it close to the vest."

"Playing it close to the vest with the media is one thing," said McGuire. "Doing it with the commissioner's office is another."

"We've had leaks in the past, you know," Morgan reminded him.

McGuire pursed his lips thoughtfully and nodded. "Yeah. I guess I see your point. But I still don't like it. I haven't been on the streets in a long time, Ed, and my ass is getting fat from sitting on it, but my nose still works and it's telling me that something is all wrong here."

"Like what?"

"Like why didn't he want to bring his own investigative team in? The Bureau trusting our lab boys to come up with everything? That would be a first."

"It's probably just politics," said Morgan. "His people screwed up. He doesn't want to ruffle our feathers any more than he has to."

"Maybe," said McGuire. "But I think whatever he wanted here, he already got it. He wasn't exactly dragging his heels getting out of here. I think I'd like to have one of our own special forensics people in here."

"Steve . . . if you'll take my advice, you'll leave it alone," said Morgan.

McGuire smiled at him. "Duly noted," he said.

Morgan grimaced and shook his head. "You're never going to get the old man's job unless you learn how to play ball."

"I can only think about one job at a time, Ed," McGuire replied. "And right now, somebody's telling me how to do mine and getting on my nerves."

"Screw you, McGuire," Morgan said with a wry grimace. "Don't take my advice. I was a cop in this town when you were still getting potty trained, but what the hell do I know? Do what you have to do. Just keep me out of it, okay? I don't need any turf battles with the Bureau. I'm only six months from my pension."

"Sure thing, Ed. It's my decision; I'll take whatever heat comes down."

"The Bureau can generate an awful lot of heat," said the older man.

"Well, you know what they say. If you can't take the heat . . ."

"Yeah, yeah. Just don't say I didn't warn you."

"My best to Gloria, Ed."

Morgan grunted. "Thanks. I'll pass it on." He turned and headed for the elevator.

McGuire beckoned to one of the investigators. "Get on the horn and get the Gypsy down here, right away."

"Yes, sir."

McGuire looked around, wrinkling his nose as if there were a bad odor in the air. "Okay, Case," he mumbled to himself. "I'll see your adept and raise you one psychic."

"Where the hell are we?" Kira asked, looking around at the unfamiliar surroundings.

"Sebastian's," Billy said. "It was the only place I could think of in a hurry."

They had materialized in the living room of a third-floor walk-up above a bar in the Village, near the corner of MacDougal and Fourth Street, within view of Washington Square Park. The apartment was not very large, but high ceilings gave it the illusion of greater space. Still, what space there was had been crammed full, mostly with books. Almost every inch of wall space was taken up with bookshelves, and in addition to the books, the shelves held all manner of strange bric-a-brac. There were small, fantastic sculptures made of bronze and pewter; various magical amulets and talismans; tarot decks and incense burners; brass and glass votive candle holders; various small black iron caldrons and ceremonial daggers; tobacco humidors and pipe stands; strangely shaped polyhedral dice and curious, little ceramic pots filled with herbs and powders. . . . The whole resembled a cross between an antiquarian bookshop and an occult notions shop. Books spilled out of the shelves onto the carpeted floor, where they were piled in precarious stacks in the corners and underneath the coffee and end tables and just about anywhere else there was any room.

Kira had never been to the home of Dr. Sebastian Makepeace before, though Billy obviously had. The eccentric New York University professor was one of the few who shared their secret and knew all about the runestones. Makepeace was not in, so they carried Wyrdrune to the sofa, an old Queen Anne that had been battered into submission and covered with tobacco burns and beverage stains. He was still unconscious and breathing raggedly. Billy started carefully removing his shirt.

"Oh, my God," said Kira as she saw how badly he was burned. "Is he going to be all right?"

"I don't know," Billy replied. "Modred took that blast full force. It should have gone right through him. His runestone must have saved him."

"The runestone!" Kira said, staring at Wyrdrune's blackened chest with sudden realization. "It's gone!"

"You noticed that," said Billy tensely.

"You don't think it was . . ."

"Destroyed?" said Billy. He shook his head. "I don't know. Your guess is as good as mine. But I suppose it's possible."

"Then that would mean Modred is gone, as well," Kira said in a hushed voice.

"It would mean much more than that," said Billy with a hard edge to his voice.

Kira swallowed hard as the full import of his words sank in. If the runestone had been destroyed, it would mean more than just Modred's death, but the deaths of all the animating spirits that inhabited the enchanted gem. She stared at her own runestone, the sapphire magically bonded to the flesh of her right palm, then raised her gaze to the emerald embedded in Wyrdrune's forehead. The third runestone, the one that had been Modred's, had been embedded in his chest. Now it was gone. Through Wyrdrune, Modred had lived on, sharing consciousness with him, and the spell of the Living Triangle had survived intact. But now, she thought . . . What would happen now?

Billy took a deep breath, gathering his energies, and held his hands over Wyrdrune's injured chest. "Merlin could have done this," he murmured to himself. "And Gorlois could have done it. That should mean that I can do it, too. Except I've never tried."

"You can do it, Billy," Kira reassured him. "You know you can. You *have* to."

Billy closed his eyes and moistened his lips as he held his hands out, palms down, over Wyrdrune's burn-ravaged chest. As he inhaled deeply and concentrated, blue thaumaturgic energy crackled around his outstretched fingertips like electrical discharges. Kira bit her lower lip as she watched silently, barely able to breathe. It appeared as if she had already lost Modred. She could not bear to lose Wyrdrune, as well.

A blue aura formed around Billy as he sat there, concentrating intently. It pulsated, expanding and contracting, strobing slightly, then wide beams of thaumaturgic force streamed out from Billy's palms, bathing Wyrdrune's chest and enveloping him in a blue aura as well. As Billy's aura dimmed, the aura around Wyrdrune grew brighter, a visible manifestation of the healing exchange of life energy. Then the blue glow suddenly faded and Billy collapsed.

"Billy!"

Kira caught him before he fell and eased him to the floor, leaning back with him against the front of the sofa.

"I'm . . . all right," he murmured, resting his head on her shoulder. "Just . . . weak." His eyelids fluttered. "Did it . . . work?"

Kira glanced at Wyrdrune's bare chest, from which the burns were already disappearing. The skin of his upper torso was red and fading even as she watched.

"Yes, Billy, it worked. You did it."

"Good." He sighed and closed his eyes, utterly exhausted by the effort. "I wasn't sure . . . I could . . . ." His voice trailed off and seconds later his chest was rising and falling rhythmically as he slept.

"I wasn't sure you could, either," Kira said softly.

There was still a great deal about Billy that she didn't know. Not even Billy knew. Not anymore. A great deal had happened to him in a relatively short time. He had gone through more changes than most people could be expected to survive, much less understand. From a troubled, young, multiethnic street urchin living by his wits in London's East End, he had gone to being an avatar of a legendary archmage, possessed by the spirit of his ancestor, Merlin Ambrosius, who had involved him in a struggle dating back to the very dawn of time.

It had not been an entirely benevolent possession. The two personalities, Billy and Merlin, had often been at odds with one another, a situation that was further complicated when Billy came into possession of an enchanted ring that held the spirit of a sorcerer knight named Gorlois, Duke of Cornwall, the last surviving member of the Council of the White—and Merlin's father.

Gorlois had been one of the Old Ones, an immortal race

of magic users who had been the dominant race on earth when humans were still walking on all fours. It was from them that human legends of gods and supernatural beings came, for they had regarded primitive humans as nothing more than animals, sources of life energy to empower their thaumaturgic spells. In time, however, as humans started to evolve, many of the Old Ones came to feel that it was wrong to use them in this manner and so the ruling Council of the White decreed that humans could no longer be ritually sacrificed for their life force, as they were developing into intelligent creatures. This was the beginning of white magic, thaumaturgy that called upon the life force of the spellcaster or else employed life energy from other living creatures only in a way that would allow that energy to be naturally replenished.

However, not all the Old Ones had obeyed the dictates of the Council. There were those who had rebelled and refused to give up necromancy—the sorcery of death. These were the Dark Ones, and the conflict between them and the Council led to war. It was a devastating struggle recalled in Norse legends as the Ragnarok. In Germanic myth, it became known as the Götterdämmerung, the Twilight of the Gods. The upheaval had its counterpart in many creation myths, because from it humans had emerged as dominant. Not many of the Old Ones had been left alive. The Dark Ones were defeated and entombed in the Euphrates Valley, held in a magical state of half-life by a powerful spell devised by the surviving members of the Council of the White, all of whom—save one—gave up their lives, or at least their corporeal existence, to infuse their life energies into three enchanted runestones that held the Dark Ones prisoner. These stones became the spell known as the Living Triangle, and they were placed within the Eternal Circle where the Dark Ones were confined. The one who placed them there was Gorlois, the youngest and the last surviving member of the Council, who then went out into the world to live among the humans.

As the ages passed, Gorlois made his way to the lands of the north, where he became a warlord. He took a De Dannan witch to wife and had a son with her named Merlin, who inherited the sorcerous powers of his father. When his wife began to age, Gorlois abandoned her and found another, a young Welshwoman named Igraine, with whom he had three daughters. He named them Elaine, Morgana, and Morgause. And each of them inherited his powers, too. One day, a rival warlord saw Igraine and fell in lust with her. Aided by Merlin, Uther Pendragon overcame Gorlois, who realized too late that Uther had magic on his side, and as he died, he infused his life force into the fire opal ring he wore, a ring that passed on to his daughter, Morgana, who became known as the sorceress Morgan Le Fay.

To revenge herself on Merlin and his pupil, Arthur, son of the man who had brought about her father's death, Morgana cast a spell on Arthur and took him to her bed. The issue of this union was a boy named Modred, part human, part immortal mage. Then Morgana tricked Merlin with the aid of a young witch whom she sent out to seduce him. She cast a spell on him, immuring him within the cleft of a large oak, where he would sleep for the next two thousand years. Arthur and Modred then faced each other on the field of battle and both fell, but being part immortal, Modred had recovered from wounds that would have killed an ordinary man. He left Britain and for the next two thousand years traveled the world as an embittered mercenary, living many different lives and amassing a huge fortune. When Kira had first met him, he was a shadowy hit man known as Morpheus, who had accepted a contract on her life.

In the meantime, the world forgot the ways of magic. Thaumaturgy became relegated to storybooks and legends until the day technology came grinding to a halt in the global disaster known as the Collapse. It was then, when anarchy reigned at the close of the twenty-second century, that Merlin awoke from his long sleep and brought back the old knowledge. It was the beginning of the Second Thaumaturgic Age. Merlin founded schools throughout the world, training adepts in the discipline of magic, and the old infrastructure of technology revived, supported by thaumaturgy as a new energy base. But the return of magic to the world awoke the Dark

Ones in their tomb, and with the aid of one of Merlin's pupils, who had removed the runestones, they managed to escape. And ever since that day, Kira's life had no longer been her own.

She recalled the day it started for her, the day she chose to steal the runestones from Christie's auction house. It was not her usual sort of job. She was a cat burglar, not a snatch-and-grab artist, and the idea of stealing the gems in broad daylight, in a roomful of adepts, seemed crazy—yet she had been unable to resist. From the moment she had read about the auction in the paper, she had felt strangely compelled to make the heist. In fact, she had been quite literally compelled, both by fate and magic, though she had not realized it at the time.

That was the day she had met Wyrdrune. She smiled as she recalled her first impression of him. It had been far from favorable. A scruffy, young warlock with a mass of curly blond hair and the look of a boy caught with his fingers in the cookie jar. He had been born Melvin Karpinsky. Wyrdrune was his mage name. Most adepts had by then dispensed with the tradition of using mage names, but Wyrdrune had received his from his old teacher, none other than Merlin Ambrosius himself, and he preferred it to his birth name. But legally, he could not lay claim to being an adept. He had been expelled from the College of Sorcerers in Cambridge, Massachusetts, for practicing magic without certification. He had returned to his native New York City, where he lived in a railroad flat located on East Fourth Street, along with the most unusual familiar Kira had ever seen—a straw broom that he had animated and that had become impressed with the irascible personality of his late mother.

As an adept, Wyrdrune possessed great natural talent, but it was undisciplined and unrefined. With his education interrupted, he had been casting about for some way to complete it on his own, but that required money, and for some peculiar reason, he had also become fixated on the auction of the Euphrates artifacts being held at Christie's.

They had both tried to steal the runestones at the same time and circumstances had forced them to team up for the theft.

Thereafter, despite their initial dislike of one another, they had been unable to break up the team. Each time they tried to fence the runestones, the gems had magically returned to them, which led to at least one well-connected fence putting out a contract on them. With the police pursuing them as well, they had been forced to turn for help to Wyrdrune's old professor, Merlin, who had been the first to realize the true nature of the runestones. When they encountered Modred, who had been sent to kill them, the living runestones had forged a link between the three of them, magically bonding with them, making them avatars for the spirits of the mages whose life energies imbued the stones. From that point on, their lives had changed irrevocably.

It was fate that they, the descendants of Gorlois, should have all been brought together to align themselves against the threat posed by the Dark Ones. It was fate that after Merlin died, his spirit should have possessed his sole surviving relative, a young English delinquent by the name of Billy Slade, and it was fate that Morgan Le Fay's enchanted ring, which had held the spirit of her father, should have come into Billy's hands, bringing the spirit of Gorlois to his descendant. Fate, magic, synchronicity, whatever it was, thought Kira, they had all become caught up in it.

As she watched Billy sleep, Kira thought about all that they had gone through. She thought about what they had risked, what they had won, and what they had lost. Billy had lost not only his individuality, but he no longer even looked the same. He had become a completely different person. The Billy Slade who came back with them from London had died in Santa Fe, New Mexico, killed by a necromancer. The spirits of Gorlois and Merlin had fused their life energies with his as he lay dying and the result had been a sorcerous mutation. Merlin was now gone, and Gorlois was gone. The Billy Slade she knew was gone, as well. But elements of all three of them had been magically combined to give birth to the young man whose head now rested on her shoulder. He looked about nineteen years old, but in a sense, he had lived for thousands of years. And in another sense, he was a newborn. Spellborn. There had probably never been anyone like him before. He was unique. Kira wondered what it felt like. And at the same time, she didn't really want to know.

Wyrdrune and Modred had changed, too. The enchanted, living gems had wrought changes in their molecular structure, changes that were, according to the laws of science, utterly impossible. When Modred died, killed by a Dark One's acolyte in Tokyo, Japan, his runestone had absorbed his life force and bonded with Wyrdrune, so that the integrity of the spell uniting them could be preserved. The two men she had loved wound up sharing consciousness in the same body, a body that could shapechange. Wyrdrune could physically manifest as Modred and both of them were present all the time. It had made her love life interesting, to say the least, and she had wondered if she would not be the next to undergo some sort of sorcerous mutation.

Kira clenched her fist, feeling the sapphire runestone embedded in her palm. She had not asked for any of this. She had never been given any choice. The runestone was a part of her now, and yet she had never grown completely accustomed to it. She wondered if she ever could. It frightened her. It gave her strange, disturbing dreams that defied her comprehension. Often, in the middle of the night, it seemed as if she could hear voices murmuring to her, and she was never certain if it was a dream or if she really heard them. And each time she tried to remember what they said, the memory slipped away.

She had no idea what would happen now. Had Modred's runestone been destroyed, and Modred along with it? Or had his life force fused with Wyrdrune's, as the life energies of Gorlois and Merlin had fused with Billy's? The only thing she knew for sure was that she bore the blame for what had happened. She had allowed her guard to slip and that was inexcusable. It had all happened so fast . . . She suddenly smelled hot cocoa. She frowned. *Hot cocoa?*

"One marshmallow or two?"

She looked up and saw Sebastian Makepeace standing over

her, holding a steaming hot mug of cocoa in one hand and a bag of marshmallows in the other.

"Sebastian! I didn't hear you come in . . . ."

"Well, you didn't exactly use the door yourself now, did you?" Makepeace replied.

He made an imposing sight, as usual. He stood six feet six inches tall and weighed close to three hundred pounds. He wore a black beret at a jaunty angle, and his long white hair cascaded to the shoulders of his ankle-length, black leather coat, beneath which he wore a red and white striped shirt, a bright blue, Flemish style cravat, a purple tweed jacket, khaki pants, and suede desert boots. For a university professor, it was quite a flamboyant outfit. On the other hand, for a man who claimed to be a fairy, it was probably conservative.

"Sebastian, we were hit," she said.

"So I gathered," he replied, setting the mug down on the coffee table. "Two, I think." He waggled his index finger and two marshmallows obligingly floated up out of the plastic bag and plopped themselves into the cocoa.

"You *knew*?"

"No, but when I come home to find two of you unconscious in my living room, the energy residue of a healing spell permeating the entire place, and you sitting there with your aura palpitating like a strobe light, it doesn't take a great leap of deduction to figure out you've had some trouble. Now drink your cocoa."

She stared at him. "How the hell can I drink cocoa at a time like this?"

"You simply lift the mug up to your lips and sip," said Makepeace. "Careful, though, it's hot."

"Sebastian, are you *listening* to me?"

"Drink."

With a sigh of frustrated resignation, she raised the mug to her lips and took a sip. It tasted indescribably good. She took another, larger sip. The warmth of the hot cocoa seemed to spread slowly throughout her entire body. She felt herself starting to relax as a sense of calm contentment came over her.

"Good, isn't it?" Makepeace said.

"Mmmm, it's delicious." She drank some more. She felt as if she were floating on a warm and fluffy cloud. A crooked smile played across her lips. "I must be really tired. I think I'm getting a buzz off this . . . ."

"Drink up."

She finished off the mug, then gave a small belch.

"Better?" Makepeace said.

"Mmmm. Much." Her eyes crossed and she keeled over onto the carpet, unconscious.

"I make the best hot cocoa in town," said Makepeace.

CHAPTER TWO

THE YOUNG WOMAN who came into the penthouse apartment did not look like anyone who would be part of a police investigation. Her long and wavy hair was naturally blond, or so McGuire seemed to recall. He had also seen it brunette, henna red, and silver. At the moment it was violet. She wore large hoop earrings and a gold butterfly stud in her nose. Dark violet eyeshadow, dark violet lipstick, dark violet fingernails out to there, McGuire noted, taking inventory. She had on a puffy-sleeved blouse of dark blue silk, a black and gold embroidered velvet vest, tight, faded blue jeans, and knee-high leather boots with high heels. To complete the ensemble, she wore a profusion of necklaces and amulets, a dark blue silk scarf tied around her head, like a Barbary pirate, and she carried a paisley blue and purple wool serape draped over one shoulder.

Natasha Ouspenskaya, better known simply as "the Gypsy," had no formal connection with the N.Y.P.D. Most department officials would get blank looks if her name was mentioned, though they all knew about her. They simply weren't very comfortable admitting it. The Gypsy was not an adept. At least, she was not certified as one, though McGuire could not swear she abstained from practicing magic without a license. To the best of his knowledge, she had never tried to pass herself off as an adept. "I'm just a simple gypsy fortune-teller," she would say with a look of wide-eyed innocence that looked as genuine as it was misleading. However, whether she practiced any illegal hocus-pocus on the side or not, any talents she might have had in that area were not what interested Deputy Commissioner Steve McGuire, or anyone else in the N.Y.P.D. for that matter. What interested them was the fact that she was a highly gifted psychic, the strongest and most reliable they had ever encountered.

McGuire had dated her briefly shortly after they first met. The memory of that experience still made him wince inwardly. The Gypsy had just helped the department solve a difficult murder case and the press had gotten wind of it. McGuire got caught right in the middle and had to take care of the spin control. Considering her flamboyance, it hadn't been an easy job. He had felt attracted to her from the beginning. She was so completely different from any woman he had ever met. She had immediately sensed his interest and announced, in a thick, Transylvanian accent, "You find me interesting, no? Something different, an unusual experience, eh?" She had drawn out the word "un-*you*-shoo-all" the way Count Dracula might have done. "You wonder if you can maintain control with such a woman. *Hah!*"

The melodramatic Balkan accent was merely an affectation, of course, something she trotted out from time to time merely to amuse herself. Natasha Ouspenskaya, despite her name, hailed not from the Carpathians, but from Roslyn, Long Island. And if McGuire had any remaining doubts about her psychic abilities, they were gone after that first dinner date. She had been able to read him like an open book, something he had found extremely disconcerting. Their relationship, if it could even be called that, had not lasted longer than two or three dates, but they had remained friends and McGuire continued to call on her whenever the department was faced with a particularly baffling case.

He had expected her to come sweeping flamboyantly into

the room when she arrived, making one of her usual grand entrances, but instead she *staggered* in, supported by a police officer. Her face was white and she looked shaken.

"Natasha!" McGuire said, moving toward her quickly. "What happened?"

"She threw up in the elevator," the patrolman said.

"Are you all right?" said McGuire.

"No," she said, shaking her head. "Give me a minute." She straightened up with effort and took a deep breath, pressing her fingers to her temples, then exhaled heavily. She repeated the deep breathing several times before she spoke again. "Whoo. That's better. It's not so bad now. Damn, what the *hell* have you got here, Mac?"

"I was hoping you could tell me," McGuire said. "You're picking something up already?"

"Picking it *up*? It's practically knocking me *down*! The vibrations in that elevator just about floored me. I've never felt anything like it."

McGuire frowned. "And that was just in the elevator?"

"Somebody died in that elevator, Mac. Died horribly."

"Yes, two Bureau agents," said McGuire, nodding.

"No . . . there was only one."

McGuire shook his head. "There were two. Agents Silver and Whelen. And one police officer. He survived, but he's in the hospital, in critical condition."

Natasha shook her head. "No. . . . No, that can't be right," she insisted. "Only *one* man died in that elevator. The psychic impressions are extremely strong. I could almost *hear* his mind screaming."

McGuire pursed his lips thoughtfully. "Well, I suppose it's possible. One of them might have died in the elevator; the other one might have died in here and Angelo may have pulled him back in, not realizing he was already dead. I guess it could have happened that way. In any case, I've got two dead Bureau agents and one cop in intensive care. I want to know what happened here."

"Magic," said Natasha as she started to circle around the

apartment, walking slowly with her arms slightly spread out from her sides, her eyes wide and alert, glancing all around, her breathing shallow. "Magic happened."

"We already knew that much," said McGuire.

"I'm talking *heavy* magic, Mac," she said. "Mage-level stuff."

"*Mage* level?" said McGuire. "That's impossible."

"I'm telling you," she insisted. "There were several extremely powerful adepts here."

"Both Agents Silver and Whelen were eighth-level adepts, Natasha," said McGuire. "But they certainly weren't mages."

"No. . . . No, I'm talking about the people who were living here. And the one who came for them."

"It was a raid, Natasha," McGuire said. "Silver and Whelen came here to make an arrest."

She shook her head. "No. . . . He came here to kill."

"*Who* came here to kill?" McGuire asked, frowning and watching her intently as she moved around the room.

She stopped for a moment and squeezed her eyes shut, trying to concentrate. She let her breath out in an exasperated sigh and shook her head. "I don't know. It's all so confusing . . . . There's just so *much* here. . . . It's all getting muddled."

"Okay, take it easy," said McGuire. "Take your time."

"I need to have everybody out of here," she said. "There's too much interference. I'm getting distracted."

McGuire nodded to one of the detectives, who quickly ushered the forensics team out. Several of them glanced at the Gypsy and shook their heads with resignation, but nobody said anything in McGuire's presence. The deputy commissioner was, after all, the second-highest ranking official in the department. A few moments later only McGuire and Natasha remained in the penthouse.

"I don't understand . . ." Natasha said, staring down at the floor and cocking her head to one side, as if listening to something. "I'm getting the impression that there were only three people living here, but at the same time, I'm registering more. And *both* impressions feel right. But that doesn't make any sense.''

"Don't worry about it for now," McGuire said. "Just give me whatever you pick up. We'll sort it out later. If a few details seem contradictory, don't concern yourself about it."

"That's just the thing," she said with a puzzled frown. "I keep getting *completely* contradictory impressions. All over the place. I get the sense that the people living here were young . . . and then, at the same time, I'm picking up a feeling of old age."

"Like . . . how old?"

"Extremely old. Ancient. Thousands of years. . . ." She stopped and frowned. "Well, now how the hell can *that* be?"

"But that's what you're getting?"

She nodded. "Yes, but . . . it's crazy. How could anybody be thousands of years old?"

"But you said you also had the sense the people living here were young."

"Well, yes, that, too. It's very peculiar. . . ."

"What else can you pick up about them? You said there were three?"

"Two males and a female," she said immediately. Then she frowned again and shook her head. "No, that isn't right. I'm getting one female and *one* male." Another headshake. "No, that's only two, and there were three . . ."

"Well, which is it?"

"I don't *know*! Be quiet, Mac, I can't focus. . . ."

Her frustration was clearly evident. McGuire had never seen her react this way before. Her psychic impressions were usually so right on the money that she had a tendency to get cocky. This was a new experience for her. He could see that she was thrown by it.

"It's the strangest thing," she said. "I'm picking up different impressions, but they all seem to contradict each other and most of them are completely illogical."

"Is it possible that could have been done on purpose?" asked McGuire.

She glanced at him with a puzzled expression. "What do you mean?"

"I don't know, exactly. Maybe a spell of some sort, to confuse anyone who tried to get a reading on this place."

She thought about it for a moment. "I suppose that's possible," she said. "It's not really my area of expertise, you know. You'd have to ask an adept. But if there was some sort of spell that . . ." Her voice suddenly trailed off.

"What is it?"

"A spell," she said slowly, her voice scarcely above a whisper. "Yes, a *spell*. . . ."

She was on the verge of something. McGuire wanted to press her for details, but at the same time, he didn't want to say anything that might throw her off. Come on, Gypsy, he thought, you can do it. Come on. Tell me what went down here.

"The living triangle . . ." she said suddenly.

McGuire quickly took out his notebook and started writing. The Gypsy closed her eyes and spoke again, in a sort of chant:

> "Three stones, three keys to lock the spell,
> Three jewels to guard the Gates of Hell,
> Three to bind them, three in one,
> Three to hide them from the sun,
> Three to hold them, three to keep,
> Three to watch the sleepless sleep."

McGuire wrote quickly, getting it all down in his notebook. On the surface, it sounded like some sort of nursery rhyme. Natasha opened her eyes, blinked, and shook her head, as if to clear it. She looked dazed. "What was that?" he asked.

"I have no idea," she replied. "It just came to me. It must be some kind of spell."

"A living triangle . . . What does that mean?"

"How the hell am I supposed to know? This place is full of more powerful vibrations than I've ever encountered anywhere before. I'm being flooded with so much, I'm having a hard time making sense of anything. It's like listening to several different pieces of music, all played at the same time. It's like a psychic cacophony, and it's driving me crazy!"

"You want to get out of here for a while?"

She shook her head. "No. It's exasperating, but I'm all right. I was sick back there in the elevator, but the feeling in here is different. There's been a tremendous amount of energy released here."

"Thaumaturgic energy?"

"Unquestionably. Have you had forensic adepts in here to scan for trace emanations?"

"Not yet. You kicked everybody out."

"Well, when they do get around to taking a reading, don't be surprised if it knocks them for a loop," she said. "Does the name Morpheus mean anything to you?"

"Morpheus? No. What's that?"

"It's not a what, it's a who," Natasha said. "And it's not his only name."

"What about Michael Cornwall?"

"Yes, that resonates . . . and Modred," said Natasha. "He's also known as Modred."

McGuire wrote it down. "Now we're getting somewhere."

Natasha frowned. "But he's dead. I think." She shook her head. "I don't know, I'm not sure. . . . I'm getting something about a rune. . . . It has something to do with the spell." She cocked her head to one side. "Weird."

"What's weird?"

"The rune. It's a weird rune."

"A weird rune?"

"A runestone."

"A weird runestone?"

She frowned. "No, that's not right. . . ." She exhaled heavily. "I need some time alone in here, Mac."

He looked dubious. "The Bureau is going to start getting antsy about that forensics report. They don't know about you yet and I'd just as soon they didn't find out. How long are you going to need?"

"I don't know. I'm picking up the strangest impressions, Mac. I've never experienced anything like this. Either I'm

losing it or somebody's trying to confuse the hell out of me.
I'm getting something about a weird rune and a *talking broom*,
for crying out loud. It's like psychic word salad and it's giving
me a headache. If I can have a couple of hours alone in here,
I should be able to make some sense of it all."

"Okay," McGuire said, "two hours, and then I've got to
send the forensics team back in." He checked his watch.
"I'll be back for you by six."

"If I don't have something more concrete for you by then,
I'll trade in my tarot deck for *The Wall Street Journal*."

McGuire grinned and took the elevator back downstairs.
The forensics team was waiting for him down there, along
with the detectives. There was also a crowd of reporters
waiting outside, on the sidewalk, desperate to get a story in
before the evening newscast.

"The Gypsy come up with anything?" asked Detective
Hank Sloan, from Homicide.

"She's still up there," replied McGuire.

"Alone?" asked one of the forensics adepts with concern.
"Sir, we haven't even had a chance to go over the place yet
and—"

"Don't worry, she's seen enough crime scenes to know
not to disturb any evidence," McGuire said.

"Media's in full howl," said Robinson, Sloan's partner.

"Tell them I'll have a statement for them at the hospital,"
McGuire said. "I want to check on Detective Angelo, and at
the same time, I want to get them away from here, if possible.
The last thing we need is to have them see the Gypsy."

"Too late," said Sloan. "Bunch of 'em saw her going in.
They've been asking about her involvement."

"Hell, that's all I need," McGuire said. "The boss is
going to throw a fit."

"Bringing her in was your idea," Sloan said.

"She gets results, Hank," said McGuire. "And right now,
we need some results, because we haven't got squat. I'm
going over to the hospital. I'll be back in a couple of hours.
See that nobody disturbs the Gypsy while she's up there. Oh,

and, Hank, run these and see what you come up with." He tore a couple of pages out of his notebook and handed them to Sloan.

"Morpheus, Modred, Living Triangle, Weird Rune, Runestone . . . and what's this? Some kind of nursery rhyme?" asked Sloan.

"It's what the Gypsy picked up," McGuire said. "She thinks it might be some sort of spell. Morpheus and Modred might be aliases of Michael Cornwall. The others . . . I don't know what the hell they are. See if you can come up with anything."

"It's not much," said Sloan.

"It's a beginning, Hank. Get on it, okay?"

"You got it."

McGuire slipped out through the basement to avoid the press and had a squad car drive him over to the hospital, so that he could check on Detective Angelo. All he knew so far was that Angelo was in critical condition. He wanted to have all the details. When he talked to the press, he wanted to have at least some answers for them. He was hoping that Angelo could supply them. Assuming he could talk.

At the hospital, he identified himself by producing his shield at the desk, then asked to speak to the doctor in charge of Angelo's case. He noticed that the nurses exchanged nervous glances when he mentioned Angelo's name. That wasn't a good sign. A few moments later a white-coated physician approached him.

"Deputy Commissioner McGuire? I'm Dr. Ronald Fuller, Chief of Medicine."

"Thank you for coming, Doctor," said McGuire. "What can you tell me about Detective Angelo's condition? Is he able to talk?"

"Well," Fuller began uneasily, "up until a short while ago, I wouldn't have thought he was capable of anything. Detective Angelo was in a coma when he was brought into emergency."

"*Was* in a coma? You mean he didn't make it?"

"Well, apparently, Detective Angelo not only came out of his coma, but he left the hospital," said Dr. Fuller, looking rather upset.

"What do you mean he *left the hospital*? You mean he was in a coma when he came here several hours ago and now he's been *discharged*?"

"No, no, that would be quite irregular," said Dr. Fuller. "I mean he apparently took it upon himself to leave."

"Wait a minute," said McGuire. "What the hell is this? You're telling me that a man who was in a *coma* a mere matter of hours ago suddenly gets up and just *walks out* on his own steam?"

"He was seen leaving the hospital," said Dr. Fuller.

"And nobody tried to *stop* him?"

"Well, I'm afraid I was a bit imprecise there," Dr. Fuller said. "In point of fact, he was seen leaving his room and going into the elevator. Apparently, no one actually *saw* him leave the hospital, but we've conducted a thorough search of the entire building and he isn't on the premises."

"This is the craziest thing I've ever heard of," said McGuire.

"It gets crazier," the doctor replied.

"Who saw him leave?" McGuire demanded.

"One of the nurses—"

"I want to speak to her, right now."

"I'm afraid that's not possible," said Dr. Fuller. "She's under sedation."

"Why?"

"Because she went into hysterics when she saw him coming out of his room," Dr. Fuller replied. "You didn't quite let me finish. Detective Angelo was in a coma when he arrived in E.R. He was moved into a private room and placed on life support. Shortly after that, he was pronounced brain dead."

"*What?*"

"Look, I know how this sounds," said Dr. Fuller.

"Does the word 'nuts' ring a bell?"

"My first response was to ream out the doctor who pronounced him brain dead," Fuller said, "except he insisted I check out the patient's E.E.G. myself, which I did, and frankly, I would have made the same diagnosis. Anybody would. It was flat, all across the board. Naturally, I assumed the machine was faulty, so we tested it and it checked out."

"So what are you saying, Doctor, Angelo was brain dead, and then he suddenly came back to life and just strolled out of here?"

"I can appreciate your sarcasm, Mr. McGuire," Fuller replied. "Believe me, I would have the same reaction in your place. In fact, I did. Until I called in our thaumaturgic pathologist."

"Your what?"

"Our thaumaturgic pathologist," Fuller repeated. "Almost every hospital has a department of thaumaturgic medicine now, or they'd better have if they wish to remain competitive. There's a great demand for it. People are opting more and more for magical healing instead of more traditional medical therapy. It's less invasive, insurance companies like it because it involves less drugs and is consequently less expensive over the long run, and—"

"Right, get to the punch line," said McGuire impatiently.

"I had Dr. Marconis, our staff thaumaturgic pathologist, examine Detective Angelo's chart and then check his room for trace emanations. Dr. Marconis is a seventh-level adept, with degrees from Johns Hopkins and the College of Sorcerers in Cambridge. He is highly respected, both as an adept and a physician."

"The *point*, Doctor, please," McGuire said.

"The point is that Dr. Marconis was not only able to detect thaumaturgic trace emanations in Detective Angelo's room, but he said they were the strongest he had ever encountered. The energy in the residue of the trace emanations alone, he said, would have been enough to power our entire hospital for six months. On the recommendation of Dr. Marconis, we have since moved three patients in and out of that room. All three were terminal. All three were left in there for no longer than ten minutes, and all three are now showing signs of complete recovery."

"You mean just being in that room for ten minutes cured them?"

"It certainly looks that way," said Dr. Fuller. "Unfortunately, the effect is only temporary. The trace emanations will probably dissipate by tomorrow. In the meantime, we're moving as many terminal patients in and out of there as possible, and charting everything. I don't know what happened, or how it happened, but it seems to be working and I'm not going to look a gift horse in the mouth."

"Where is Dr. Marconis now?" McGuire asked. "Can I speak with him?"

"I'm afraid not," Dr. Fuller replied. "For the time being, he's in charge of this phenomenon, and he is going to be investigating it to the best of his ability for as long as it lasts."

"I would very much like to speak with him as soon as he's available, and discuss the results of his investigation," said McGuire.

"I'll be sure to pass it on," said Dr. Fuller. "Meanwhile, there was one thing that Dr. Marconis wanted me to ask the police. Exactly what was Detective Angelo exposed to?"

McGuire took a deep breath and exhaled heavily. "Doctor, I wish to hell I knew."

The Gypsy took the stairs down from the penthouse. It was a long way down, but she had no intention of getting into that elevator again. She had removed her boots and carried them in her left hand as she descended in her stocking feet. Exercise had never been her strong suit, and it was hard enough going down all those flights of stairs without having to do it in high heels. There was the added benefit that with her boots off, her feet made no noise on the stairs. She did not wish to attract any attention, especially since she was sneaking evidence out of a crime scene.

"*Must* you carry me upside down?" said Broom.

"I'm sorry," said the Gypsy, taking the enchanted broom off her shoulder, where she'd been carrying it like a rifle, and holding it down at her side in her right hand. "There, is that any better?"

"Just be careful and don't hit my head on the railing," Broom replied.

"You don't have a head, so far as I can see."

"*Nu*? I don't have a mouth either, but you hear me talking, don't you, Miss Smarty Pants?"

"Listen, bad enough I'm sneaking out with evidence from a crime scene, I don't need any *tsuris* from you."

"Evidence? Who're you calling evidence? Wait a minute . . . where does a gypsy fortune-teller who dresses like a stolen car get off using a word like *tsuris*?"

"I'm Jewish. So sue me."

"You're Jewish? That's funny, you don't look Jewish."

"Oh, and I suppose you do?"

"I must admit you have a point there," Broom said. "Where's the cat?"

Natasha looked over her shoulder. "She's coming down behind us. You *sure* she's not a thaumagene?"

"Nope. Shadow is a perfectly ordinary house cat," Broom said. "Which is to say, no magic. She doesn't talk, but she's smart as a whip."

"I can't believe I'm doing this," Natasha said. "If McGuire finds out, he'll kill me."

"For what, stealing a broom?"

"A thaumaturgically animated, *talking* broom, who can probably answer all his questions," said Natasha.

"Trust me, *bubeleh*, you're doing the right thing. Those policemen would've asked me lots of questions that I couldn't really answer and then I'd have wound up in some dark closet in their property room."

"Somehow, I doubt that," said Natasha with a grin. And then her smile faded. "What I'm worried about is how I'm going to get out of here with you. They're liable to ask *me* lots of questions I can't really answer if I go traipsing through the lobby with you."

"Go down to the basement and out through the parking garage," said Broom. "Then you can walk over to First Avenue and hail a cab."

"McGuire said he was going to come back and pick me

up in about two hours," she said. She checked her watch. "Boy, he is *not* going to be happy about this. Just remember, Broom, we've got a deal. I expect some serious cooperation in return for this."

"You'll get it, don't worry," said the broom. "You may not want it when you got it, but you'll get it. Boy, will you ever get it. And boy, are you not going to want it. Maybe you should just put me and the cat in that cab and go back up to the penthouse so you can meet your friend. You really don't want to get mixed up in this *farpotshket* situation. You look like a nice girl. A little too much with the makeup, maybe, and the purple hair I could do without, but you should just live and be happy and not get yourself involved. Trust me on this, okay? I know from what I'm talking."

"Forget it, Broom, we made a deal. I get you out of there and take you where you want to go, and in return you let me know what the hell went on up there. Half the things I picked up in that place scared the daylights out of me and the other half I flat out don't believe."

"Okay, but don't say I didn't warn you," said the broom. "Now where exactly are we going from here?"

"The Village," Broom said. "If anybody knows what's going on, it'll be Sebastian."

"Sebastian?" Natasha frowned. "I'm not getting anything off that name. Who is he? Is he an adept?"

"No, he's a fairy."

"In the Village? There's a big surprise."

"Not *that* kind," said the broom.

"What other kind is there?"

"The kind in fairy tales."

Natasha stopped. "Now, *wait* a minute, you don't mean to tell me . . . A *fairy*? You mean, like Tinkerbell? Glow in the dark, magical sprite with gossamer wings, *that* kind of fairy?"

"Well . . . no. Not exactly."

"Well, then *what*, exactly?"

"Maybe we'd just better wait until you meet Sebastian,"

Broom said. "He's not really the easiest person to describe. You sort of have to experience him firsthand."

"You're not doing very much to clear things up," the Gypsy said.

"Don't worry about it, dear," said Broom. "I promise you, it'll only get worse."

CHAPTER
THREE

THE ENTRANCE TO Lovecraft's Cafe was below street level, down a narrow flight of steps and through a heavy steel door painted black and covered with electric yellow runes. The uninitiated often thought the dramatic-looking runes spelled out some sort of ward or cabalistic message, but in fact they merely spelled out the phrase "Mixed drinks, fine food."

The interior of the cafe was a whimsical blend of the occult and Rebeat, a retro movement harkening back to the coffeehouse tradition of the Village in the days prior to the Collapse. The decor was spare and black. Black walls, black ceiling, black booths, black everything, including the lycras, jeans, and turtlenecks of the waiting staff, most of whom were young dancers and actors waiting for their big break. Everyone who worked at Lovecraft's, and many of the patrons, wore the obligatory Rebeat black eye makeup that completely encircled the eyes. Some of the patterns were round, like painted-on sunglasses; others were diamond-shaped, giving a harlequin effect; while still others ran down the cheeks like tear tracks, making the wearers look like weeping raccoons. Save for this masklike eye shadow, no other makeup was worn, and a vampiric pallor was cultivated by avoiding sunlight. The heavy-duty Rebeats, the real purists, also affected a flat monotone, speaking in a bored and detached way, all the time keeping a completely neutral facial expression. Emotional displays of any kind were frowned upon. In fact, frowns themselves were frowned upon, and smiles were definitely uncool. It was impossible to shock or get a rise out of a true Rebeat. Nothing surprised them; they had seen it all, and none of it was very noteworthy. They dismissed most things with jaded catchphrases such as "Been there, done that," and "It's all nickel-and-dime."

Lovecraft's was not a trendy bar, because the Rebeat lifestyle was not very amenable to trendiness. It was a bit too odd and difficult to maintain for the terminally au courant. It was not enough to simply look the part, one had to do one's homework. Rebeats were not hedonists; they were diehard intellectuals, masters of the hip sub-reference. Their drug of choice was reading and their recreation was composing and listening to poetry. They were also antimusic, regarding it as superficially emotional and too distracting. They liked their poetry performed to the percussive beat of bongos or the electronic syncopations of their rhythm boxes . . . or, better yet, done "hardcore"—with no accompaniment at all. Rebeat was an antitrend, and so Lovecraft's was not trendy. It was essentially a hangout for bohemian adepts and the intellectually disaffected—in other words, alcoholic wizards and college students.

Dr. Sebastian Makepeace dwelled comfortably, if rather ostentatiously, in this environment. His doctorate was in Pre-Collapse History, which he taught at New York University, but he also held graduate degrees in Metaphysics and Occult Studies. Such esoteric qualifications made him eminently acceptable not only to his academic colleagues but to the Rebeats as well. Both groups appreciated him for his intellectual abilities and his originality. Even in a place like Greenwich Village, the mecca of the odd and the bizarre, Makepeace was unique. In a world where everyone who ever took an undergraduate course in Thaumaturgy liked to pose as an adept, Makepeace adamantly refused the title. He was, he insisted, neither a wizard nor a sorcerer. He was a fairy.

It irked him that dictionaries defined the term as either "a small, imaginary being with magical powers" or "a male homosexual." Use of the word "fairy" to describe male homosexuals was something to which Makepeace took strenuous exception. It was, he claimed, offensive to both gays *and* fairies. He was on a personal crusade to redefine the word and his ongoing battle with the compilers of the *Oxford English Dictionary* had become something of a legend in academic circles. He obviously took issue with the word "imaginary," and insisted that his size certainly gave the lie to the word "small." At a height of six feet six, and with a rather considerable girth, he would not be considered either small or imaginary by anyone's definition. That left the "magical powers," and there was no question that he had them. How he came by them, however, was a subject of considerable debate among his students.

At N.Y.U. he was considered an amiable, if somewhat volatile, oddball, and each year some of his students stubbornly set out to prove that old Professor Makepeace was nothing more than a traditionally trained adept. To date, however, none of them had managed to prove any such thing. He did nothing to discourage their efforts to "expose" him. He knew that no amount of research on their part would turn up any record of anyone named Sebastian Makepeace ever taking any postgraduate courses in Thaumaturgy, much less a degree from any College of Sorcerers. The Bureau of Thaumaturgy, under the aegis of the International Thaumaturgical Commission, administered all programs of magic study and certification throughout the world, but the name Sebastian Makepeace did not appear in any of their records.

However, to the skeptics, this did not constitute proof of his assertions. Tuition at a College of Sorcerers was expensive and the admission process was highly selective and competitive, but all the texts used in the advanced courses could be had at reasonable prices at virtually any used bookstore in the country. This had created certain problems that the B.O.T. had not foreseen. In other nations, where freedom of information was not always regarded as a right, laws had been passed to prohibit the unauthorized sale and possession of thaumaturgy texts, but in America, such prohibitions would not be constitutional.

Anyone with access to an occult supply store, claimed the skeptics, could easily obtain all the necessary knowledge and materials to practice magic. However, such home study was not without its hazards. Hospitals and psychiatric wards were full of people who had tried to teach themselves how to perform magic without the supervision of a certified adept. Makepeace always pointed out that it required natural ability, enormous discipline, and proper training. Nevertheless, the skeptics chose to believe that Makepeace was either a rare exception to the rule or else had received his training under another name. No one had ever seen a real-live fairy, they insisted, and there was no proof of their existence. They conveniently overlooked the fact that none of the spells Sebastian Makepeace used could be found in any textbook.

Lovecraft's was the one place where Makepeace was accepted at face value. The Rebeats didn't care one way or the other what he was. Supernatural being? Sure, whatever. Pass the pitcher, Dad. Some people found such blasé hipness irritating. Makepeace found it remarkably refreshing.

"Hey, dad," a young Rebeat regular greeted him as he made his way toward his usual table at the back.

"Hey, daughter," he replied. The waitress was not, of course, his daughter, but if they called him "Dad," he always replied in kind, addressing them as "Son" or "Daughter," whatever seemed appropriate. Sometimes it was difficult to tell. He knew that it was not the proper "hip" response, but it seemed to amuse the young people.

He had left Kira upstairs, keeping an eye on Wyrdrune, who was still unconscious, and Billy, who was fast asleep, exhausted by the healing spell. Kira had looked pretty tired herself, but she would not sleep, nor would she leave the others. He did not have anything in his refrigerator that would make a decent meal, since he ate out all the time, so he came down to Lovecraft's to get them something to eat and ponder what Kira had told him.

"The usual, Doc?" said a pretty, young, dark-haired waitress with heavy black eye shadow. She was wearing a black sheath dress that looked as if it had been painted on.

"Yes, please, Morticia," Makepeace said. "And please tell Eduardo that I would like some of his excellent fettucine Alfredo to go. Enough for three or four generous portions. I have some unexpected company."

"Sure thing, Doc," said the waitress.

"Oh, and by the way, dear, is Gonzago in tonight?"

"He's at the bar."

"He is?" said Makepeace with a frown. "Where? I don't see him."

She merely pointed up.

Makepeace raised his gaze toward the ceiling and said, "Ah. Well, be a love and ask him to come down, would you?"

The man who was plastered up against the ceiling did not respond at once when the waitress called to him. His voluminous blue robes draped from his figure like funereal vestments, and his long white hair and beard hung down like Spanish moss while he remained pressed up against the ceiling like a torpid fly. Taking a nap on the ceiling was rather unusual even in a bar like Lovecraft's, Makepeace thought, but then Dr. Morrison Gonzago was an unusual human being. He was the only member of the faculty at N.Y.U. who was considered even more eccentric than Makepeace, but then he seemed to work at it much harder.

The fourth time Morticia called his name, Gonzago started and woke up . . . and promptly plunged straight toward the bar. Several of the patrons immediately leapt aside in alarm, upsetting their drinks in the process, but what looked to be a very messy crash landing was narrowly averted at the last instant when Gonzago's body came to an abrupt halt in midair, less than an inch above the bar. Hovering there, his nose barely touching the bartop, Gonzago started to slowly drift down the length of the bar, noisily slurping up the spilled drinks. Then he turned over in midair, like a man in bed turning over onto his back, belched loudly and profoundly, sat up, and, with a slight thump, dropped down onto a bar stool.

"A pint of ale, my good publican, and put it on my tab," he slurred.

"Your tab hasn't been paid in two months, Gonzo," said the bartender. "Sorry, but I've been told to cut you off."

"Cut me *off*? Why, you impertinent young whelp, I was running up a tab at this fine establishment while you were still sucking on your mother's tit! My tab pays the bloody mortgage on this place! Now draw me a pint of ale!"

"Sorry, Gonzo. No can do."

"Give him his pint, Tony, I'm buying," Makepeace said.

"Ah," said Gonzago, noticing Makepeace for the first time. "Saved by the good fairy! You are a gentleman and a scholar, sir." He made a wide, sweeping bow to Makepeace and fell off his stool. Before he hit the floor, however, he levitated and floated back up to the level of the bar. To anyone not well versed in the principles of thaumaturgy, it was a sight that was merely comical. To Makepeace, however, who knew something of the thaumaturgic arts, it was a testimony to Gonzago's skills as an adept that he could work these spells so quickly and so effectively, even while thoroughly in his cups.

"You are an incorrigible reprobate, Gonzago," Makepeace replied, "but I forgive you because you have character."

"Why, bless your heart, Sebastian," Gonzago replied. "That is the first time anyone has spoken of my character since . . . when was it? Ah, since that symposium at Columbia last year."

"The writing conference? I thought they kicked you out," said Makepeace.

"I did not say they spoke favorably."

The bartender set a pint of ale down in front of Gonzago. The wizard promptly levitated it to the level of his face, where it obligingly floated up to his lips, tipped slightly, and dispensed a gulp of brew. Gonzago sighed and smacked his lips with satisfaction, then came back down to the floor and sauntered over to join Makepeace at his table. His pint of ale obediently floated along behind him, followed by a bowl of beer nuts.

While the regulars at Lovecraft's were all well accustomed to Gonzago's antics, others couldn't help but stare. Which was partly why Gonzago did it, Makepeace thought. Even high-level corporate adepts were conservative in expending their powers, because magic had a price, but Morrison Gonzago did not seem to know the meaning of the word "conservative." He was a study in excess. He drank enough booze to pickle the innards of an elephant and he was always using magic profligately, at enormous cost to his life energy. Most people would have long since burned out from such relentless self-abuse, but when it came to life force, Gonzago seemed to have enough for at least a dozen men.

He had graduated from Columbia with a degree in English Literature, then took a Masters in Occult Sciences at Harvard. He was awarded his Th.D. by the Cambridge College of Sorcerers, where he had studied under none other than Merlin Ambrosius himself, and he had been the first to achieve a perfect score on his certification exams, a feat unmatched by anyone to date, so far as Makepeace knew. He had received a stream of lucrative job offers, but instead of joining the corporate sector, Gonzago went back to school on a graduate fellowship. While teaching English at Yale, he took a Masters of Fine Arts in Creative Writing, during which time he also won three major poetry awards and published his first novel, which was promptly awarded the Pulitzer. Colleges and universities throughout the country fell all over themselves offering him positions on their faculties. However, that was before they had a chance to get to know him. Afterward, their initial enthusiasm waned rather quickly. Gonzago had wound up at N.Y.U. after bouncing around from one school to another throughout most of his career, with long stints in between where he had tried to write, without success. He was never able to duplicate that surge of incandescent energy with which he had blazed onto the literary scene . . . and so he drank, instead. He had worn out his welcome at most of the colleges where he had taught, and so he came to New York City, where faded literary lions with somewhat scandalous reputations were not the exception, but the norm. And at a faculty reception shortly after his arrival, he had made an astonishing discovery. There was someone in the History Department who was not only as flamboyant and eccentric as he was, in his own way, but who was actually capable of drinking him right under the table . . . all without ever getting even slightly tipsy. The two men became instant best friends.

Neither one of them looked even remotely professorial. Makepeace, in Gonzago's words, "dressed like a stolen car," while Gonzago affected dark blue robes emblazoned with cabalistic symbols, similar to the ones Merlin Ambrosius had worn many years ago. Despite the fact that most adepts no longer wore the traditional sorcerer's robes, Gonzago insisted it was the way a proper wizard *ought* to look. Together, he and Makepeace made quite a spectacle. Morticia brought a pitcher of beer to the table, and Makepeace proceeded to drink from it as if it were a mug.

"Bring a second one for my esteemed colleague," Makepeace told her. "Have you eaten yet, Morrison, or did you forget again?"

"I ate yesterday, I think."

"He'll have a pastrami on rye, with hot mustard," added Makepeace. "Man cannot live on alcohol alone, although Lord knows, he tries."

"Stop mothering me, Sebastian."

"You don't need a mother, you need a keeper," Makepeace replied. "I shudder to think what your liver must look like."

"It's growing and crowding out my other organs," said Gonzago. "I can feel the pressure. Or perhaps I merely need to piss. But you should talk. For a man who imbibes as prodigiously as you do, the very least you can do is have the good grace to get inebriated on occasion."

"Fairies don't get drunk, old boy," said Makepeace.

"Then I fail to see the point."

Makepeace grinned and raised his pitcher. "Cheers."

"*L'chayim*," said Gonzago.

"Are you sober enough to have this conversation?" Makepeace asked.

"That depends on how many functional brain cells I have left," replied Gonzago. "You don't need all that many to teach Freshman Comp. What's on your mind, old friend?"

"How long have we known each other, Morrison?"

Gonzago considered for a moment.

"Entirely too long. Why?"

"Have you ever known me to prevaricate?"

"Is this a serious conversation?"

"Deadly serious."

"*Deadly* serious? Dear me. What have you done, Sebastian? Don't tell me you've gotten involved with one of your nubile, young students. I thought you knew better than that."

"This is considerably more serious than that, I'm afraid," said Makepeace. "I consider you one of my closest friends, Morrison, and yet . . . there is a great deal about me you do not know."

"Oh-oh. I sense a grave confession coming on."

"I'm serious, Morrison. There are things I've never told you, and with good reason, I might add. However, I am going to tell you now, because I need your help. I need someone I can trust."

Gonzago raised his bushy eyebrows. "This *does* sound serious. Are you in some sort of trouble?"

"Not I," said Makepeace. "But a very good friend of mine is."

"I see. What can I do?

"Before I tell you," Makepeace said, "you should know that it could be very dangerous."

"Indeed? Define dangerous."

"Potentially life-threatening."

"I would call that an accurate, if somewhat alarming, definition," Gonzago said with a nod. "Do go on."

"It's rather a long story," Makepeace said.

"Finals are over, dear boy, and I have no immediate plans other than to curl up with a case of Scotch and pass the summer in a pleasant stupor. So let 'er rip."

"You studied with Ambrosius, Morrison," Makepeace said. "You knew him. You were one of his prize pupils, were you not?"

"I am proud to say I was, yes. Why?"

"Well, you remember when his mansion in Beacon Hill burned down several years ago?"

"Yes, of course," said Gonzago, looking down into his ale. "It made headline news not only in Boston, but throughout the world. A tragic loss."

"What if I were to tell you that Merlin did *not* die in that fire?"

Gonzago looked up at him with surprise. "Good Lord. You don't mean to say he's still alive?"

"You are familiar with the spell of life force transference?" Makepeace replied.

"Well, yes, naturally, but it would be beyond the capability of most adepts. It would take nothing less than a mage to . . ." His voice trailed off as comprehension dawned.

"His corporeal self died, although not in that fire," Makepeace replied. "But his astral self survived. However, the whole story is even more complicated. In fact, it began even before Merlin was born, when—"

Makepeace stopped abruptly.

"What is it?" asked Gonzago.

"I'm not sure," said Makepeace. Gonzago followed his gaze. Makepeace was looking toward the entrance.

A stunning young woman with flowing, violet hair was making her way toward their table. Yet, as striking as her appearance was, she was not what everyone was looking at. Everybody in the bar was staring at her companion, an ambulatory broom holding a black cat in its rubbery-looking arms as it swept across the floor, preceding her and heading directly toward Makepeace with alacrity.

"I take it back," Gonzago said. "I am *not* sober enough to have this conversation."

John Angelo stood looking around at his surroundings, feeling they were vaguely familiar, yet at the same time having no idea where he was or how he had arrived there. The last thing he remembered clearly was waking up in a hospital. He had no memory of how he came to the hospital in the first place, or even why. He had checked to see if he was injured, but so far as he could tell, he seemed to be all right.

Barefoot and wearing nothing but the white hospital gown he awoke in, he had walked out into the hallway and encountered a nurse carrying a tray. When she saw him, she dropped the tray and screamed. He bolted past the nurses' station and into the elevator, ignoring their shouts for him to stop. He remembered pushing the button for the lobby . . . or had he pushed the button for the lobby? It seemed as if that was what he would have done, must have done, but though it was starting to come back to him in little bits and pieces, none of it was linear. The very next thing he remembered was standing in the living room of the apartment where he now found himself. Only how in the world did he get here?

I got into the elevator, he thought, and I pushed the button for the lobby . . . and then . . . Then what? Then I was here. Only how the hell did I *get* here? And where the hell *is* "here"? He walked over to the window and looked out. He was in a high-rise apartment building on the Upper West Side. The street was far below, perhaps twenty floors down. Only what street was it? He had the feeling he should know, but he couldn't seem to make things fit together somehow.

He turned and glanced around at the apartment. It puzzled him that he could not remember how he got here. He could not remember anything after entering the elevator. He did not remember coming out into the lobby or hailing a cab. . . . Surely someone would have tried to stop him if he came out of the elevator and into the hospital lobby looking the way he did. But why couldn't he remember?

He tried to organize his thoughts and concentrate. Where the hell am I? And then, an even more chilling thought. Who the hell am I? With a shock, he suddenly realized that he had absolutely no idea. God, he thought, what happened to me? Why can't I remember? And how did I get here from the hospital? It seems as if I got into that elevator only seconds ago, and now I'm in this strange apartment. Do I live here?

Something about the place sort of vaguely felt like home, and then again, it didn't. Perhaps, he thought, there was something in the apartment itself that would clue him in. There was nothing in the living room that seemed to help. Black leather sofa and easy chair, gray carpet, steel and glass coffee table, end tables, lamps, entertainment center, several paintings of nude women on the walls . . . He frowned. Did he really like that sort of thing? The whole place seemed rather tasteless. There was nothing in the living room to give him any clue as to his identity—if, in fact, this was even his place. He didn't seem to like it much.

He went into the bathroom and looked into the mirror. He stared at the face he saw reflected back at him. He wasn't even sure he recognized it. The man in the mirror had shaggy black hair, neatly trimmed to just above the collar; a full black beard, also neatly trimmed; brown eyes, vaguely almond-shaped and sleepy-looking, what women often called "bedroom eyes." He frowned at the thought. Did that mean he was a ladies man? Or was he married? Did he have a family? He checked his left hand. No wedding ring. Would they have taken it off at the hospital? He didn't think so. And there was no telltale ring mark. So he probably wasn't married. But did he live alone?

The toilet articles in the bathroom suggested that he did—assuming, again, that this was his apartment. A check of the closets in the bedroom revealed no women's clothing. Just suits, shirts, slacks, and sport coats, flashy and well tailored. He found clean underwear in the bureau drawers. It fit. The clothes fit, too, like they were made for him. Perhaps they were. The jacket had a tag sewn on the inside, stating that the garment had been custom tailored by Zangarra and Son for Giovanni Angelico. That must be me, he thought. Or is it? The name seemed vaguely familiar somehow. But only vaguely.

While he was getting dressed, he had noticed a strange gemstone implanted in the skin of his chest, over his heart.

A ruby. It looked real. Then again, why would anyone bother to have an artificial gem made a part of their body? He stared at it in the mirror, seeing its peculiar highlights, touching it lightly, wondering why it was there. Purely a bit of decadent ornamentation, apparently. Whoever I am, he thought, I must be quite a character.

In the drawer of the end table by the bed, he found a roll of cash large enough to choke a horse, but no wallet, no ID and not a single credit card. He found a small, black enamel jewelry box that contained a large and flashy diamond ring set in gold; an expensive Swiss watch, also gold; and a heavy, gold ID bracelet engraved in fancy script with the name "Johnny Angel." He also found a gun.

It was a 9-mm semiautomatic of Italian manufacture. He picked it up, removed the magazine—fully loaded—and racked the slide back. The motions seemed very natural and familiar to him. It seems I know about guns, he thought. A pricey gun, custom-tailored suits, expensive jewelry, a lot of cash, but no ID and no credit cards. Two names, one of which sounded like an alias . . . Johnny Angel. Sounds like a cheap hood. He considered the gold jewelry, the expensive suits, the large roll of cash. Maybe not so cheap. If I *am* Giovanni Angelico, he thought, then I may be some sort of criminal. And, somehow, that thought seemed very familiar, too.

"What do you mean you don't know where he lives?" McGuire said with disbelief. "How can you not know where he lives? He works for the department, doesn't he?"

"He's detached to special duty, Organized Crime Task Force," said the young sergeant, staring at her monitor screen. She looked up at McGuire. "His current operational files are restricted."

McGuire gave a long, exasperated sigh. Was *anything* going to work out normally on this case? The commissioner wanted facts, because the mayor wanted to know what was being done and the media was driving him crazy. So the commissioner was driving McGuire crazy. He wanted answers, except that McGuire had no answers to give him. Whatever answers were available, the Bureau had, and they were not disposed to share. The press wanted to know why they had been told essentially nothing about one of the largest police raids in the city's history. They were screaming that the people had a right to know. And now they had gotten hold of the fact that an officer who had been injured in that raid and was supposedly brain dead had simply gotten up out of bed and walked out of the hospital. It had sent them into a feeding frenzy that made a school of piranha fish look like a bunch of sardines. The whole thing was driving McGuire nuts.

"Angelo's files have been transferred to the O.C.T.F. database," the sergeant said. "Without proper authorization, we're locked out. He's one of the D.A.'s people."

"No, Sergeant, he's one of *my* people, on *loan* to the D.A. And she's managed to rig things so that I can't even find out where one of my own people is supposed to live. Jesus. Get her on the phone."

About an hour later, he had finally gotten through to District Attorney Mathews. "Christine," he said, "I've got a problem. I require access to the files of one of my people on loan to your Organized Crime Task Force."

"Sorry, Steve, you know I can't do that," she replied.

"Christine, look, I've got a situation here—"

"Steve, I told the mayor when we set this whole thing up that in order to safeguard the lives of the officers and maintain the integrity of our investigations, I had to have complete and absolute control over all files and all internal policy and communications relating to the task force. As I recall, your office supported me in this undertaking and promised full cooperation."

"I know that, Christine, but this is a special case. I need—"

"I'm sorry, Steve, I can't make any exceptions. There have been leaks in the past and officers have died as a result."

"Don't you think I know that, Christine? Now will you listen to me, please?" And he quickly brought her up-to-date.

"All right, now wait a minute," she said when he had finished, "just let me get this straight. You're telling me that Angelo arrived at the hospital in a coma, was pronounced brain dead, *then got up and walked out?*"

"That's right."

"That's impossible."

"That's what I said."

"Well, obviously, there must be some mistake."

"I only wish there were, but Angelo had a living will stipulating that no heroic measures should be taken to keep him alive in the event of something like this, so not long after he was officially pronounced brain dead, they took him off life support in the presence of the department physician. And that was all she wrote. There was no heartbeat, no respiratory function, no brain waves, nothing. Only the fact remains that while they were getting ready to take him to the morgue, Angelo got out of bed and was seen leaving his hospital room, barefoot and wearing only a hospital gown. He got into the elevator and was never seen again. He simply disappeared."

"What do you mean he disappeared?"

"I mean he disappeared. Flat out vanished. The people on duty in the lobby swear they never saw him get off the elevator. He may have gotten out some other way, like maybe through the maintenance corridors in the basement or something, but either way, nobody saw him. He's gone, and no one knows what's happened to him."

"Well, I'd say their diagnosis left something to be desired," D.A. Mathews said dryly.

"Christine, the man was *stone cold dead.*"

"Or so they claim, at any rate," she replied. "Sounds to me as if somebody's trying to cover their ass."

"There were witnesses, Christine," McGuire said. "They took Angelo off life support and all his vital functions stopped, period. The nurse who saw Angelo leaving his room had a nervous breakdown. She saw a dead man walking. The doctors over there are seriously upset about this. I had one of our forensic adepts check the room out. He said there were enough thaumaturgic trace emanations in there to light up Yankee Stadium.''

"Not even magic can bring a man back from the dead, Steve," the D.A. said.

"Well, then I guess Angelo must be dead, but he doesn't seem to have the sense to lie down."

"What was he doing on this big raid of yours, anyway?" she countered. "The task force is under my authority."

"A, it wasn't *my* raid," McGuire said "and B, he was commandeered by the Bureau agent in charge, who claimed to have received your personal okay."

"Well, he didn't."

"I didn't think so. Either way, he's dead now; the local Bureau chief is telling me to keep my nose out of it; and you and I have both got a mess on our hands."

"What do you mean, 'you and I *both*'? What have I to do with it?"

"Well, Angelo was undercover with your task force, wasn't he? I don't know what the hell he was working on, presumably you do, but he's out there somewhere, walking around, with God only knows what going through his brain. Do *you* know what he's going to do?"

"I see your point," she said. "All right. What do you want me to do?"

"Release his files to me," McGuire said. "I need his current address, to start with. Who knows, maybe we'll get lucky and find him at home, having a beer and watching TV."

"This sounds absolutely crazy, you know that, don't you?"

"I know," McGuire said. "Believe me, I know. But there is one possible explanation. Angelo might be a zombie."

"A *what*?"

"A zombie. A body that's being thaumaturgically animated and controlled by someone. Our adepts tell me that it's possible. It would take some pretty advanced sorcery, and it's highly illegal, of course, but they say it can be done, theoretically. This whole thing has got necromancy written all over it.''

"Brother, that's all we need," she said. She sighed heavily. "All right, where are you calling from, your office?''

"Yeah.''

"Okay, I'll pull the file and meet you there in twenty minutes. I want to go along on this personally, and the file doesn't leave my hands.''

"Fair enough. I'll be here.''

"This better be on the level, Steve.''

"Come on, you know me better than that.''

"Yes, I guess I do. If anybody else were telling me this, I'd say they had been drinking.''

"Right about now, I could use a drink. A stiff one.''

"I think I'll join you. Okay, I'll be there as soon as I can.''

"Thanks, Christine.'' McGuire hung up the phone and put his head in his hands, rubbing his temples. He was starting to get a migraine. He picked up the phone again and dialed. "This is McGuire," he said. "Any word on the Gypsy? No, huh? Damn that woman. All right, put out an A.P.B. on her. I want her picked up and booked on interfering with a homicide investigation and any other goddamn thing you can think of. I don't care if she pulls in a dozen lawyers. I want her held until I can get a chance to talk to her personally.'' He hung up the phone again.

"Are you all right, sir?'' asked the sergeant with concern.

"No," replied McGuire. "No, I'm not all right. I wish to God someone would tell me what the *hell* is going on here.''

"Sir, I've got Channel Seven on the line.''

"Terrific," he said with a grimace. "Tell 'em I died and went out for a walk.''

CHAPTER
FOUR

"BELIEVE ME, IT would be far better for you if you did not become involved," said Billy.

"It's a little late for that, I already *am* involved," Natasha replied.

They were sitting in the living room of Makepeace's apartment, drinking coffee. Makepeace was in the bedroom, on the phone. Gonzago sat quietly, sipping from his mug and listening to their conversation. Wyrdrune had recovered fully from his injuries, though he still looked a little drawn and pale.

"It would bring you nothing but trouble," he said.

"I've already *got* trouble. If I know McGuire, he's probably got the whole department out looking for me by now," said Natasha. "But I picked up enough in that penthouse of yours that it's going to drive me crazy if I don't learn all the answers."

"Curiosity killed the cat," said Kira. "You took a pretty big risk coming here. The police think we killed those Bureau agents. How do you know we'll even let you out of here alive?"

"I'm psychic, remember?" said the Gypsy. "I trust my instincts. And they tell me you people aren't murderers. But you're mixed up with some powerful black magic, and I don't understand why you won't go to the authorities."

"Because it wouldn't do any good. We're mainly concerned with keeping the authorities out of it," said Wyrdrune. "And you work for the police."

"I *consult* for the police," she said. "That makes a big difference. I don't carry a badge and I'm not on their payroll. They can't tell me what to do."

"Maybe not, but they can arrest you for being an accessory," said Kira. "Just sitting here with us makes you guilty of a felony. Aiding and abetting."

"I know the law," Natasha replied. "What I don't understand is why you won't go to the police or the Bureau if you're innocent."

"Neither the police nor the Bureau would be capable of handling this situation," Billy said. "Even the Bureau's topranking adepts would be no match for the forces we're up against. Besides, there would still be the matter of convincing them."

"Well, you can start by trying to convince me," Natasha said. "For openers, who's Modred?"

"You're the psychic, you tell me," said Wyrdrune.

"I'm not a telepath," she replied. "I pick up psychic impressions. Sometimes they come through real clear, sometimes they don't. Sometimes I just get feelings and I have to try to make sense out of them. And in this case, I can't make much sense of anything."

"For instance?" Wyrdrune said.

"Well, for one thing, you look about twenty-five, but you read like you're positively ancient. I get the feeling that you're *centuries* old."

"Try millenniums."

"That's crazy."

"I'm also twenty-five. Go on."

"What is this, a test?"

"Humor me."

Natasha sighed. "All right. You don't read like you're one person, but a whole bunch of people. Kira, too. As for

Billy, I simply can't get anything out of him at all. He's shielding.''

"What else?" said Wyrdrune. "Exactly how much have you been able to pick up?"

"You want me to go over the whole thing?"

"Please."

She sighed. "I'm not sure where to start. It's all a jumble. With the exception of Sebastian and Gonzago, here, the rest of you are putting out incredible amounts of energy. You've got the most powerful auras I've ever seen."

"You can actually *see* them?"

"I don't even have to try. The air around you seems to vibrate."

"Go on."

"Back in your penthouse, I got something about somebody called Morpheus. And Modred. I think they're both the same person. And I got a lot of pain associated with him. I also picked up something about Merlin being there, but he's supposed to have died when his house burned down in Boston several years ago. And there were some incredibly malevolent impressions associated with somebody or something called the Dark Ones. There's more. Should I go on?"

"No," said Wyrdrune. "You already know more than enough to cause us a great deal of trouble."

"The question is, what are you going to do about it?" she asked.

"The smart thing to do would be to make you forget everything you know," he said.

Billy shook his head. "We can't do that," he said.

"Why not?"

"She's a psychic. A spell like that could easily destroy her gift. That's not what we're about."

"No," Wyrdrune agreed glumly, "it's not."

"You could actually do that?" Natasha asked with alarm.

"Yes, but we won't," said Billy. "It would be a violation of the path. I'm afraid we don't have any choice but to tell you everything. As you said, you already are involved. But you're going to wish you weren't."

"You want to tell her?" Wyrdrune asked.

"Why don't you start?" Billy said. "After all, it began with you and Kira."

"It began a lot longer ago than that," said Wyrdrune. "It's a long story. I'll try to make it brief. Being psychic, you can probably pick up a lot of it yourself as I go along. A long, long time ago, when humans were still walking on all fours, another race of beings lived on this planet. We call them the Old Ones. They looked a great deal like us, except that they had golden skin and they all apparently had fiery red hair. They were magic users. To them, humans seemed little more than animals, and they used us much the same way we use animals. That is, they didn't eat us, but in a sense, they did consume us. Humans provided the life force for their rituals."

"Necromancers," said Natasha.

Wyrdrune nodded. "As humans evolved into more intelligent creatures, the Old Ones gradually abandoned the practice of sacrificing them in their magical rituals, regarding it as being too cruel. For a long time, they simply didn't think of humans as sentient, but as a sort of subrace. The way we might regard monkeys. They started to use their magic in a more conservative way; that is, they would still practice their rituals, but they no longer killed. They would draw off only a portion of the subject's life force, so that recovery was possible. This was the beginning of white magic, or thaumaturgy. However, there were those among them who refused to give up the old ways. These were the Dark Ones, the necromancers."

"The ones who wouldn't give up killing," said Natasha.

"Right. They could get more power faster by absorbing all the life force of a subject instead of only part of it, and they insisted that it was our natural function to serve that purpose, and that killing humans in their rituals was necessary to keep their population in check. In that sense, I suppose, they had a point, because humans reproduced much more quickly than they did. Compared to them, we were like rabbits. The question created a rift between them that eventually led to war, a mage war that devastated their population. It's probably where the human myths of the Ragnarok, the Twilight of the Gods, came from. In fact, we can trace much of our mythology back to the Old Ones. Stories of sorcerers and shape-changers, vampires—in a sense, that's what they were—the gods of the Greeks and Romans, the Norse pantheon, it all probably dates back to them.''

"That's amazing,'' said Natasha. "Why didn't any trace of them show up in the fossil record?''

"We're not really sure. It would probably be very difficult, if not impossible, to differentiate the remains of modern Homo sapiens from theirs, for one thing. For another, the Old Ones were immortal. If they were not killed, they lived forever. Their cells apparently had no limit to regeneration. In any case, when the Dark Ones were defeated by the Council of the White, the ruling body of the Old Ones, they were entombed in a subterranean cavern in the Euphrates Valley, held there in a sort of comatose state by a spell the Council had devised. It was the most powerful spell they had ever cast. The Living Triangle. By that point, the Council realized their time was past. The human population had been growing steadily and their own population had declined. The war had reduced them even further. So the Council cast their spell in such a way that they infused their own life energies into three enchanted runestones, the keys to the spell.''

"Three stones, three keys to lock the spell, three jewels to guard the gates of Hell,'' Natasha said. "So that's where that came from!''

Wyrdrune nodded. "Only one member of the Council was left alive to put the living runestones in place and seal the cavern. He was the youngest member of the Council, a mage named Gorlois, and when he was done, he cast off his sorcerer's robes and went out into the world to live among the humans, passing as one of them. The rest of the surviving Old Ones had to go underground and pass as human, too, because the humans outnumbered them and they had started hunting them. It was the end of the First Thaumaturgic Age. Well, not quite the end. Gorlois eventually made his way to what are now the British Isles, where he married a De Dannan witch and had a child with her. That child was Merlin. But Gorlois was immortal, and when his wife grew old, he left her, became a warlord in Cornwall, and took a younger wife, a Welshwoman named Igraine. With her, he had three daughters—Elaine, Morgana, and Morgause. Kira and I are descended from them. And, being half-breeds, they all inherited the ability to do magic. Merlin never forgave his father for abandoning his mother, so he helped a rival warlord named Uther Pendragon to defeat him. By the time Gorlois realized that Uther was being aided by magic, it was too late and he had been dealt a mortal blow. At the last instant, he flung his astral spirit from his dying body and it entered the fire opal in the ring he wore. That ring then passed to his daughter Morgana, and it became the source of much of her power. She became known as the sorceress Morgan Le Fay. And to take revenge for her father's murder, she seduced her half brother, Uther's son, Arthur, and had a child by him named Modred.''

"*That's* who Modred is?'' Natasha said with astonishment. "King Arthur's son?''

"The same,'' said Wyrdrune. "You know the story from there on, or at least the mythic part of it. Modred exposed the affair between Arthur's champion, Lancelot, and Queen Guinevere, and brought down Arthur's kingdom. By that time, Morgan Le Fay had already taken her revenge on Merlin. She posed as his pupil to learn everything he knew, then arranged to have him seduced by a young De Dannan witch named Nimue, who slipped him a sleeping potion. While Merlin was asleep, Morgan Le Fay had him placed in the cleft of a large oak tree and sealed him up inside it, under a spell to sleep for the next two thousand years. A living death. According to the legend, Modred and Arthur killed each other on the field of battle, but Modred had the blood of the Old Ones flowing in his veins. He recovered and survived for the next two thousand years, mainly as a mercenary in one war after another, amassing an incredible fortune over the centuries. Although he was a sorcerer, he gave up magic. It had never brought him anything but pain, and as the years passed, he grew more embittered and more cynical, dying by inches on the inside, even though he was practically immortal. He didn't know how much life he had, he was a half-breed and he knew he wouldn't live forever, but his life span was many times the human norm. In time, he became known as Morpheus, a predator who preyed on other predators, but always for a price. The world's top professional assassin. The law enforcement agencies of the world believe that it's a family tradition, handed down from generation to generation, and that there have been many different men named Morpheus, when in fact, it's been Modred all along. He had survived for all those years, up to the beginning of the Second Thaumaturgic Age, when Merlin awoke from his enchantment and brought back magic to the world.''

"We first met him when he accepted a contract on us," Kira said. "I was working as a cat burglar in Manhattan, and I read an article in the newspaper about the auction of the Euphrates artifacts, which had been unearthed in a dig. An Arab sorcerer who was one of Merlin's pupils had detected magical trace emanations coming from a subterranean cavern. He found the runestones and removed them from the circle where the Dark Ones were confined. And they possessed him. But in the meantime, the runestones were placed with the other artifacts that were discovered and they were to be sold at auction in New York, to licensed adept bidders. I read about it, and for some reason, I knew I had to have those stones. It was crazy; it was not my sort of job at all. A robbery in broad daylight, in front of a roomful of adepts, I don't know how I thought I'd pull it off. But I simply *had* to do it. I figured I'd steal the stones and fence them. Only it turned out Wyrdrune had the same idea."

"I was a graduate student of thaumaturgy in Cambridge," Wyrdrune said, "and I'd just had my scholarship yanked for practicing magic without a license." He grimaced. "I was low on money, and I was always looking for shortcuts back then. I came back home to New York, thinking to raise some money somehow so I could finish school, and I read that same article. And, like Kira, I was seized with an irresistible compulsion to get those stones. We both wound up hitting the auction at the same time. Kira snagged the stones while I effected our escape with a teleportation spell—''

''Which you couldn't do worth beans,'' Kira put in. ''I almost wound up materializing inside the wall of his apartment building.''

''Well, anyway, we were stuck with each other until we could fence the stones,'' said Wyrdrune, not anxious to dwell on the subject. ''At least, that's what we thought. Only the stones wouldn't stay fenced. We sold them to one fence, and they came back. We sold them again, to another fence, and they came back again. On top of that, the Dark Ones had sent their acolyte after us to get the stones back and destroy them. The police were after us; the B.O.T. was after us because magic had been used in the commission of the crime, and one of the fences that we sold the stones to was well connected. He couldn't afford having it get around that he could be ripped off, so he was willing to spend the money to put out a contract. He wanted to get the best man in the business for the job, partly so he could say he'd gotten the best man in the business, and he got him.''

''Modred,'' said Natasha.

''Exactly. Except when Modred finally caught up to us, something happened that nobody could have expected. By that time, I'd swallowed my pride and gone to Merlin for help. He was my old teacher, and I knew I was involved in something magical that was way over my head. It was Merlin who first figured out what the runestones were. But it looked as if Modred was going to take us out before Merlin could do anything to help. Of course, we didn't know it was Modred at the time. We just knew there was a hit man on our trail. And when Modred found us and came to make the hit, the runestones worked their magic. The spirits of the Council had been manipulating things all along, because we three were the descendants of Gorlois—Modred through his mother, Morgan Le Fay, and Kira and I through his other daughters, Elaine and Morgause. They had chosen us for that reason as their avatars, the ones through whom they would manifest their power. When we came face-to-face with Modred, the runestones became spellbound with us." He took off his headband, revealing the emerald stone. "Mine became magically embedded in my forehead. Kira's became implanted in her palm. And Modred's stone fused into the skin over the left side of his chest."

"Head, hand, and heart," Natasha murmured. "So that's why you read like you're so much older than you really are. You've become united with the spirits of the Council, in the stone. But where do Billy and Sebastian fit in?"

"I was getting to that," said Wyrdrune. "The Dark Ones weren't able to escape right away. They were weak from all those centuries of confinement, and they were using their acolyte to kill for them and funnel the life energies of his victims to them. When we became united with the stones, we suddenly knew the whole story and we realized we had to stop them. We had no choice. We almost got there in time. Merlin got there just ahead of us. He tried to fight them off until we could arrive and manifest the power of the Living Triangle, but they overwhelmed him and he died. We managed to get some of them, but some escaped. We don't know how many. But we thought we had lost Merlin."

"What they didn't know was that Merlin had left his body in his astral spirit, in a last-ditch effort to save his soul," Billy said. "He drifted for a while, until he found me. I was an orphan living on the streets in London, in and out of jail most of my young life. I was just fourteen. And then suddenly, one day, I awoke to find myself possessed. I thought I was going crazy. But it was Merlin's spirit. He had entered me because I was his descendant. Nimue, the witch who had seduced him for Morgana, had borne his child. In the beginning, we did not exactly get along too well. I wanted no part of him. It was just as difficult for him, suddenly finding himself in the body of a juvenile delinquent." Billy smiled. "Eventually, I met these two, and immediately knew who they were, because Merlin had known them, of course.

And we've been together ever since, trying to track down the surviving Dark Ones. As for Sebastian . . . well now, trying to explain Sebastian is a bit of a trick.''

''Modred and Sebastian have known each other for years,'' said Wyrdrune. ''A *lot* of years.''

''And Gorlois?'' Natasha said. ''Why do I have the feeling he's here, too?''

''Because he is,'' said Billy, tapping his chest. ''In here. Magic often works in mysterious ways. Call it fate, call it serendipity, or forces we don't completely understand, but his ring came into my possession and once I put it on, I couldn't get it off. I became the repository of both Merlin's spirit and that of his father, whom Merlin had helped Uther kill. It was not exactly the happiest of family reunions. It was like being a split personality until I was attacked and mortally wounded by one of the Dark Ones in New Mexico. I would have died, but Merlin and Gorlois gave up their life forces to fuse them with mine, in order to save my life. You might say I'm sort of a magical mutation, three different personalities blended into one. I aged in the process, and my entire physical appearance changed rather dramatically.''

''And Modred? What became of him?'' Natasha asked. ''I somehow get the impression that *you* were Modred,'' she added, looking at Wyrdrune with a puzzled expression. ''But after what you've said . . .''

''Your impression is right on,'' said Wyrdrune. ''I *was* Modred. We tracked one of the Dark Ones to Tokyo, Japan, and while we were there, Modred was attacked and killed. His runestone absorbed his life essence and bonded with me. Up until yesterday, we shared the same body, and Modred was able to manifest physically through me. But when we were attacked, Modred manifested and took the brunt of it. We thought it killed him. It almost killed me. But now we know he's still alive and out there somewhere.''

''What makes you so certain?'' asked Natasha.

''The runestones,'' Wyrdrune said. ''If he were dead, Kira and I would feel it. There's a link between us. And then there's what you told us about that police detective who participated in the raid on our penthouse. There was a story about him on the news this evening. He was supposedly brain dead, but right after they disconnected the life-support machinery, he got up and left the hospital. When we heard that, we knew that if he really *was* dead, then the only way he could have revived is if Modred's runestone bonded with him.''

"On the other hand, it could be a trap set by the B.O.T. to draw us out," said Kira.

"They did not release his name," said Billy. "If it was a trap, the Bureau would have given out more information."

"Angelo," Natasha said suddenly.

"What?" said Billy.

"The detective who was taken to the hospital. His name was Angelo. I just remembered that McGuire mentioned it, but I don't know his first name. I wasn't trying to read McGuire, and even if I was, all the impressions I was being bombarded with would have distracted me."

"Well, at least that's something," Wrydrune said. "It's certainly more than we had before."

"More coffee?" asked Broom.

"Thanks, Broom," said Wyrdrune wearily, holding out his cup.

"Oh, so now it's 'thanks, Broom,' is it? Where was all your gratitude when you just took off and left me?"

"Broom, not *now*, okay?"

"Sure, never mind me. I'm just a servant around here; I don't count for anything. Nobody ever thinks of me. So what if I have to drag my old bristles all over the city trying to find you?"

"Drag *what* bristles? You took a *cab*, for crying out loud!"

"You ever try riding in a taxicab when you can't bend over to sit down? And the way that cabbie drove, it's lucky we made it here in one piece, I'm telling you."

"Broom, put a lid on it, will you?" Wyrdrune said with exasperation.

"You hear the way he talks? That's the thanks I get for slaving over a hot stove for his supper, doing his laundry, mending the holes in his socks, making his bed every day, and fluffing up his pillows . . ."

"*Broom!*"

"All right, all right, I'm going already," said Broom, sweeping back into the kitchen in a petulant huff. "So what if I get dishpan hands and dustballs in my bristles? I'm only a poor, old broom, just prop me in the closet and leave me there, all alone in the dark. . . ."

"Are they always like this?" asked Gonzago.

"No, sometimes they're really a pain," said Kira with a grin.

"I *heard* that," Broom said.

"Astonishing piece of conjuring, that broom," Gonzago said. "Really quite amazing. Tell me, what spell did you use?"

"If I could remember, then maybe I could figure out how to undo it," Wyrdrune said sourly.

"I heard *that*, too!" Broom called from the kitchen.

"Can we get back to the situation at hand?" said Billy.

"Right," said Wyrdrune, turning to Natasha. "Well, you've heard the whole story, in a nutshell. So you still think we ought to go to the Bureau with it?"

Natasha gave a small snort. "I must admit I see your point. If I wasn't psychic and didn't know that you were telling me the truth, I'm sure I wouldn't have believed it, either. But surely, there's got to be a way to convince them."

"Convincing an individual is a lot easier than trying to convince an entire entrenched bureaucracy," said Billy. "Besides, the Bureau is vulnerable. After all, we were attacked by a Bureau agent who had been possessed."

"This time we've run into a Dark One who is real smart," said Wyrdrune. "A B.O.T. agent makes the perfect acolyte. They can command considerable resources, as you've seen."

"How can you stop them if the Bureau can't?" Natasha asked.

"Through the power of the runestones," Wyrdrune said. "The only problem is, without Modred, we can't manifest the Living Triangle. And without the power of all three rune-stones acting in concert, we don't know if we *can* stop them.''

"But if you knew to come here," she said, "and Modred has taken over Angelo's body, then wouldn't he know to come here, too?"

"That's the question we've been asking ourselves," said Wyrdrune. "If that was the case, he would have been here by now. Something's wrong. We're going to have to find him.''

"You realize we have more than just the problem of finding Modred," Billy said. "We were hit in our own place. That means we've been compromised. And Natasha told us that she felt only one man died in that elevator. It wasn't Angelo, so it must have been the other Bureau agent. I'd guess that the acolyte killed the other agent in the elevator and compelled Angelo to do his bidding. Then, when the attack failed, the necromancer abandoned the body he was inhabiting and fled.''

"So you're saying that a *dead man* organized the entire police raid?" Natasha said.

"No, not necessarily," Wyrdrune replied. "Remember that although they both employ the same principles, necromancy is inherently a great deal more powerful than thaumaturgy. The Dark Ones are capable of things that ordinary human adepts can't do. Magic is a demanding discipline, and they've had thousands of years to refine their art. Hell, it was theirs in the first place.''

"But . . . raising the dead?" Natasha said.

"It's not exactly raising the dead," said Billy. "Essentially, an acolyte, as we call them, is anyone who has been possessed by the Dark Ones, either placed under a spell of compulsion or literally taken over. They can do that with either a live body or a dead one. If they do it with a corpse, then the body doesn't actually come to life. Basically, it's a zombie that moves at the will of the necromancer. It continues to decay, of course. Take away that will and it collapses. But if it's done with a live person, then the individual could be possessed, enchanted, and controlled by the will of the necromancer, or else the person could enter the service of the necromancer of their own volition.''

"What probably happened with that Bureau agent was the necromancer possessed him, invaded his will, and then when he was through with him, he absorbed his life force," Wyrdrune said. "That probably happened just prior to the attack on us. The necromancer needed an extra boost before he launched the attack, so he used the agent's life force. Simply consumed it.''

"Jesus," said Natasha.

"That only gives you a glimpse of what we're up against," said Kira.

At that moment, Makepeace came back into the room and announced that Jacqueline was leaving Paris on the next available flight for New York. "I think we're going to need all the help that we can get," he said. "Which is why I've asked my friend, Morrison, to join us. And I also thought Ms. Ouspenskaya could be quite helpful, considering her special gift.''

"I don't know how special it is," she said. "It hasn't told me a single thing about you. I don't sense that you're shielding, but I still can't get a reading on you.''

"Ah, well, that's because I'm a fairy, my dear," Sebastian said.

Natasha frowned. "What does being gay have to do with it?''

Wyrdrune winced and said, "Ouch.''

"Not *that* kind of fairy," Makepeace said stiffly.

"Then what . . . Now wait a minute, you don't mean to tell me that . . . *You?*''

"What did you expect, Tinkerbell?''

"This has to be the strangest day of my life," Natasha said, shaking her head.

"I have a feeling that things are going to get much stranger before this is over," said Gonzago. "But I must say, it beats hell out of grading papers.''

"Some crew," said Natasha. "A dropout warlock, a cat burglar, a former juvenile delinquent, an alcoholic wizard, an overgrown fairy, and a psychic gypsy. Oh, and a talking broom, as well. The only thing we're missing is a witch with a pointy hat."

"Correction," Makepeace said. "We *have* a witch. Only I wouldn't mention anything about a pointy hat when Jacqueline arrives. It might offend her fashion sense."

Natasha rolled her eyes. "Please let this be a dream," she said.

"It's liable to be a real nightmare," Kira said. "Are you quite sure you want to be a part of this?"

"Suppose I said no?" Natasha replied. "Then what?"

"Then you'd be free to go," said Wyrdrune.

"With everything I know now?"

"What would you do, tell the deputy commissioner? And what do you think his reaction would be?"

"Knowing McGuire, he'd think I've gone off the deep end," she said. "No, I don't think this is something I can turn my back on. Knowing what I know now, I don't think I'd ever get a good night's sleep. But I do think I should go back to McGuire. I could be more help to you if I kept you posted on what the police were doing in this case."

"An excellent idea," Billy said. "But you realize what would happen if you were caught collaborating with us?"

"I don't imagine it would be anywhere near as bad as what would happen if one of those Dark Ones got his hands on me," she said.

"Good point," said Wyrdrune. "We can certainly use your help. But how will we keep in touch? We're safe enough here for the time being, but we may have to leave on very short notice."

"Allow me," said Makepeace. He went over to one of his bookshelves and selected an amulet from the shelf. It was a large amethyst mounted in gold, on a matching chain. He placed it around Natasha's neck. "It matches your hair," he said with a smile.

"What does this do?" she asked.

"It's keyed to me," he said. "If you want to reach me, simply take hold of it and think of me."

"That's all?"

"That's all."

"But what if I should lose it?"

Makepeace smiled. "See that window over there?"

"Yes?"

"Toss it out."

"What, you mean just throw it out the window?"

"As far as you can."

"Are you *sure*?"

"Trust me."

She did as he requested. She went over to the window, took the amulet from around her neck, glanced back at him uncertainly, and, when he nodded, threw it out the window as hard as she could. Then she turned around to face him once again. "Well, it's gone. What now?"

Makepeace simply lowered his gaze to her chest. She looked down. The amulet was hanging around her neck, between her breasts.

"Now *that's* what I call a good trick," she said. "Is this a runestone?"

"No, it's a blarney stone," said Makepeace.

She raised her eyebrows. "I thought that was a rock in Ireland."

"That is a blarney stone, as well," Makepeace replied. "A blarney stone is any mineral that has been infused with fairy glamor."

"Looks like you're stuck with it now," said Kira. "And with us, as well."

CHAPTER FIVE

"I CAN'T BELIEVE you actually had the nerve to come here," Case said, staring at the dapper-looking man seated across from his desk. Except, of course, he wasn't a man. Case knew that.

He looked perfectly normal, sitting there very calm and self-possessed in his custom-tailored suit, with his legs casually crossed. The golden coppery tone of his skin might have been a carefully cultivated suntan. His well-groomed hair was an uncommon, fiery shade of red, but it only served to accentuate his striking appearance. His eyes were a brilliant emerald green, so bright they almost seemed to glow, but it was hard to tell because of the tinted glasses that he wore. He looked like a highly successful young businessman. People might stare at him on the street, especially women, but only because he looked so fit and handsome. There was something about him, what most people would call presence, but Case knew it was the aura of a predator. A predator who was not human. And he actually had the nerve to come to his office.

"Why is that so difficult to believe?" the necromancer asked with a disarming smile that sent a chill through Case.

"You just walked into Bureau headquarters, as calmly as you please?" said Case.

"What of it? The so-called adepts on your staff are like somnambulists. Their abilities are paltry and ludicrously stunted, as are yours. What have I to fear from them?"

Or me, thought Case grimly. "I don't like it," he said. "It's taking a big chance. You promised me I'd be protected."

"The only protection you need to concern yourself with is protection from myself. I could easily destroy your will or drain you of your life force. You exist at my indulgence, Case. Never forget that."

"There's not much chance of that," said Case with weary resignation. He sighed. "That little escapade of yours has brought a hornets' nest down around my head. Why did you have to kill those men?"

"Because it was necessary. I could hardly have allowed witnesses."

"Well, it was all for nothing. You let them escape."

"If the police had done their job properly, the avatars would be dead by now and the runestones would have been destroyed. As it is, I had to cover my tracks as best I could."

"What was the plan? To frame them for the death of Whelen?"

"And the police detective, Angelo. If the S.W.A.T. team had arrived on time, they would have seen two bodies and me engaged in magical combat with the suspects, as I believe you call them. They would have opened fire and it would have been finished in a matter of seconds. But they were delayed and I was forced to drain energy from Angelo and Silver and retreat. I should have known better than to depend on humans."

"What the hell, we're merely mortal," said Case with a grimace.

"Spare me your sarcasm. What have you managed to learn?"

"Not much," said Case. "The police are still holding on

to their forensics report. McGuire's a cagey bastard. He might prove a problem."

"Then he shall have to be disposed of."

"That would cause an even greater problem. You don't just off the deputy police commissioner. McGuire's got a lot of friends in this town, a lot of pull. He's been around for a while and he's well connected. You don't mess with somebody who's got clout like that."

"Then he shall be your responsibility. Make sure he doesn't interfere."

"I'll do my best."

"Remember that you have just as much to fear from the avatars as I do," said the necromancer. "You are in my service now. They shall not differentiate between us."

"You're saying they could come after me?" said Case uneasily.

"If they are not stopped first."

"And I'm expendable, is that it?"

"Not so long as you remain useful."

"Right. And what happens to me when they're dead?"

"That depends entirely on you. If you continue to remain useful to me, you would benefit highly from our relationship, I can assure you. If not . . . Remember what became of Agent Silver."

Case moistened his lips. "Yeah. I'm not likely to forget."

"What is the current situation?"

"I've got to let McGuire finish his preliminary investigation. He's taken a personal interest in this, because of all the attendant publicity. I could order him to back off completely, but if I flex my muscles too much, it would only aggravate the situation. I've got to at least pay lip service to the idea of working with him. In any event, whatever his forensics people come up with, it'll be forwarded to me. That's standard operating procedure in a case like this. The N.Y.P.D. forensics adepts aren't idiots. They're bound to come up with something. Obviously, they'll realize Silver and Whelen were killed by necromancy, but they'll think that Cornwall did it.

If that's even the name he's using currently, which I strongly doubt. He'll realize that alias has been compromised.''

"So what you're telling me is that you have no idea where they are now?"

"Not at the moment. But they're not likely to be leaving town. We're watching all the bus terminals, train stations, and airports. We're keeping tabs on all rentals. We've got their descriptions circulated all over the city. Those people are hot as coals right about now. They're not going anywhere.''

"That is not good enough. I want them found.''

"We're working on it, believe me. It's our top priority case. I've had every field agent in this office drop everything else to concentrate on this exclusively. And the police are out combing the streets for them, as well. It's only a matter of time, believe me."

"Do not make the mistake of underestimating them," the necromancer said. "Remember that they are not ordinary humans. They are united with the spirits of the runestones. When that power is manifested, they are far more dangerous than you can imagine.''

"I'll keep that in mind. In the meantime, what have you done with Detective Angelo?"

The necromancer frowned. "Angelo? Angelo is dead.''

"Well, for a dead man, he sure seems pretty spry,'' said Case. "He had himself a walk, right out of the hospital.''

The necromancer stiffened. *"Why didn't you tell me this before?''*

"Well . . . I thought you knew. You mean . . . you weren't responsible?''

"No. No, I was not responsible.''

"I don't understand.''

"Fool! It can only mean one thing. One of the runestones must have bonded with him. Angelo is now an avatar. That means they are still at full strength. He must be found, at all costs.''

"That may not be easy," Case said. "Angelo was on the D.A.'s Organized Crime Task Force, working undercover. That means his files are restricted.''

"Restricted? What does that mean?''

"It means only the D.A.'s office has access to them."

"Does not the Bureau have authority in crimes involving magic?"

"It does, but we don't have proof of any crime here. That is, any crime involved in Angelo leaving the hospital. The media is treating the story the obvious way, as if the hospital screwed up in pronouncing him dead prematurely. Getting hold of Angelo's files could be tricky."

"Why are his files so necessary?"

"Because without them, there's no way of knowing where he's been living, or what he's been doing, or with whom he's been associating. That's the whole point of O.C.T.F. Specially selected police officers go undercover, acting as criminals in order to infiltrate organized crime operations in the city. They quite literally go underground. New lives are manufactured for them, and they establish new residences and entirely new patterns of behavior. They don't check in with their superiors at the police department; they're on loan to the D.A.'s Office of Special Investigations."

"All this is of no consequence," the necromancer said. "If Angelo has bonded with a runestone, then he will seek to join the others. Find them and you will find him, as well. How you do it makes no difference to me. Just see that it is done, and soon, or else I shall take matters into my own hands." He got up. "The next time I see you, I expect more progress. Or else . . ."

Case suddenly felt a blinding pain in his skull, as if it were being crushed. He opened his mouth to scream, but no sound came forth. He grabbed his head in agony, gasping for breath, his eyes bulging. Then, just as abruptly as it came on, the pain vanished.

"Merely a small reminder," the necromancer said. "Do not disappoint me, Case."

The telephone rang in the apartment. Angelo stared at it for a moment. After three rings, the answering machine clicked on. A moment later, there was a beep, and the message began to record.

"Angel? Where the hell are you? You were supposed to meet me an hour ago, for chrissakes! You think I got nothing better to do than cool my heels waitin' on your ass? You'd better have some damn good excuse, that's all I gotta—"

Angelo picked up the phone. "Hello?"

"Johnny? What the Christ? Do you know what time it is?"

"Who is this?"

"Who is it? What, are you kidding me? It's me, Vinnie, asshole! Where the hell have you been?"

"I've . . . had some trouble."

"Trouble? What kind of trouble? With the police?" The word "police" seemed to ring a bell. "Are you okay? Did they bust you?"

"Uh . . . no . . . no, they didn't bust me. It wasn't that. It . . . uh . . . was personal."

"Personal, my ass. I ain't got time for personal. What's the deal, are you gonna make it down here, or what?"

"Where are you?"

"Where do you think I am? I'm at Luigi's, waiting for you, you clown. You were supposed to be here an hour ago! We've got business and I haven't got all night. If you queer this deal, I'm not gonna be a happy man, you get my drift? I don't care how well connected you are, nobody screws with Vinnie Maldonado, got me? *Nobody!* Now get your ass in gear and get down here."

The receiver was slammed down on the other end. Angelo frowned. Vinnie Maldonado? Was he supposed to know that name? Apparently, he was. They had a meeting scheduled at Luigi's. Only where the hell was Luigi's? During the call, he had heard noise in the background, people talking, laughing, music playing . . . A bar or restaurant, most likely. He looked around for the phone book and found one on the lower shelf of the nightstand where the telephone was. He opened it and, a moment later, found what he was looking for. Luigi's Clam and Oyster Bar. The address was in Little Italy.

Okay, he thought, I recognized the address. That's something. And whoever Vinnie Maldonado was, he certainly seemed to know him. Apparently, they were business associates. *Why couldn't he remember?* The obvious thing to do was go meet Vinnie Maldonado and see if it jogged loose any memories. For some reason, he had a strong feeling that Vinnie Maldonado was not a friend, not someone to be trusted. He opened the drawer where the gun was. It was in a shoulder holster. He took off his jacket and slipped the holster on, then secured it to his belt. It felt good. Familiar. He put the jacket back on and checked the mirror. There was no telltale bulge. The jacket had been tailored to conceal it. Whatever "business" he had with Vinnie Maldonado, he had a good hunch it wasn't legal.

"Sir, I have Ms. Ouspenskaya on the phone," the sergeant said.

McGuire snatched up the receiver. "Natasha? Where *are* you?"

"I'm at the Frog and Dragon," she said.

"The coffeehouse down in the Village? What in God's name are you doing there? Do you realize I've got an All Points Bulletin out on you?"

"On *me*? Why?"

"Are you serious? I bend the rules by leaving you alone at a crime scene and you simply disappeared! Do you realize the position that put me in?"

"I'm sorry, Steve," she said, "I just had to get out of there. I was on overload. The psychic impressions in that place were making me sick."

"None of the officers down in the lobby and nobody else saw you leave."

"I took the stairs down. I couldn't go back in that elevator again. It was just too much. My head was spinning and I missed the first floor. I got mixed up, I guess. I kept going down the stairs until I got to the basement, so I went out through the parking garage and hailed a cab."

"Wonderful. Why didn't you call and let me know where you were?"

"Because I was drunk, that's why."

"You were *drunk*?"

"I had to numb my brain out. It happens sometimes, when I absorb too much. The only thing that takes the edge off is alcohol. It fogs my brain and dulls out my receptivity. I'm sorry, I didn't mean to cause you any trouble, but don't you think you overreacted just a bit? I mean, you really have an order out for my arrest?"

McGuire sighed. "Hell, I didn't know if something happened to you or if you were trying to pull something."

"What did you think I'd done?"

"I didn't know *what* to think," he said. "I never should have left you alone up there. For all I knew, something happened to you, or maybe you took it in your head to do something stupid."

"Why would I do that?"

"It wouldn't be the first time, Natasha. I still remember the time you picked up one of your impressions in the East Side Strangler case and decided to check it out for yourself. It almost got you killed."

"Yeah, but you caught him, didn't you? So is this going to be a lecture, or do you want to know what I found out?"

"All right, go ahead."

"No, I think maybe you'd better cancel that A.P.B. first, before some off-duty cop comes in here and hauls me off in handcuffs. If that happens, I swear to God, I'll sue."

"Okay, okay, I'll take care of it. But you stay right where you are. It's not that I don't trust you, Natasha, but . . . I don't trust you. Stay put. I'll meet you down there in about an hour. I have to meet somebody first."

"Take your time. I'm not going anywhere. I just ordered dinner. I'm always hungry when I'm getting off a drunk. I'll see you when you get here. Oh, by the way, how's that detective who went to the hospital?"

"You mean you haven't heard? It's been on all the news shows."

"No, what happened?"

"I'll fill you in when I get down there. Just sober up and don't go wandering off."

She hung up. "I'm pretty sure he bought it," she said.

"But that was taking a bit of a chance, wasn't it? What if they had traced the call?"

"It would have led them to a public telephone in Brooklyn," Makepeace said.

"How did you manage that?"

"Fairy magic."

"Right. I had to ask. Anyway, the detective's full name is John Angelo. I picked it up from McGuire when I asked about him. He's easy when his guard is down. I also picked up something about how he had to get Angelo's file from Christine. That's Christine Mathews, the district attorney. He's on his way to meet her now."

"Why would the deputy police commissioner need to get a police officer's file from the D.A.?" asked Wyrdrune.

"Angelo's with the Organized Crime Task Force," said Natasha. "It's a special unit Mathews put together with the backing of the mayor's office. A specially picked group of police officers assigned to work undercover to infiltrate organized crime activities in the city."

"And he doesn't have their files?" Wyrdrune asked.

"They're all working deep cover," Natasha replied. "Only Christine Mathews and her immediate staff administering the task force have access to the details of the operation. It was a big controversy in the department. She said there had been too many leaks in the past, so the current operational files are all restricted. Only two or three people have access to them."

"It makes sense," said Kira. "There's a lot at stake. It wouldn't be the first time police officials had been corrupted."

"So what happens now?" Natasha asked.

"You go and meet McGuire at the coffeehouse," said Wyrdrune. "Stick with the story we worked out. And try to find out as much as you can without seeming too obvious."

"That shouldn't be a problem."

"Oh, right. Of course."

"I wish we still had Archimedes," Kira said. "He would've had no trouble getting us Angelo's file."

"What happened to Archimedes?" asked Makepeace.

"Unfortunately, he took a sniper's bullet back in the penthouse," Billy said. "I'm really going to miss that little guy."

"We're not talking about a person, are we?" Natasha said.

"No, but he was very much alive. Archimedes was a very special little computer," Wyrdrune said. "He could have broken into any data bank in the country as easy as you please. But without Archimedes, we're going to have to do this the hard way."

"We follow McGuire?" Kira said.

Wyrdrune nodded. "In the meantime, we'll need to set up a new base of operations. We obviously can't go back to the penthouse, and I don't want to compromise Sebastian. It's too risky for us here. Too many people coming and going."

"Leave that to me," said Billy. "Sebastian will need to meet Jacqueline at the airport."

"What about me?" Gonzago asked. "How can I help?"

"By staying here and holding down the fort," said Wyrdrune. "If any of us runs into any problems, we'll contact you. Until we know more, we can't really make any other plans. We'll have to play this on the fly. And Modred, or Angelo, might show up here while we're gone. I hope. That would solve our biggest problem at the moment."

"What worries me is why he hasn't come here by now," said Kira. "You'd think this would be the first place he'd go."

"Unless he doesn't remember that," said Billy.

"What do you mean?" asked Wyrdrune.

"He took the full force of that attack and Angelo was brain damaged. There's also no way of knowing to what extent the runestone itself may have been affected. In order to protect itself, keep both of you alive, and then effect the bond with Angelo, the runestone had to have expended a great deal of energy. The laws of magic can't be violated. Even the runestones can be depleted."

"In other words, it's possible that Angelo may not have recovered fully," Wyrdrune said.

"And with the trauma, he may not be able to remember

anything," said Billy. "Which puts him into even greater danger. We know there's at least one necromancer out there, and he knows who Angelo is."

"And if he's been following the news, he knows the cop who was injured in that raid has left the hospital," said Kira.

"Exactly," Billy said. "It wouldn't take much for him to put it all together."

They were all silent for a moment, until Wyrdrune swore softly.

"I couldn't have said it better," Billy said. "We don't have any time to lose. If the Dark One finds him before we do, he may not even be able to defend himself."

"And if the Dark One takes his life force, he'll absorb the life force of the runestone, too," said Wyrdrune. "And then there'll be no stopping him."

The cab dropped him off in front of Luigi's. He paid the cabbie with money from the roll he'd found. There was more than enough left to support him for a while, but it would not last forever. And he was not sure where he would get more. He did not even know what he did for a living. By the look of things so far, whatever it was, it was probably illegal. He was not sure how he felt about that. It bothered him that he didn't know, but it did not seem to disturb his conscience. Perhaps this Vinnie Maldonado, whoever he was, would be able to shed some light on matters. But he was not sure how much to tell him. I'll simply have to play it by ear, he thought, as he went into the restaurant. Now the question was, how would he recognize Vinnie Maldonado?

Luigi's was hardly a fashionable, upscale restaurant. For all the working-class aura of its name, however, it was a very clean and pleasant, middle-income sort of place, small and intimate, with a long bar running along the right side and square-tabled booths covered with red and white checkered tablecloths along the left side. There were tables in the back, with Chianti bottles acting as candle holders in the center of each, and silverware neatly folded up in crimson napkins.

There were posters depicting scenes of Italy and Sicily framed on the walls and the place seemed to do a brisk business. A nice little neighborhood Italian restaurant.

"Johnny! Over here!"

A man was waving at him from a booth along the back dividing wall that separated the rear section from the lounge. He was looking right at him, with an impatient expression. Apparently, this was Maldonado. Angelo made his way over to his booth and slid in opposite him.

"Jeez, it took you fuckin' forever to get down here," Maldonado said. "I was starting to get real nervous about you, Johnny boy. There's a lot ridin' on this deal. You eat yet?"

"Uh . . . no, actually."

Maldonado raised his hand and snapped his fingers loudly several times. "The linguini with clam sauce is real good tonight. Go ahead, it's on me."

"Sounds fine. Thank you."

A waitress came and Maldonado gave her the order like an impresario. "And bring us another bottle of this nice Chianti," he added, "and a glass for my friend, here."

The waitress said, "Certainly, sir, coming right up," then turned, smiled at Angelo, and gave him a wink.

"Hey, I think she likes you," Maldonado said as she left. "You oughtta get yourself some of that. Sweet. Anyway, here's what it is." He leaned forward and lowered his voice. "The shipment's coming in soon, but I don't trust those bastards. They're actin' like they're tryin' to do business, but I wouldn't put it past 'em to pull a fast one. And the padrone wouldn't like that, you know what I mean? We already lost those two big shipments last month and that stuff doesn't come cheap. Once maybe, they get lucky, pick up some noise on the street, who knows? Twice in a row, it doesn't look so good. Somebody's got a big mouth. Word is you did good work up in Detroit. You came highly recommended and Tommy says you made a real favorable impression. He's got his eye on you for bigger things. Anyway, the thing is, he thinks we may have a problem with Joey."

"Which Joey is that?" asked Angelo.

"Joey Battaglia, you know, you met him. Cocky little son of a bitch, with the attitude and the fuckin' earring, likes to talk big?"

"Oh, him," said Angelo, not having any idea who he was.

"Yeah. Tommy wouldn't have taken him on, but he's Franco's sister's boy and, well, you know how it is. But the kid's a punk. He's got no class, and not much smarts, either. He's taken up with a goddamn whore, for Christ's sake. She got a place over in Soho, works the lounges over on Spring Street, pickin' up on the gallery crowd. Makes like she's an artist. Bullshit artist, if you ask me. Personally, the kid wants to make it with a hooker, it's no skin off my nose. It's his gonads that are gonna fall off, not mine. But maybe he's been talkin' too much. He ain't exactly subtle, and they've been seen around together a lot. It's bad for business, if you know what I mean. Like, it wouldn't take much for some cop to lean on her a little. Tommy thinks Joey's got a mouth on him, and he wants to find out if he's been talking to the broad. And if she's been talking to anybody else."

"And you want me to find this out?" said Angelo.

"You got the picture. Tommy's real anxious about this, so if Joey is the leak, we gotta find out now. I figure you and me take a ride over to Soho. I know where she's gonna be tonight. She's got habits like clockwork, that broad. I point her out, then you take it from there."

"I'm not sure exactly what it is you want me to do," said Angelo.

"Whatever it takes," said Maldonado, looking him directly in the eyes.

"Right," said Angelo.

The waitress brought the food.

"Enjoy your meal," Maldonado said.

McGuire sat leafing through the folder. "Angelico, huh? Wasn't that a little obvious?"

"Maybe, to somebody who knew him. But he worked street-level undercover vice before, under a number of different names, and he wasn't in contact with any of the people he's been investigating on this assignment. We worked with the F.B.I. to manufacture a cover identity for him as Giovanni Angelico, alias Johnny Angel, former mob muscle from Detroit. They had a mob lieutenant there nailed cold and turned him into an informer. They set it up so Angelo was able to use him as a reference. Besides, Angelo looks completely different now. When he was working Vice, he looked like a real dirtbag. Even his own mother wouldn't have recognized him. He's got a real talent for changing his appearance." She paused. "Or should I say had?"

McGuire shook his head. "I don't know. This zombie thing . . . it gives me the creeps. Sounds like something out of a horror movie. Magic is one thing, but this . . ."

"If his body is being controlled by someone, you don't think he . . . it . . . would have gone home, do you?"

"I don't know what to think. I'm still not really sold on the idea, but at least it will give us a place to start. Our adepts tell me that when someone is possessed like that, theoretically, the controlling adept has access to his memories. Of course, none of them have ever tried it, so they don't know for sure. It's not the sort of thing they teach in graduate programs of thaumaturgy."

"So then how do they know?"

"The B.O.T. holds periodic briefings for police adepts in necromancy. Apparently, they've encounted it before. But our people tell me they're not sure how it works with a corpse. If he were still alive when the possession occurred, or very recently deceased, then possibly the controlling adept would be able to have access to his memories, but that sort of thing is really beyond their level of expertise."

"Then shouldn't we be bringing the Bureau in on this?" she asked.

McGuire pursed his lips. "Technically, we should. It's their jurisdiction. But then, technically, as deputy commissioner, I shouldn't even be involved directly in a police investigation."

"Except?"

McGuire sighed. "Except I don't have the sense to mind my own business."

"This thing really got to you, didn't it?" she said.

"I don't like not knowing what the hell is going on," he said. "And I don't like the feeling I have about this case. I also don't like the feeling that the Bureau knows a lot more about this than they're admitting to. My department was played for a bunch of suckers, and I especially don't like that."

"You know, I just had a real unpleasant thought," said Mathews. "If your police adepts are correct in their supposition that whoever is controlling Angelo's body might have access to his memories, then what happens if he goes back to being Johnny Angel?"

McGuire shook his head. "I don't know. How much about your operation does he know, beyond just his end of it?"

"A lot."

"Then I guess you'd have a real problem."

"Are you done looking at that file?"

He handed it back to her. "I got the gist."

"Okay, let's go."

McGuire raised his eyebrows. "Go where?"

"To Angelo's apartment, where else?"

"I don't think that would be smart," McGuire said. "Let me take it from here."

"No way, Steve. I've got to know. I've got to find out if the task force has been compromised. If so, then we're going to have to move very, very quickly to pull all our people out."

"Chances are we won't find anything at that apartment," said McGuire. "And I don't want to put you at risk. You're an attorney, Christine, not a trained police officer. And I've got just as much of a stake in this as you do. Your task force people *are* my officers, after all. Look, I promise to keep you personally posted on everything we learn, as soon as we learn it. Fair enough?"

She moistened her lips nervously. "I suppose it will have to be. But I want you to know I'm not very comfortable about leaving the Bureau out of it. If anything goes wrong, you'll have your head handed to you.''

"Don't you think I know that? Thanks for the help, Christine.''

"Don't mention it. And I *do* mean, don't mention it. We never had this discussion.''

He smiled. "Would you perjure yourself by swearing to that under oath?''

She did not return his smile. "Just watch me.''

He watched her leave and then glanced at his watch. He still had twenty minutes to meet the Gypsy. He hoped Natasha would still be there. She was a gifted psychic, no question about that, but when it came to things like keeping her appointments, she was not very responsible. Come to think of it, she was not very responsible about a lot of things, he thought.

The drive down to the Village was expedited by the siren and the flashing light, one of the perks of being deputy police commissioner. Another perk was carrying a gun. He hadn't carried a gun in a long time, but before he left, he had taken his old semiautomatic out of its box in the desk drawer and strapped on his belt holster, though as he drove down to the Frog and Dragon coffeehouse on Bleecker Street, it occurred to him that there might not be much point to shooting a man who was already dead.

A part of him did not want to involve Natasha in this any further, but another part of him knew he'd *need* a psychic to figure out this crazy case. He already had several detectives working on it, assisted by police adepts. Why was he getting involved personally? It probably wasn't smart. But Christine had been right. This thing had gotten to him. And for some reason, he didn't trust Case.

He couldn't put his finger on why, but his cop instincts had always been good. They hadn't had a workout in quite a while, true, but his nose was telling him that there was something wrong with Case. Part of it, he had to admit, was personal prejudice. He simply didn't like the man. Ever since he took over the New York Bureau office, Case had maintained a condescending attitude toward the department, as if they were mere scut workers while it was the Bureau that handled all the important matters. To some extent, of course, that was true. The department was neither trained nor equipped to deal with magic crime, except for minor misdemeanors and the like, but Case had an attitude problem. He was a petty power junkie.

McGuire had seen his type many times before and they were always the same. Little men who sought comfortable niches in bureaucracies that would enable them to lord it over people. Unlike people who had *real* power, they could not discriminate. They took refuge in things like policy and regulation and were utterly inflexible. More often than not, they could be found holding down a desk at a public utility or in an administrative branch of some hospital or corporation, where the pecking order was rigidly established and their authority was clearly defined. At best, they could be merely irritating. At worst, they could be maddening impediments to progress. There was usually only one way to deal with them, and that was to go over their heads to someone with more clout, play the game their way, and either use a connection or become a mild irritant to someone in a position well above them. Suspend an anvil on a string above their heads and then draw their attention to the scissors in your hand. Then suddenly they became very cooperative and polite.

Case, however, was one of the worst examples of the breed, a man who had actually managed to worm his way into a position of some significant power. The only way to go over his head would be to go to Bureau Headquarters in Washington, and McGuire had no legs to stand on. No one in the Bureau owed him any favors, and while there were some favors he could call in with people who would have some influence, this was not the time or the situation for that. He was clearly out of bounds. He had purposely delayed in having the forensics reports submitted to the Bureau office, and instead of turning the entire matter over to Case, as he was supposed to do, he was poaching on the Bureau's turf, to say nothing of acting outside the limits of his office by playing detective.

"You've lost your objectivity, McGuire," he mumbled to himself. The proper thing to do was tell the driver to turn this car around, levitate it right back to the garage, then get those reports to Case and just forget about the whole damned thing. That was exactly the right thing to do. "Screw that," he said.

CHAPTER
SIX

~~~

THE LOUNGE, AS Maldonado called it, was really no more than a bar and nobody seemed to be lounging. It was a large, high-ceilinged room with a heavily varnished wood floor and a long mahogany bar behind which three bartenders were kept busy. The place was crowded and few people were sitting. Everyone was milling about, dressed very fashionably in outfits of neo-Edwardian and renaissance punk, seeing and being seen, posing and deprecating other poses. There was music playing, some kind of high-stress, metronomic, syncopated dirge punctuated by inner-city noises such as sirens, shots, and jackhammers. The undertone of conversation blended with it in a strange, ethereal way. It gave the atmosphere of the place a decided edge.

"That's her over there, with the legs," said Maldonado, pointing out a young woman in a chain-mail and black leather jacket, a short red skirt slashed clear up to her hips, so that it was practically a loincloth, and graceful, high-heeled sandals. She had long blond hair artfully streaked with blue, and she wore bright, wet-looking lipstick. She was rocking her head slightly in time to the music and, at the same time, casually looking all around the room. She had, thought Angelo, the look of a hungry tigress.

"Her name's Donna, but she calls herself Blue," said Maldonado. "Rents a loft just down the street, calls it her studio. Has a roommate, an artist's model or something, but she never seems to be around. Joey's been bragging that both of 'em have pulled the train for him. Who knows, maybe they have. If you like what you see, nothing says you can't have yourself a little fun before you start takin' care of business. Do what you gotta do. Nobody's gonna cry over a slut like that. Call me tomorrow and let me know what you found out."

Maldonado clapped him on the shoulder, got up, and left. Angelo simply stood there, not knowing what to do. Maldonado's words had been ambiguous, but the implication was clear. He was expected to at least rough her up, "whatever it takes," to get information out of her about Joey Battaglia, whom he didn't even know, or if he knew him, he could not remember. And Maldonado had even hinted that if he killed her, no one would shed any tears.

What kind of people was he mixed up with? What was this shipment that was coming in? It sounded like drugs, or something equally illegal. Jesus, I must be with the mob, thought Angelo. What was this work he was supposed to have done in Detroit? Was he a killer? That thought brought him up short. He suddenly felt certain that he *had* killed before, not once or twice, but many times. And at the same time, he felt repugnance for the thought.

I can't go through with this, he told himself. But at the very least, I've got to warn this woman. Simply because she was a prostitute, that was no reason for her to be beaten up or even killed. And if he didn't do it, someone else probably would. And what would happen to *him* if he didn't do it? Maldonado expected to be called tomorrow. He didn't even know Maldonado's phone number. Perhaps it was somewhere in the apartment. He suddenly decided he would not go back there. The place had felt vaguely familiar, but it wasn't home, and there was nothing there he wanted. And when he did not do what was expected of him, it was the first place they would look for him.

He waited until there was an empty space at the bar and walked up next to her. Her eyes slid over him as he took his place at the bar. She smiled. "Well, hi," she said, and slowly moistened her lips. "What's your name?"

"Johnny."

"Hi, Johnny, I'm Blue."

"I'm sorry to hear that. Will it cheer you up if I buy you a drink?"

She laughed. "Hey, that's original, I like that. I like guys who are quick. But not *too* quick."

"What are you drinking?" he asked.

"Vodka and tonic."

"A vodka and tonic for the lady," Johnny said, "and I'll have . . ." What did he drink? "I'll have your best single malt Scotch," he said, which was the first thing that came into his mind.

"Oooh," she said, "a man who's serious about his Scotch."

"So . . ." He wasn't quite sure how to begin. "I see you're alone here. Are you waiting for someone?"

"No, just hanging out. Why, what's on your mind?"

"That could be a dangerous question," he said.

"So give me a dangerous answer," she replied. "What do you like?"

"Are you working?"

"Everybody works. Why, you a cop?"

"Do I look like a cop?"

"Cops dress sharp and grow beards these days," she said.

"Maybe you're a cop," he said.

"Then where am I hiding my gun?"

"Under that jacket, maybe."

"The jacket comes right off," she said, slipping out of it. Underneath, she wore a chain-mail halter that left nothing to the imagination. "So, you like what you see?"

"Nice," said Angelo.

"I've got a place just down the street. You interested?"

The bartender brought their drinks. Angelo took out his roll to pay for them. Her eyes got big when she saw it.

"Well, I guess you do all right," she said, staring at the roll greedily. "Two hundred and I'm off for the whole night."

"Okay," he said, and started to peel off the bills.

"Hey, not *here*, all right? Come on, we'll go to my place."

She tossed back her drink, put her jacket back on, took his arm, and walked him outside. On the sidewalk, she snuggled closer to him and bumped her hip up against his side. Abruptly she pulled away.

"Hey, that's a gun!" she said. "You *are* a cop, you scumbag!"

She started to move away, but he grabbed her arm. "Wait . . ."

"Let go of me!"

"I'm *not* a cop," he insisted. But for some strange reason, that sounded wrong somehow.

"Yeah, bull—*shit*!"

"Listen to me, you're in danger."

"Yeah, from *you*, asshole. Let *go* of me!" She tried to jerk away.

He kept his grip firm. "Not from me. From Joey Battaglia's friends."

She stopped struggling suddenly and stared at him. "What the hell is this? How do you know Joey?"

"Joey ever talk about any of his friends?" said Angelo. "Tommy? His uncle Franco? Vinnie Maldonado?"

"What are you, a narc? Who the hell are you?"

"I don't know," he said.

"What do you mean, you don't *know*?"

"I mean something happened to me and I woke up in a hospital the other day and I couldn't remember a thing. I seem to be somebody named Johnny Angel and Maldonado just brought me here to work you over so I could find out if Joey's been talking about the shipments. Maybe even kill you. But I'm not going to do it, I swear. I just wanted to warn you."

"Holy shit," she said, turning pale. "Holy fucking shit."

"Look, I'm not going to do anything," said Angelo, "but I'm supposed to call Maldonado tomorrow and let him know what happened. When he doesn't hear from me, he's probably going to come looking for me. And Joey's friends are going to come looking for you."

"Oh, God. Oh, Jesus, no. . . ."

"They know where you live. You've got to get away somewhere."

"Christ. Why are you doing this?"

"I told you, I lost my memory somehow. All I know is that I'm supposed to be somebody named Angelico, who's also known as Johnny Angel, and apparently I'm involved with the mob. But if that's who I was, I'm not that person now. I don't want any part of it."

"This is on the level, isn't it?" she said.

"It's a nightmare, that's what it is," Angelo replied.

"They're going to come after you, too, when you don't do . . . what you're supposed to do. You know that, don't you?"

"I know. I don't care. I just can't go through with it. I simply can't believe I was someone like that, but Maldonado seemed to know me, and he said something about some work I did up in Detroit. . . . I think I must be losing my mind." His head was starting to hurt.

"Hey, you all right?"

"No. I don't think so. I feel dizzy."

"Come on, we'll go to my place."

"Didn't you hear what I just said?"

"I heard, believe me. But you're supposed to be working me over tonight, or maybe dumping my body somewhere. They're not gonna come looking until tomorrow, at least. Meanwhile, I gotta get some stuff together so I can split and you look like you're about to fall down. Come on, lean on me."

He suddenly felt weak. It seemed to him as if he were hearing voices in his head, like a distant chorus of whispers, but he could not make out what they were saying. She helped him down the street about two blocks to her building. They took an old freight elevator up to her loft. There wasn't much to it. It was spacious, but very sparsely furnished. There was a black leather couch and loveseat, a coffee table, a few potted plants, a kitchen table and some chairs by the kitchenette at the back, an expensive entertainment system, a large futon bed with a mirror on the wall beside it, but mostly the place was bare, save for the paintings on the walls and an artist's easel set up on a large, paint-spattered canvas dropcloth underneath the skylight. She helped him to the couch and headed for the kitchen, where she opened the refrigerator and took out a bottle of vodka.

"You look like you could use a drink," she said, bringing it to him with a glass. "Sorry, I don't have any Scotch."

He poured himself a glassful and took a healthy slug. It warmed him and he seemed to feel a little better. She sat down on the chair beside him.

"You really don't remember who you are?"

"I can't seem to remember anything."

"How do you know you're Johnny Angel?"

"I found myself in his apartment. I found the gun, the money, his ID bracelet, his suits . . . they seemed to fit like they were made for me. And then Maldonado called and recognized my voice. He said we were supposed to meet at Luigi's and when I got there, he recognized me and waved me over. I didn't know him from Adam. That's where I learned everything else, listening to him while he told me what I was supposed to do. It seems the police have seized several of these shipments they're bringing in—drugs, I guess—and somebody named Tommy thinks Joey's got a big mouth. They know Joey's been seeing you and they don't like it. They think he's been bragging to you, talking big and boasting about what they were doing, and they suspect you've been tipping off the police. And that's about all I know."

"Jesus Christ," she said. "We're fucking dead. They'll probably kill Joey, too."

"No offense, but for some reason, I'm not too worried about Joey."

"To hell with Joey. He's a real sick puppy. Here I think I've met myself a real high roller and turns out all he wants to do is watch me with my tricks and then slap me around and call me names. He gets into my life and then I can't figure out how to shake him. He scared me, with all his talk about his connections."

"So he did talk to you?"

"Yeah, but I didn't say nothing to nobody. Like I said, he scared me. I was trying to find another place so I could move and maybe lose him, but it looks like I waited a little too long. Damn, we've gotta get out of here." She got up, removed her heels, and started running around the place, collecting her belongings and throwing them into a suitcase. "You better call us a cab," she said as she ran around, wasting no time.

"Us?" he said.

"Well, I can't just run out on you after you saved my life," she said. "You've got amnesia. Where you gonna go?"

"I have no idea."

"That's what I mean."

"You believe me?"

She didn't stop moving. "Yeah, I believe you."

"Why?"

"Who'd make up a story like that?"

"What if it's just a bluff to get you to leave with me?"

She stopped for a moment and looked at him, then shook her head. "No, I don't think so. If you wanted to do me, you'd do it right here. Who's around to see? Besides, you're hurtin', honey. I can tell."

"I appreciate your trust," he said wearily.

"Hell, the mess I'm in, I've gotta trust somebody," she said, throwing things into a suitcase. "Besides, we've both gotta split and you're the one with all the cash. Call that cab."

"Where are we going?"

"To a hotel. Someplace they won't think to look for us." She thought a moment. "The Plaza. What the hell, you can afford it. We'll figure out what to do when we get there."

Angelo reached for the phone.

"He's been here," said Natasha, looking around the bedroom.

"Are you sure?" McGuire asked, checking the drawers and the closets.

"I'm sure," she replied, picking up the white hospital gown from the floor beside the bed.

"Oh," said McGuire, a little sheepishly. "I would've found that, eventually." He shook his head. "How the hell did he get all the way here from the hospital dressed like that?"

"Maybe he took a cab," Natasha said.

"Is that right? Where did he keep his wallet?"

"I'm picking up a real feeling of confusion," she said, squeezing the gown in her hands. "He's lost. He doesn't seem to know who he is. I don't think he even knew how he got here."

McGuire saw the light blinking on the answering machine and punched the playback button. *"Angel? Where the hell are you? You were supposed to meet me here an hour ago, for Christ's sake! You think I got nothing better to do than cool my heels waitin' on your ass? You'd better have some damn good excuse, that's all I gotta—"* The message tape clicked off.

"He must have picked up the phone," McGuire said.

"Do you know who that is?" Natasha asked.

McGuire shook his head. "No."

"Don't touch the phone," she said. "Let me see it."

He moved away. She rewound the tape and played it back again while she held on to the receiver, her eyes closed.

"Maldonado," she said, her eyes still closed as she held on to the receiver.

"Vinnie Maldonado?" said McGuire.

She opened her eyes. "Yes, I think that's it."

"You're good," he said with admiration.

"Yeah, you only want me for my mind. So you do know him."

"I know *of* him. He's one of Tommy Leone's chief lieutenants in the Lucchese family. Christine's not going to like this. Did you get anything else?"

"Something about a meeting."

"Well, *that* part's on the tape," he said wryly.

She grimaced. "Let me try again."

She rewound the tape and played it back again while she held on to the receiver, concentrating. "Luigi's."

"I know the place. It's in Little Italy. You done with that phone?"

"I guess."

He took it from her and called in, ordering a stakeout on the apartment, then he hung up and said, "Let's go."

"Where are we going?"

"Luigi's Clam and Oyster Bar."

"Great, I'm hungry."

"I thought you just had dinner."

"All this psychic stuff gives me an appetite," she said.

He shook his head. "You're an expensive date."

"Yeah, but on the other hand, I know exactly what you like."

"I don't want to talk about it."

She started making clucking noises, like a chicken.

"Hell, come on," he said with exasperation, taking her arm.

"Oooh, I love it when you're masterful," she said as he pulled her out of the apartment.

"They're leaving," Kira said, watching from the cab double-parked across the street as McGuire and Gypsy came out of the apartment building and got into their car.

"That didn't take long," she said.

They watched as McGuire's car sped off.

"They found something," Kira said. "They seem in an awful hurry."

"Follow them," said Wyrdrune to the cabbie.

Without a word, the cabbie levitated the car and it skimmed off about a foot off the ground after McGuire's unmarked unit. The cabdriver was a lower-grade transportational adept, which meant he only knew the basic spells of low-level levitation and impulsion, enough to get him his hack license. He would have been no match for Wyrdrune, even without his runestone. Wyrdrune had no real qualms about placing him under a spell of compulsion. It was strictly unethical, of course, but he told himself the cabbie wasn't doing anything he wouldn't have done anyway, more or less. He would simply find himself in another part of town much later, unable to account for a block of his time, and with nothing on his meter. But he would have a very large tip.

"We're heading toward Little Italy," Kira said. "I wish I knew what they found out up there."

"They found out Angelo got a call from a hood named Vinnie Maldonado," Wyrdrune said, "and he was supposed to meet him at a place called Luigi's Clam and Oyster Bar in Little Italy."

Kira stared at him. "How the hell did you know that?"

Wyrdrune pulled an amulet out from under his shirt. It was an exact match of the one Makepeace had given Natasha. "The reception is particularly good," he said, tapping his head with his forefinger. "I guess her being psychic helps."

"Very sneaky," Kira said. She punched him in the arm. "Why didn't you tell me?"

"I didn't have a chance. Sebastian only slipped this to me as we were leaving," he said, tucking the amulet back underneath his shirt. "We worked up the spell together about two weeks ago, as a way of trying to keep in touch with our friends. The only problem is, it's limited by distance. There's only enough resonance to broadcast clearly for about three miles, and the reception starts getting rapidly weaker after that until it fades out completely at about five. We were hoping to find a spell that would increase its strength, but the trouble is, you'd need larger and larger stones to a point where it gets impractical. But in this case, it comes in real handy."

"You don't trust her?" Kira asked.

"No, it isn't that," he replied. "Gypsy's okay. She understands what we're up against. I just don't think she fully appreciates the danger. She's impulsive and she strikes me as a risk taker."

"I guess it takes one to know one, huh?"

"You should talk."

"Why would Modred go to meet some hood?"

"Modred wouldn't," Wyrdrune said. "Angelo might,

though. Gypsy told McGuire she picked up something about Angelo feeling confused and lost, not really knowing who he was. It fits with what Billy suggested. Modred's probably got amnesia from the trauma. Either that or he's just out of it. Maybe he's not even Modred anymore, but someone new, a combination of Angelo and himself, the way Billy's a combination of himself, Merlin, and Gorlois.''

"So that means we've lost Modred?"

"Not necessarily. We didn't lose Billy when he changed, did we? He simply became something more than what he was.''

"But he suffered a severe trauma, as well," said Kira. "He almost died. Why didn't the same thing happen to him?"

"Hard to say," said Wyrdrune. "For one thing, don't forget both Merlin and Gorlois were a lot stronger than Modred. And then there's the fact that Modred's already died once before, in a manner of speaking. I don't know. There's also the fact that Angelo had been possessed by the Dark One and it sounds like he had his life force drained. There seems to have been enough left to sustain him for a while, until he got to the hospital, but he was pronounced brain dead shortly after he got there. The runestone had already bonded with him by then. It had to have happened just after the Dark One siphoned off Angelo's life energy through his acolyte. The runestone bonded with a host that was hanging on by a bare thread. And Modred had been hurt. That's a lot of damage to overcome and even the runestones have to have their limits.''

"Can you pick up what they're talking about now?" asked Kira, looking ahead of them through the windshield at McGuire's car.

Wyrdrune nodded. "McGuire's worried that this thing is escalating more and more out of his control, not that he had any control to begin with. He didn't tell the D.A. he was bringing Gypsy in on this, and he's concerned about how he's going to explain the whole thing to the commissioner. Gypsy's picking up a lot from him, too, and I'm getting that, as well. It's real interesting.''

"How so?"

"He knows she can read him, but he doesn't seem very concerned about it. He likes her and apparently they've got some history."

"Oh, it's like that."

"Sort of. Push never really came to shove, apparently. The thing that's really interesting is that he doesn't seem to trust Case, the local Bureau chief. He doesn't like him to begin with, but he also thinks Case knows more about this than he's letting on. At least to him."

"Well, we know that's true enough," said Kira. "The Bureau's got a file on us, except they've got it backward. They think *we're* the necromancers."

"McGuire could be useful," Wyrdrune said. "I realize that part of what I'm getting is filtered through Gypsy's perception of him, and she likes him, but look at what he's doing. The deputy commissioner is not supposed to be working on a case himself. He's got detectives assigned to this thing, but he's decided to handle this personally. He took the book and tossed it right out the window, because he's got his own way of doing things. Remind you of anyone we know?"

"Mike Blood of Scotland Yard," she said.

"Bingo. Seems like they're both cut from the same cloth."

"You're thinking of bringing him in with us?"

"Maybe. Let's see what he does. But having the deputy police commissioner of New York City on our team would certainly make things a lot easier for us in this town."

"They're stopping," Kira said.

"Yep, there's Luigi's," Wyrdrune said. He had the cabbie stop a short distance down the block. "Okay, let's see what happens now."

"McGuire, commissioner's office," he said, showing the bartender his shield and ID.

"I know who you are, Mr. McGuire," the man said. "What can I do for you?"

"Was Vinnie Maldonado here today?"

"He sure was, but you didn't hear it from me."

"Did he meet anyone?"

"Yeah, some guy. Don't know his name. Dark hair, beard, flashy clothes. They were sitting over in the back booth there. Don't know what they talked about, though. Don't want to know."

"How long ago did they leave?"

"I dunno. Couple hours, maybe. Can't say for sure. Place was busy. Toni waited on 'em."

"Can I speak to her?"

"Sure." He called the waitress over. The waitress essentially corroborated what the bartender said, except she gave a better description of the man Maldonado had met. It was undoubtedly Angelo. She pointed out the booth where they were sitting. It was occupied. McGuire went over to the middle-aged couple sitting there.

"Excuse me, folks," he said, showing his shield and ID to them. "I'm sorry to interrupt your meal, but there were some felony suspects sitting here a little earlier today and I'd like to ask you to let us examine this booth for a moment. I'm sorry for the inconvenience; if you'll wait over by the bar, the department will pick up your tab."

The man looked at his wife. "Sounds like a good deal to me," he said, sliding out of the booth. "Help yourself."

As the couple left, McGuire and Gypsy slid into the booth. "Well, can you get anything?" he asked her.

She shook her head. "I don't know. They've changed all the silverware, of course, and there've been people sitting here since then. That'll muddy everything out."

"Try."

She closed her eyes and sat very still for a moment. Then she made a face and shook her head again. "I'm sorry, Steve. I'm picking up more about the couple who just left than anything else."

"Damn. Wait a minute." He waved the waitress over. "Toni, you still have the check for those people we asked you about, don't you?"

"Sure thing. Got it right here," she said, taking it out of her apron pocket.

"Would you give it to her, please?" McGuire said, indicating Gypsy.

She handed the check to Natasha.

"We'll give it back when we're finished looking at it, thank you," said McGuire.

The waitress shrugged. "Don't know what there is to see. They had some wine and linguine is all. Take your time, though." She went off to see to her other tables.

"Anything?" McGuire said.

Gypsy held the check in her hand, frowning slightly. "Angelo didn't touch it," she said. "I'm getting the other guy, Maldonado. And the waitress. She's having boyfriend trouble."

"I don't want to hear about the *waitress*," said McGuire.

"Something about shipments," said Natasha, frowning. "And somebody named Joey. Mean anything?"

McGuire shook his head. "Could be anybody. Can't you get anything else?"

She crumpled the check up in her fist and closed her eyes. After a moment she opened them quickly. "Oh, boy," she said.

"What is it?"

"Maldonado wants Angelo to take care of somebody, a woman," she said. "A hooker, I think, or maybe he just thinks of her as being a whore. Something to do with Joey and these shipments. I'm not really getting anything else." She flattened the check on the tabletop and smoothed it out a little with her hand. "Somebody named Tommy," she said.

"Tommy Leone?"

"Maybe. He's angry about the shipments. And Joey." She shrugged. "Joey Something. Something Italian, with a B. That's all I can get. I'm sorry, Steve."

"Maybe it's enough," he said. "Let's cross our fingers. I've got to make a phone call."

They relinquished the booth back to the people who were sitting there, McGuire took care of their bill, then asked to use the phone in the office. He looked at his watch, then dialed.

"Christine? McGuire. Look, I'm at Luigi's. I found out Angelo met with Vinnie Maldonado here a few hours ago. Does Tommy Leone know anybody named Joey, last name something with a B, Italian?"

"Joey Battaglia," she said immediately. "Franco Maranallo's nephew. A real sleaze. Likes to beat up women, especially hookers."

"Was there someone in particular he was associating with? A hooker, I mean, or some other woman?"

"Hold on a moment, I can check Angelo's most recent reports," she said. "Why, have you got something?"

"Yeah, I think so. Tommy Leone's upset about losing some shipments. And he's angry at Joey. It looks as if he thinks Joey's been talking too much to some woman, a hooker, perhaps."

"Yeah, we had the D.E.A. seize two of their shipments last month, street value of over two million dollars. Angelo gave us the tip. It must have really hit Leone where it hurts. Let me see, Battaglia, Joey . . . here we go." He heard the rustling of papers in the background. "Known associates . . . hmmmm . . . I'm sorry, Steve, nothing here about any women, hookers or otherwise. Apparently Angelo didn't think there was anyone significant."

"Shit," said McGuire.

"Why, what have you come up with?"

"You're not going to like this. I think Maldonado sent Angelo out after some woman this Joey Battaglia's been associating with."

"What do you mean, he sent him *after* some woman?"

"Maybe to work her over, possibly even kill her."

"Wait a minute," she said. "Are you *sure*? I thought you said Angelo was being controlled by some adept?"

"That's how it looks," McGuire said.

"So what the hell is he doing taking orders from Maldonado?"

"I don't have the faintest idea. It's possible he's not being controlled, after all."

"I thought you said he was a zombie?"

"I said that my people said it was possible," McGuire said. "There may be some other explanation for why he died and didn't stay dead. Maybe the hospital really did screw up, I don't know. But there's a chance he may not know who he really is. That is to say, he may actually think his cover identity is his real identity."

He heard her sigh. "You're telling me that Angelo might think he's really Johnny Angel and he's taken a contract on some woman?"

"I'm afraid it's possible."

"Dear God. You've got to stop him."

"I will, if I can find him. But you were the best lead I had. I can check with some of my people, but it would be a crap shoot. They won't have your intelligence, because you've played it so close to the vest with your task force."

"Get off my back, Steve. Hell. I'm sorry. Look, I'll see what I can do. I'll check with some of my people, see if anybody knows more about who Battaglia's been seeing. It might take some time, though."

"We may not have much."

"Then get the hell off the phone." She hung up.

CHAPTER
SEVEN

"WHAT THE HELL is this?" said Case, staring at his terminal monitor screen. "The files on Angelo are restricted?"

"Detective John Angelo has been detached to special duty with the Organized Crime Task Force," the computer replied. "I am unable to access his personnel files."

"Did you inform the N.Y.P.D. data bank that this is a B.O.T. priority request?"

"I am programmed to do that as standard procedure," the computer replied. "Clearance is required for access to all N.Y.P.D. personnel files."

Case sighed with exasperation. "All right. Make the request again, we'll do it by the numbers. Give my full name, title, ID, shield number, and clearance authorization code."

"Working," said the computer. A moment later the same "Restricted" message appeared on the terminal screen. "Request denied," the computer said.

Case swore. "What the hell do you mean, *request denied*?"

"I mean that access to Detective John Angelo's personnel file has been refused," the computer replied.

"I *know* that," Case said irritably. "It's not *supposed* to be refused. Can you determine if this is a computer error?"

"Do you wish me to request a diagnostic run for confirmation?"

"How long would that take?"

"The police department computers use thaumaturgically etched chips only. They are not thaumaturgically animated, as are mine. A complete diagnostic run would require downtime for a period of at least one hour."

Case sighed. "I can't order their computers down for a whole hour," he said. "It would paralyze all their operations. There's got to be another way. Find out *why* the request has been denied."

"Working," the computer said. A moment later it replied, "Access to Organized Crime Task Force files requires special clearance from the district attorney's office."

Case frowned. "How can D.A. Mathews deny access to the Bureau?"

"One moment, please . . . . The authority for special access clearance for Organized Crime Task Force files is by order of the mayor," the computer replied.

"So that's it," Case said. "Damn politicians. All right, two can play at this game. Get me the director's office at Bureau headquarters in Washington, D.C."

"Working," the computer said. A moment later it said, "I have the director's office on line."

Case picked up his phone. "This is Agent Case, New York Bureau chief. Who am I speaking to?"

"This is the director's personal secretary, Agent Michaels. What can I do for you, sir?"

"I've got a problem obtaining certain police department files necessary in an ongoing felony magic crime investigation this office is conducting," Case said. "It seems these files have been transferred to a special unit designated as the Organized Crime Task Force here in New York, and access has been restricted solely to the district attorney's office by special order of the mayor. Our Bureau clearance is being refused and I can't get access."

"They don't have the authority to deny the Bureau access to their files," the secretary said.

"I *know* that," Case said, "but the way they've set these particular files up, all clearances except those obtained directly from the D.A. are being automatically denied. I'd have to go through the D.A.'s office to get special access clearance for what I'm already authorized to have. It's a snafu and I don't have time to put through all the official paperwork or get into a pissing contest with the local D.A. I need that information *now*."

"I understand, sir. Which files do you require?"

"I need access to all personnel and operational files for the New York City Organized Crime Task Force," Case replied.

"I'll get on it right away, sir. I'll have the attorney general's office contact the New York City district attorney and straighten this matter out."

"Very good. Please arrange to have all the files downloaded directly to my office as soon as possible."

"That should be no problem. Will that be all, sir?"

"Yes, thank you very much," said Case. He hung up the phone and smiled. "So much for D.A. Mathews. Now, let's see what we can do about our friend McGuire."

"You hungry?" Blue asked, picking up the room phone. "What the hell, this is the Plaza. Might as well enjoy ourselves."

"No, I don't want anything," Angelo said, staring out the window at the shadows of Central Park. He seemed to remember a view of the park, only from a different direction. The memory nagged at him. "You go ahead and order something, if you like."

"You sure?"

"Yes, I'm sure." He went into the bathroom and threw some water on his face. He opened his shirt and stared at the gem embedded in his chest. He touched it. It felt strangely warm. When did he have that done, and why? Again, he seemed to hear a chorus of whispers in the back of his mind, but they came and went before he could discern anything. He rubbed his temples. Great, he thought. Now he was hearing voices. That couldn't be a good sign.

Why couldn't he seem to think straight? He was practically dead on his feet, yet he hadn't really done anything that he should feel so utterly exhausted. It must be stress, he thought. Or perhaps the aftereffects of whatever trauma he'd sustained that had made him lose his memory. He came out of the bathroom to find Blue stretched out on the bed. She had taken off everything except her panties.

"I ordered some champagne and caviar," she said with a sultry smile. "But we can start working up a thirst until it gets here." She patted the bed beside her.

"Don't take this the wrong way," said Angelo, "but I'd really rather not."

"What's the matter?" she asked, a touch defensively. "Is it me? Or don't you like girls?"

"It's neither one," said Angelo, sitting down wearily on the other bed. "For one thing, I don't really know you, and for another, I couldn't even if I wanted to. I wouldn't have the energy. I'm absolutely dead on my feet and I've got a splitting headache."

"Not tonight, I've got a headache, huh?" she said. She got up and came over to sit beside him on the bed. "Here, stretch out and lean back against me," she said.

"Really, Blue, I appreciate the gesture, but—"

"Gesture nothing, I also happen to be a licensed masseuse," she said. "Here, put your head back . . . ." She started to massage his temples.

"Ahhh," he said. "That feels wonderful."

"Yeah, it helps me get better tips," she said wryly. "I took a course in acupressure at the free university. Here, let's get your shirt off. I'll give you the full treatment." She helped him off with his shirt and her eyes widened when she saw the runestone. "Hey, wow, is that a *ruby*?"

"I suppose so," he said. "I don't remember how it got there, though."

"Jeez, look at the *size* of that thing!" she said, leaning closer to examine it. "It must be worth a fortune!" As she reached out to touch it, her bare breasts brushed Angelo's face. "Hey! It feels warm!"

Angelo cleared his throat slightly. "Body temperature, I guess."

She shook her head. "No, I don't think so," she said. "Trust me, one thing a girl knows about, it's jewelry, and your body temperature wouldn't warm it up like that. It's got these little symbols carved in it."

"It does? I hadn't really noticed."

"They look like runes," she said. "You sure you don't remember anything about this?"

"No," said Angelo. "I'm not really sure of anything."

"Here, turn over," she said.

He turned over onto his stomach and she straddled him to work on his neck, back, and shoulders. Angelo felt himself starting to relax a bit. She really was a very good masseuse.

"You know what?" she said. "I think this is a magic stone. Maybe you're an adept."

"I wouldn't know," Angelo replied. "What would an adept be doing with people like Joey Battaglia and Vinnie Maldonado?"

"You got me there," she said, kneading the muscles in his back. "You know something, you're really in great shape. You must work out a lot."

"If I do, I don't remember," Angelo replied.

"You really don't remember *anything*?"

"Not really. Little bits and pieces of things. Like just now, I was standing by the window, looking out at the park, and it seemed for a moment as if the view was somehow familiar, only the angle was wrong."

"So you think maybe you used to live around here?"

"I don't know."

"God, it must be terrible not to be able to remember anything. Maybe if we work on it, we can jog something loose."

"I imagine you've got your own problems to worry about right now," said Angelo. "You can't go back to your place. Maldonado and his friends will be looking for you. What are you going to do?"

"I don't really know. I haven't exactly had much chance to think about it."

"You have any money?"

"I've got some squirreled away in an account," she said. "A few thousand. I was saving up to open my own gallery. I guess now I'll go to the bank tomorrow and take it all out. I'll need it to get out of town."

He grunted.

"Maybe I'll go to L.A. Or maybe Chicago, who knows? I didn't leave anything behind I can't replace. Like my whole life," she added sourly. "You know, as long as I can remember, I wanted to be an artist. It's not as if I *wanted* to be a hooker, you know. Things just get kind of complicated sometimes. A girl's gotta do what she can to get by. This town will chew you up and spit you out. Way it started out, a guy propositioned me and I was broke and hungry and I figured, well, just this once, you know, what can it hurt? And it was easy money. I just sort of turned my head off and got through it and afterward I felt like hell, but then the next time it was easier, and then the next time after that and the next time after that, and well, you know how it is. You just find yourself in these situations."

There was a knock at the door.

"That's room service," she said. "Just relax a minute, I'll be right back."

She got up and threw on a robe, then went to let in the room service waiter with his cart. She signed for it and poured herself a glass of champagne. She picked up the bottle and the other glass and went back into the bedroom.

"You sure you don't want some of this champagne?" she said. "It's really good."

Angelo was fast asleep.

"No, thank you, Blue," she said. She shrugged and emptied the glass. She stood over the bed, staring down at him. He was breathing deeply and heavily. "Angelo?" she said. He did not respond.

She repeated his name again, but he seemed sound asleep. Moving slowly and carefully, she went through his pockets until she found the roll of bills. She put the roll into the pocket of her leather jacket and got dressed. Her gaze fell on the semiautomatic in the shoulder holster he had left hanging on a chair. She took the pistol out of the holster. It felt large and heavy in her hand.

She considered whether or not she should take it, as well. If Joey's friends came after her . . . but then, about all she would really know how to do was point it. She knew nothing about guns, except that automatics were more complicated than revolvers. She knew that much from the entertainment programs she had seen and from watching Joey with his gun. He used to like to show it off. He would do this thing with the top part of it, where he would sort of slap it back, and the top part would move. It had something to do with loading it or getting it ready to fire. There were also little levers or something on it and she had no idea what they did. She put the gun back in its holster.

She had the money, that was all that counted. She didn't know how much was in the roll, but it was a lot. Enough, certainly, to buy her a ticket out of town. She looked back at Angelo's sleeping form and hesitated. Guy saves my life, she thought, and I wind up rolling him. Great. Then she thought, Who am I kidding? I've got to think of myself. The only thing he really saved her from was himself. And Joey. And his mobster friends. She took the roll out of her jacket pocket and stared at it for a moment, then took a deep breath and replaced it in her pocket. The hell with it, she thought. Life is hard and then you die. A girl's gotta look out for herself. She started walking toward the door, but stopped before she reached it and simply stood there.

Her shoulders slumped and she sighed, looking down at the floor. "Aw, hell," she said to herself. "I can't. I just can't."

She took the roll back out of her pocket and turned around to put it back. She gasped. Angelo was gone. In his place on the bed, sitting back against the headboard, was an old man with a deeply lined face and skin that was the color of bronze. He was dressed in a white robe and long, fiery red hair hung down almost to his waist. His eyes were a brilliant, unsettling emerald green, almost like a cat's, and they were so bright they seemed to glow. And they were watching her. She dropped the roll of bills to the floor and stared, her jaw slack. Then her knees buckled beneath her and she fell to the floor in a faint.

"Well, that's it," McGuire said, leaning back wearily against the car seat. "I can't think what else to do. I've already got an A.P.B. out on Angelo. Sooner or later, we'll find him, but by then that woman he's gone after may already be floating in the river."

"There must be something else that we can do," said Gypsy.

"I'm open to suggestions," said McGuire.

"Couldn't you bring in this guy, Maldonado, for questioning?"

McGuire shook his head. "No, he's a wise guy. He wouldn't say a word and his lawyer would have him out in no time."

"Maybe if I could get a reading on him—"

"Forget it," said McGuire. "I've already stretched the rules too far involving you as much as I have. And involving myself, for that matter. Christine's trying to build a case against Tommy Leone. If there's even a hint of a psychic being involved, it will taint all the other evidence. It's too much of a gray area. Besides, you don't want to get anywhere near a guy like Maldonado. You want to wind up in a landfill somewhere?"

"So you're simply going to give up?"

"No, but there doesn't seem to be anything to do right now except wait. I've got Angelo's apartment staked out, and there's an A.P.B. out. I can question my detectives and see if any of them know anything about who Joey Battaglia's been seeing, but he's really not a major player. Maybe Christine will come up with something. The trouble is, the trail's gone cold on us, and for that matter, I don't even know who or what we're after. Is Angelo an amnesiac cop who's had a near-death experience or is he a corpse being controlled by some necromancer? This whole thing started with that crazy raid and now it's gotten completely out of hand. I should just wash my hands of the whole thing and turn it over to the Bureau. Let Case have the headache.''

"But you're not going to do that," she said.

McGuire gave a small snort. "Does your psychic's intuition tell you that?"

"No, I just know you."

"Well, you've been a big help, Natasha, and I appreciate it."

"That sounds like a dismissal."

"Don't take it the wrong way. It's an honest thank you. But you've done about all that you can do. From here on, it's straight police work. I'll go and have a talk with that adept physician at the hospital. Maybe he can give me a better picture of exactly what we're dealing with. I'll drop you off at your place."

"What will you do when you find Angelo?"

"Try to take him in. But I just don't know if we'll have that option. Whatever Angelo's become, he's clearly out of control. If he really has become a zombie, then we're going to have to bring him down. I don't even want to *think* about what's going to happen if the media gets hold of this. In any case, Angelo isn't my main problem. It's whoever's behind this, Cornwall or whatever his name is, and his confederates."

"I thought they were the Bureau's problem," Gypsy said.

"If they're turning cops into zombies, they're my problem," said McGuire grimly.

He dropped her off in front of her apartment building and as the car skimmed away, the cab with Wyrdrune and Kira pulled up. Wyrdrune opened the back door. "Get in," he said.

"We've got trouble," Gypsy said.

"I know," Wyrdrune replied. "I heard."

She frowned. "You heard? How did you . . ." And then her eyes got big. Her hand went to the amulet at her throat. "I don't believe it. You *bugged* me?"

"It was for your safety," Wyrdrune said.

"I can't believe you actually bugged me!" Gypsy said. She took off the amulet angrily and threw it out of the window of the cab. It immediately reappeared back around her neck. "Damn it!" she said. She took it off again and threw it out again. And it came back again.

"You're wasting your time," said Wyrdrune.

"How the hell do I get rid of this thing?" she demanded.

"You can't. Not unless Sebastian takes off the spell."

"I'm going to have a word or two with that big fairy!"

"I wouldn't go losing my temper with him, if I were you," said Kira. "Fairies don't get mad. They just get even."

Gypsy sighed with exasperation. "Where are we going?"

"Back to check in with Gonzo," Wyrdrune said. "Maybe we'll get lucky and he's heard something."

"What worries me is that we haven't heard anything about that necromancer," Kira said.

"That worries you?" asked Gypsy. "I should think no news is good news."

"Not in this case," Kira replied. "In the past, what's enabled us to track them is their uncontrollable hunger for power. They start killing to build up their life force. Usually, their murders have a pattern, but there haven't been any stories about a new series of killings in the city."

"And that's bad news?"

"Well, no, of course not, but what it means is that either the Dark One is committing murders in a way that they haven't been discovered, or else he's confident enough of his strength that he doesn't feel he needs to kill to grow more powerful."

"Or else he's smart and he's preparing a spell that will allow him to take in a great deal of life force all at once," said Wyrdrune.

"You mean like a mass murder?" Gypsy asked.

"Exactly."

"And if we don't find Modred in time," said Kira, "we may not be able to stop him. Without Modred, we can't call upon the full power of the runestones."

"Can't you work up some sort of spell that will enable you to find him?" Gypsy asked.

"I wish it were that easy," Wyrdrune replied. "Unfortunately, magic has its limits, even with the runestones. There is a link between us, but it isn't something we can consciously control, and the fact that we've had no feelings about Modred one way or other suggests that his runestone is either damaged or depleted."

"What happens then?"

"I don't know," said Wyrdrune. "I suppose the runestones can be destroyed, though I don't know how. The Dark Ones certainly seem to think they can be, otherwise they'd never dare to attack us. The trouble is, they can gain strength through necromancy, which is something we can't do."

"So they can get stronger faster," Gypsy said. "If Modred's runestone is damaged or down on energy, how does it get replenished?"

"I don't know that either," Wyrdrune replied. "With ordinary white magic, recovery occurs naturally. How long it takes depends upon how much energy has been expended. The runestones are a great deal more powerful than any white magic I've ever run across. The Old Ones have more life force, but if they're injured? I don't know. We are, of course, the weak link. Physically, we're far more vulnerable than the runestones. But they need us to maintain their energy."

"How? You mean, like parasites?"

"Well, I don't know if I'd put it quite that way," said Wyrdrune. "It's more of a symbiotic relationship. They make us a lot stronger than we'd be without them. For example, I've never completed my thaumaturgical training. Technically, I shouldn't even be able to pass my first-level certification exams. But the runestone has made me a wizard. But the stones themselves are inorganic. They're alive because they contain the spirits of the Council, but they're not living organisms in the same sense we are. They do not metabolize."

"So you've got to eat to keep their strength up," Gypsy said.

"Sometimes like a horse," said Wyrdrune. "The more energy they expend, the hungrier we get afterward. Under ordinary circumstances, we eat a little more than the average person. After a large expenditure of energy, we pig out like you wouldn't believe. It's a good thing Modred's fabulously wealthy, otherwise our grocery bills alone would wipe us out."

They arrived at Makepeace's apartment building and Wyrdrune sent the cabbie to the other side of town, where the spell of compulsion would wear off and he would remember nothing. When they got upstairs, they saw that Jacqueline had already arrived.

Makepeace introduced the two of them. Jacqueline had already met Gonzago, who was obviously taken by her. Gypsy could not fail to note the contrast between them. Jacqueline Monet was a study in understated elegance. She was dressed in a black neo-Edwardian suit and a white silk shirt with a lace jabot. She wore low-heeled black boots and held herself well. Unlike herself, thought Gypsy, the woman had perfect posture. She had always counted on her flamboyance to make her the center of attention. Jacqueline was one of those rare women who could do it with mere presence. She was an older woman, though how much older was difficult to tell from her appearance alone. She was in her late forties, but she looked ten years younger. Her dark hair was starting to go gray and she did nothing to hide it. The effect of the gray streaks in her hair was actually quite becoming. She spoke with a French accent, but it was not pronounced, and her English was perfect. Gypsy found herself liking her at once.

"We need a plan," said Wyrdrune, as they all took their seats in the living room, but before he could continue, Broom came sweeping in from the kitchen with a tray of coffee cups.

"Is that all who's coming? I'm out of cups. Do you realize this man has *nothing* in his kitchen? There's a thing in the refrigerator, I don't know what the hell it is, but I swear, it's growing. A *roach* couldn't survive in this place, I'm telling you."

"I do *not* have roaches," Makepeace said stiffly.

"No, but you've got dustballs you could play soccer with," Broom replied. "The last time this place had a good cleaning, subway tokens were a quarter and cabdrivers spoke English."

"So clean the place, already!" Wyrdrune said.

"Before or after I finish cooking for this army? You think maybe it would be too much trouble to ask someone to go out for groceries, or are we all going to live on pizza and Chinese?"

"Make a list of what you need and we'll call out," said Wyrdrune, "but if you don't mind, we've got things to talk about right now, okay?"

"Why should I mind? Why should you trouble yourself about the little necessities of life, like food, for instance? I understand, you're busy saving the world. I'm expected to take care of these little, unimportant things, but you'd think it would be too much trouble for me to get some cooperation. Nasty necromancers are out there, threatening the human race, but meanwhile we're out of toilet paper. You want nasty? Try wiping your *tuchis* with the *Daily News*."

Jacqueline laughed. "*Bonjour*, Broom. I have missed you, *mon ami*."

"Well, at least somebody around here notices me," Broom said. "How are you, *bubeleh*? It's good to see you, too. You're looking a little thin, sweetheart. Have you been eating well?"

"Can we get *on* with this?" asked Wyrdrune.

"Well, excuse *me*, Mr. Wizard!" Broom said. "Here's your coffee, and it should keep you up all night thinking about what a rude and insensitive person you are." The broom set down the tray and swept off back into the kitchen in a huff.

Wyrdrune gazed up at the ceiling. "Don't just look down," he muttered, "*help* me!"

"I really must find out what sort of spell you used to create that fascinating creature,'' Gonzago said. ''I simply have to have one of my own.''

''Take *that* one, please!'' said Wyrdrune.

''Oh, I couldn't possibly do that,'' Gonzago said, pouring a liberal amount of whiskey into his coffee cup from a pocket flask. ''It would be like separating a child from its mother.''

''Which is the child and which is the mother?'' Jacqueline asked, holding out her cup for some whiskey.

''Good point,'' Gonzago replied, pouring a dash into her cup. ''Cheers.''

''Are you people through?'' asked Wyrdrune testily.

''Go ahead, my boy, we are all ears,'' Gonzago said.

''Thank you,'' he replied wryly. ''Now, here's what we've managed to learn so far. . . .''

After he had brought them all up-to-date, he asked if anyone had anything else to add. Billy reported that he had found a temporary place for them as subletters of a loft on Waverly Place and he had engaged a real estate agent to start searching for more suitable accommodations. ''Getting new digs in Manhattan is not exactly easy,'' he said.

''Well, at least it's a start,'' said Wyrdrune, nodding. ''The question now is, how are we going to find Modred?''

''You have felt nothing through the runestones?'' Jacqueline asked.

''Not a thing,'' said Kira. ''But if he was dead, we'd know it.''

''No, we know he's alive,'' said Wyrdrune. ''What we don't know is what kind of shape he's in. Apparently, he doesn't remember who he is. He thinks he's a hood named Giovanni Angelico, also known as Johnny Angel. That means Angelo was not completely brain dead when Modred's runestone merged with him, taking Modred's life force along with it. So Modred had access to at least some of his memories. Angelo was an undercover cop. He must have gotten into his cover identity so deeply that it was at the forefront of his mind most of the time.''

"I guess he'd need to do that to maintain his cover," Kira said.

"Right," said Wyrdrune. "So that's what Modred is functioning on. The problem is that, in some ways, it's not all that far off from his own sense of identity. He was a mercenary for most of his life, and then a contract killer. Becoming Johnny Angel couldn't have seemed like much of a stretch. If his own memories were confused, Angelo's probably seemed familiar. Or at least those memories associated with his cover."

"So then we must try to think like this gangster, Johnny Angel," said Jacqueline. "He has been given a job to do, about this woman. How would he go about it?"

"Assuming, of course, he decides to go through with it," said Gonzago. "Your friend Modred was a killer, however much he may have changed since then. But Angelo is a police officer."

"True, but we don't know how much of Angelo is left," said Kira.

"No, he's got a point," said Makepeace. "If Angelo was still alive when the runestone bonded with him, then surely it would not have let him die. Angelo may be lost somewhere in the matrix of the new gestalt identity he has become, but he is nevertheless present and could not countenance committing a cold-blooded murder."

"So you're saying it could have set up a massive internal conflict?" Billy asked.

"It makes sense," said Wyrdrune. "Which means that if we're lucky, he hasn't gone through with it."

"And that means the people who sent him out on the job will be after him," said Kira. "So we not only have to find him before the Dark One does, but we're going to have to beat the police and the mob to the punch, as well."

"And don't forget the B.O.T.," said Billy. "They'll be looking for him, as well."

"We need to find out what Angelo was doing as Johnny Angel. The details of the operation. Gypsy, you said Mc-

Guire had the D.A.'s task force file on Angelo?'' Wyrdrune asked.

"No, he saw it, but she took it with her," Gypsy said. "He said she wouldn't let the thing out of her sight."

"So you didn't get a look at it yourself?" asked Make-peace.

"I wasn't with him when he met her," she replied.

"Well, then I guess we'll simply have to get it from the D.A. ourselves," said Wyrdrune.

CHAPTER
EIGHT

THE MANSION OVERLOOKING Oyster Bay was one of the most well appointed and luxurious on Long Island's exclusive north shore. It stood on a high bluff looking out over the bay and Long Island Sound, and on the landward side, the hill gently sloped down across the expansive and meticulously landscaped acreage to the tall, wrought-iron gates leading to the road. The owner of the mansion was a wealthy and reclusive entertainer who lived there with his new wife and a small staff of servants. They were all physically present in the house, but in a sense, none of them were really there at all.

The house was fairly isolated, and it was not the sort of residential area where neighbors would drop by. People who lived in such places valued their privacy and generally minded their own business. To all outward appearances, nothing had disturbed the routine of the place. The landscape maintenance crews always arrived on schedule, did their work, and departed without disturbing the residents. The monthly bills were always paid on time. Each week, one of the staff would drive out through the gates in one of the vehicles belonging to the estate and go into town to do the shopping or take one of the cars in for servicing to get the thaumaturgic batteries recharged. All bills were mailed directly to the accounting firm that represented the mansion's owner, all business matters were forwarded to the management firm, and all other mail was routinely picked up at the box down by the gate, the way it always had been. Inside the mansion, on the other hand, things had changed considerably.

They changed the day three strangers had arrived, two men and a woman who looked, at first glance, to be related. In a way, they were. They had simply walked into the mansion and taken over. The minds of the owner and his young wife, and of the staff, were no longer their own. When called upon, they came to do the bidding of their new masters, but otherwise, except to take care of routine, scheduled tasks, they all remained in one room in the east wing, simply sitting there and staring straight ahead of them, remaining very quiet.

"We are wasting too much time," said one of their new masters, pacing back and forth across the spacious living room. He was dressed in loose-fitting khaki slacks, a dark green polo shirt, and tan boat shoes with no socks. By his outward appearance, he looked like nothing more than a young business professional having a quiet, casual weekend at home. But he spoke in a language that predated any that were known to history. "I did not come here merely to wait in this house day after day. When are we going to *act*?"

"You have waited for several thousand years, Calador," said his companion. He was dressed comfortably in a black silk robe and slippers as he sat in a reading chair, studying a newspaper. "Is it too much to ask to wait a few days more?"

"It is if nothing is being accomplished, Beladon," Calador replied irritably. "I was well on my way to establishing my own domain when you found me."

"Yes," Beladon replied. "I *found* you. That is precisely the point. You were careless and profligate in your methods. I had little difficulty in locating you as a result. And that was fortunate. It could easily have been the avatars who found you first."

"And then where would you be?" asked Delana, lounging stretched out on the sofa, sipping a cold drink. She was wearing some of the clothes she had found in the bedroom closet of the young woman who was now her slave. They were dark blue silk lounging pajamas, and they made a stark contrast with her bright green eyes and long red hair. She was the youngest of the three, and looked no more than nineteen or twenty by human standards, though each of her years could easily have been measured in centuries.

"I would have dealt with them as they deserve," said Calador, stopping his pacing to stare at her angrily. "Which is more than either of you would have done."

"You would have died, as the others died," Delana said with a shrug. "None of us are strong enough to prevail against the Council individually. You would do well to profit from the mistakes the others made, as Beladon has done in bringing us together."

"So, we have joined our forces together," Calador replied. "And since then, what have we accomplished of any consequence?"

"Your overeagerness shall be your undoing, Calador," said Beladon. "You, perhaps, have not accomplished anything, but I have done it for you. I have found this dwelling for us, and I have enlisted an acolyte among the humans who is in a position of some power in their society. I had also found the avatars, and nearly succeeded in destroying them, all without any direct risk to us."

"Yes, but you failed," Calador said.

"Not completely," Beladon reminded him. "One of the avatars was seriously injured. His runestone has now found a new host, but that host is weak and vulnerable."

"Then now is the time for us to strike out at the others," said Calador, "when they cannot unite to form the Living Triangle!"

"Why strike at two who are at full strength when we can strike at one who is weak?" Beladon countered. "We need only to destroy that one and the spell of the Living Triangle is forever broken."

"Then by all means, let us do it!" Calador insisted.

"Before a hunt can be successful, it is first necessary to locate the prey," Beladon replied calmly. "And that shall be done soon. I have already taken steps to insure it. In the meantime, it is your task and Delana's to prepare the spell of Quickening, so that we may be at full strength when we must face the others.''

''We have been doing our part to prepare the spell,'' said Calador. ''There is little else to do here while you are gone.''

Beladon smiled. ''All those eons of confinement in the pit and now you feel trapped in this large and airy place? Patience, Calador, patience. That was what the others lacked. I know the hunger for fresh life force grows within you by the day, as it does in Delana and myself. You think we are immune? That has always been the price of necromancy, and we have always accepted it. However, things are different now. The humans are far, far greater in number than they were in our day, and though you may think them inferior still, the fact remains they have evolved considerably. Even with the avatars eliminated and the runestones destroyed, they can still pose a formidable danger to us.''

''I find that difficult to believe,'' said Calador. ''You overstate the case, Beladon. They had posed no threat to me at all.''

''That is because you had chosen to establish your domain in a remote and primitive area of their world,'' said Beladon. ''You should take advantage of your time to study them more thoroughly. Read their books and newspapers, watch the television, as Delana has been doing.''

''There is nothing on that box but mindless drivel,'' Calador said scornfully.

''You must be selective in your viewing,'' Beladon replied. ''You have learned the language of this tribe of humans, but you have learned little else about them. Watch their news programs and educational channels. And even the 'mindless drivel,' as you call it, has things to teach about their culture and society. Their weapons, for example, are far more formidable than the crude tools they had used when they were under our dominion in the old days. They can kill at a great distance, and we *can* be killed, Calador. Study their history books. I have placed a number of them in the library. You will see how the surviving Old Ones fared after we had been defeated by the Council in the Great War. For centuries thereafter, the humans persecuted them, hunting them down and killing them. Even after the last of the purebred were gone, they still continued with their persecutions in an effort to winnow out the half-breeds among them. Read about the Burning Times and the Inquisition. Read about their Holy Wars, waged to depose the half-breeds who rose to prominence among them. For centuries, they had condemned magic until they eventually came to believe that it was no more than a myth, yet now it has taken root among them and while none of their disciples individually can match our strength, together they could overwhelm us easily. Eliminating the avatars is but the first step to regaining our dominion. Conquering the humans will not be as easy as you think. We shall need to seek out our old companions, wherever they have fled to, as I have sought you out, so that we may all unite our strength together."

"With you as leader, I presume?" said Calador.

"That is a matter for the others to decide, once we have gathered them together," Beladon replied. "If someone else is chosen, or if the others all decide to rule in congress, it is all the same to me. There is no need for us to compete among ourselves. There is now plenty of the human resource for us all. That is what the others never fully understood. Or else their greed for power blinded them to practicality. They thought only of themselves, first to escape from the avatars and hide until they could recover fully, then to build up their own power as quickly as possible. They marked out their domains, as you did, some wisely, some unwisely, and those that were the greediest were the first to fall. The humans have developed intricate systems of communications of which the avatars can take advantage. Few places in their world are now so far removed that news of what occurs there is not disseminated elsewhere. If you would not disdain to examine this newspaper, for example, you would see that it reports events that occur all throughout the world, and their television programs do likewise. They have also developed networks of information that utilize devices called computers, which are more efficient than most spells, and these computers link their world, one nation with another, from the smallest village to the largest city. The Old Ones were right, Calador. The humans have developed into a highly intelligent and advanced species, just as they predicted. It means that they shall serve us better once they have been subjugated, but it shall take all the rest of us working together to accomplish that task. And if I can make you understand that and accept it, then we will have taken the first step toward our eventual victory.''

A book came floating out of the library and stopped, hovering in midair before Calador.

"Read this," said Beladon. "It is a brief history of their world, written by a man named H. G. Wells. It will make a good beginning to familiarize yourself with our new dominion.''

Calador stretched out his hand and the book obediently dropped into it.

"In the meantime, I shall proceed with our plan to find the missing avatar," said Beladon. "And this time, Delana, I shall ask you to assist me. There will be a part for you to play, as well, Calador, but for the present, as the humans say, you have your homework.''

When Blue came to, she was lying on the bed. The red-haired man with coppery skin and the bright green eyes was sitting beside her, staring down at her intently. His gaze was so direct and unsettling that she flinched from it. She sat up quickly and moved away from him, scrambling to the opposite side of the bed.

"Who the hell are you?" she demanded in a frightened tone. "What happened to Johnny?"

"Listen to me carefully," the old man said. "There is not much time. The manifestation takes strength that is required for the avatar to heal. You must tell him that he is not who he thinks he is. He must find a man named Sebastian Makepeace, who lives in a place known as the Village, above Lovecraft's Cafe. He must go to him and tell him that his name is Modred. As we gather our strength to make him whole again, his memory shall return, but there may not be enough time. The Dark Ones know that he is vulnerable now, and they shall come for him.''

"I don't know what you're talking about," she said. "I don't understand. What the hell is going—''

The bright green eyes flared with a brilliant inner light and her voice suddenly froze in her throat.

"You will remember, and you shall tell him," said the Old One. And in the next instant, he was gone and Angelo was in his place, sitting on the bed. The transformation had taken place in the blink of eye. Angelo slumped over and steadied himself with a hand on the bed.

"What happened?" he said. "I must have fallen asleep. . . .''

She blinked several times. "You're not who you think you are," she said.

"What?"

"You have to find a man named Sebastian Makepeace, who lives in the Village, above Lovecraft's Cafe, and tell him that your name is Modred. You're going to get your memory back, but there may not be enough time. The Dark Ones are coming for you.''

"What are you talking about?" asked Angelo.

She blinked again, several times. "I don't have the faintest idea," she replied. "That's what the old guy said."

"*What* old guy?"

"The old guy you turned into."

Angelo stared at her. "I turned into an old man? Were you dreaming, or what?"

She shook her head. "Not unless I'm dreaming right now. This happened like a couple of seconds ago. You fell asleep and you turned into this old guy with long red hair and a great tan. He was dressed in a white robe and he made me give you that message. He did something with his eyes. Put me under a spell, I guess." She shook her head. "One thing's for damn sure. You sure ain't Johnny Angel. You're somebody called Modred. And you're an adept. Either that or you've got somebody else living inside there.''

"Are you putting me on?"

"Okay, so it sounds pretty crazy, but it's true. You mean you don't remember anything about what just happened?"

Angelo shook his head. "No. The last thing I remember is you giving me a rubdown. And then I guess I fell asleep."

"Yeah, well, I did something else, too," she said sheepishly. "After you fell asleep, I took your roll and I was gonna split, but at the last minute, I decided I couldn't go through with it. I was halfway to the door and I changed my mind. When I turned around, you were gone and there was this old guy in your place."

"Why are you telling me this?"

"Because when you get your memory back, I don't want you thinking I wasn't a hundred percent straight with you," she said. "Mister, I don't know who you are, except that you're somebody called Modred, but we're talking major sorcery here and I ain't gonna mess with that. That stuff scares me even more than Joey's friends."

"Modred," said Angelo. "The name sounds familiar."

"It should," she said. "It's who you really are."

"So then who's Johnny Angel?"

"You're asking me? Until a few hours ago, I didn't even know you. But if you're just some hired muscle working for Tommy Leone, then I'm the Queen of England."

Angelo exhaled heavily. "This is rather a lot to deal with," he said.

"You believe me, don't you?"

He nodded. "Yes, I believe you. The name Modred rings a bell. So does the name Makepeace. And I've got a very uneasy feeling about the Dark Ones, whoever they are."

"Maybe this old guy, Modred or whatever his name is, is who you really are," she said. "Maybe you used some kind of spell to become Johnny Angel for some reason and then something happened and you lost your memory and you got stuck."

Angelo frowned. "I suppose that's possible. Still, it doesn't seem right, somehow. I don't know why. But I have to find out." He got up and stumbled, almost falling down.

"Are you okay?"

"I'm just feeling weak and dizzy," he said.

"The change probably took a lot out of you," she said. "The old guy said something about that."

Angelo started putting on his shirt. "I have to find this man, Makepeace." He stopped and glanced at her. "It was good of you to tell me about the money. Do you need some to get away?"

She grimaced. "I can always use some cash."

"Here," said Angelo, peeling off several large bills from the roll. "I appreciate your help."

"Thanks. But look, you're not going to get very far, the kind of shape you're in. Why don't we call down for a cab and I'll go with you as far as Lovecraft's. I know where it is. It's at MacDougal and Fourth. Least I can do is make sure you get there okay and find this guy."

Angelo nodded. "Thanks, I'll take you up on that. But afterward, you make sure you get out of town."

"Don't worry. Soon as we find this guy Makepeace, I'm on a plane and I'm outta here."

They called down to the front desk and asked for the doorman to flag down a cab. Within five minutes, they were on their way down to MacDougal Street. In the meantime, Makepeace, Billy, and Jacqueline had gone to prepare the loft on Waverly Place for occupancy, while Wyrdrune, Kira, and Gypsy were on their way to see Steve McGuire.

"He's already seen the D.A.'s file on Angelo," Gypsy pointed out, "and if we've got to get anything else out of Christine Mathews, he's our best bet. Besides, I don't know where she lives and I don't think we want to go waltzing into the D.A.'s office tomorrow. You guys are wanted, after all."

"There is that little inconvenience," Wyrdrune agreed. "Aside from which, McGuire is the only one in a position to lift that A.P.B. on Angelo. The last thing we need right now is for him to get arrested. No jail could hold Modred, but if Modred doesn't remember that he's Modred, things could get sticky if he was taken in."

"They probably wouldn't put him in jail, though," Kira

said. "Wouldn't they be more likely to take him to a hospital?"

"He's walked out of a hospital before," said Wyrdrune. "Besides, there's no telling what he's likely to do if they try to take him in. If he resists arrest, he's liable to get shot. No, McGuire's the man we've got to see. I just hope we can convince him without having to compel his cooperation."

"You'll have to tell him everything," said Gypsy.

"I wasn't planning on lying to the man," said Wyrdrune. "The question is, how much is he going to believe?"

"With me vouching for you, all of it, I'm sure," said Gypsy. "He doesn't consider me the most dependable person in the world, but he knows I'd never lie to him. Just lay it out for him the way you did for me. He's a good man to have in your corner."

The cab dropped them off in front of McGuire's apartment building and Gypsy buzzed up from the lobby. She did not tell him she had brought anybody with her, just that she had some new, important information about the case and had to see him right away. Consequently, McGuire was taken aback when he opened his apartment door to admit her and Wyrdrune and Kira quickly stepped in behind her.

"What is this?" he said, backing up a couple of steps warily.

"It's okay, Steve, they're friends," said Gypsy. "I want you to listen to them."

"There's no need for alarm, Deputy Commissioner," said Wyrdrune. "We're here to help."

McGuire's eyes involuntarily flicked back toward where he'd left his gun. Kira caught the quick reaction.

"You won't need your gun, Mr. McGuire," she said. "We could stop you before you tried to use it, anyway."

"I think I know who you people are," he said uneasily.

"Yes, we were the tenants of that penthouse your department raided," Wyrdrune said. "Two of them, at any rate. However, there's a lot about what happened you don't know. We're not the ones you should be after. We came here hoping to convince you of that. And to help you stop the real necromancers.''

"Listen to them, Steve," said Gypsy. "Please."

McGuire glanced at her briefly, then looked back at Wyrdrune. "How do I know she hasn't been placed under a spell of some sort?"

"You don't, I suppose," Wyrdrune replied. "But you know that *you* haven't been placed under a spell."

"At least, not yet," McGuire said, tension in his bearing.

"If I wanted to place you under a spell of compulsion, Deputy Commissioner, I could do so very easily," said Wyrdrune. "The fact that I haven't should tell you something. We just came here to talk. I'm sure you have a lot of questions about what's been going on. We're the ones with all the answers. Believe it or not, we're the good guys."

"You are, huh? You'll have to convince me of that."

"I'll do my best," said Wyrdrune. "I was hoping Gypsy's presence would help in that regard, but if you feel she's being coerced, I can provide you with the names of a number of people who will vouch for what I'm about to tell you. One of them is Captain Rebecca Farrell, of the L.A.P.D. Another is Chief Inspector Michael Blood of Scotland Yard. And there are others, such as Inspector Armand Renaud of the Paris police, and Agent Akiro Katayama of the Tokyo office of the I.T.C. And if you feel that we've somehow managed to coerce all those people, as well, you can also check with a man named Yohaku, in Japan, unless you think we're powerful enough to suborn one of the highest-ranking mages in the world."

"You drop some pretty impressive names," McGuire said. "All right, go ahead. I'm listening."

"Perhaps we'd better sit down," said Wyrdrune. "This is going to take a while."

Angelo pressed the buzzer for Makepeace's apartment. When a man's voice answered, he said, "I'm looking for Sebastian Makepeace."

"And who is it that's looking?" asked the voice over the speaker.

Angelo hesitated slightly. He moistened his lips and said, "Modred."

"Good heavens! Come on up, my boy." The door buzzer sounded and Angelo opened the door. He held it for a moment and turned to Blue. "Thanks again for everything," he said.

"Hey, you helped me out, it was the least I could do," she said. "You sure you're gonna be all right?"

"I'm not really sure of anything," Angelo replied, "but there's really nothing more that you can do. You'd best be going. The cab's waiting."

Blue nodded. "You know, part of me's real curious about what the story is with you. But another part of me doesn't really want to know, and that's the part that looks out for number one. It's kept me out of trouble all these years. Well, mostly out of trouble, anyway."

"I understand," said Angelo.

She hesitated, then leaned forward quickly and gave him a kiss on the cheek. "Good luck, whoever you are," she said.

"Good luck to you, too, Blue. And watch out for men you meet in bars."

She smiled wryly. "Yeah. Story of my life." She turned and ran to the cab without a backward glance. Angelo watched as it skimmed away. She didn't wave. She didn't even look at him. She was already gone. He turned and started walking up the stairs.

The man who answered the door was dressed in the robe of an adept. He had white hair and a long white beard. There was something about his appearance that tugged at Angelo's memory, but he couldn't seem to put his finger on it. "Sebastian Makepeace?" he said.

"No, but he should be back shortly. My name is Morrison Gonzago, I'm a close friend of his, and I know all about you. My friends call me Gonzo. Please, come in. Everyone's been quite concerned about you."

"Everyone?" said Angelo, entering the apartment and looking around.

"You don't remember?" asked Gonzago.

Angelo shook his head. "No, not really. If I tell you how I got here, I don't think you'd believe me."

"Try me. You might be surprised."

"All right. I was with a young lady . . . well, a prostitute, to be exact. It's rather a long story, but I was trying to help her get away from some people who were after her."

"Tommy Leone's people?" said Gonzago.

Angelo looked surprised. "How did you know that?"

"Never mind that for now. Please, sit down."

"Thanks. I'm about dead on my feet."

They took their seats in the living room. "Do go on," Gonzago said. "You were about to tell me how you came here."

"Well, we were in a hotel, and I fell asleep, and while I was asleep, I apparently turned into someone else. An old man with long red hair and a white robe, who told her that my name was Modred and I had to find a man named Sebastian Makepeace, who lived above Lovecraft's Cafe in the Village. And to make sure she got it right, he placed her under a spell. She gave me the message and I came straight here."

Gonzago leaned forward, an expression of intense interest on his face. *"They actually manifested?"*

"Who's they?" asked Angelo with a frown.

"The Old Ones," said Gonzago. "The spirits of the rune-stone."

Angelo opened his shirt. "You mean this?"

"Yes," said Gonzago. "You have no memory of its significance?"

Angelo shook his head. "No. I have no idea how it got there. I don't even know who Modred is. All I know is the message I was given, and the fact that this . . . transformation took a hell of a lot out of me. I'm so tired I can barely keep my eyes open."

"Would you like some coffee?" asked Gonzago. "Or perhaps something a bit stronger?"

"Thanks. I could really use a cup of coffee."

"One moment," said Gonzago. He got up and went back into the bedroom. Angelo heard him say, "We have a visitor who'd like some coffee. You'll never guess who it is."

"*More* coffee? What do I look like, a percolator? You realize we've almost gone through all the filters? You know what all that caffeine *does* to your system?"

"This is for our guest—"

"*More* guests? *Gevalt!* This place is getting to be like Grand Central Station. All right, never mind, I'll just drop everything in here and go and make more coffee. So what if the bathtub's got a ring around it that looks like a rally stripe? And that's another thing, we need more cleanser. I made a list, did anybody bother even *looking* at the list?"

"Broom," said Angelo suddenly.

A moment later Gonzago came back into the living room, preceded by a straw broom with spindly, rubbery-looking arms. "So, and who might you be?" it said.

"Broom," said Angelo again. "Your name is Broom."

"I know who *I* am, *bubeleh*," said Broom. "I was asking about you. You have a name, handsome?"

"Modred, I think."

"*Oy!*" said Broom, bringing one of its hands to where its chest would have been, if it had a chest. "Is it really you?" It shuffled closer.

"I suppose so," Angelo replied. "That is, I'm not really sure. I can't really remember. But I seem to remember you."

"Open up that shirt a little more," said Broom.

Angelo held his shirt open so Broom could see the runestone, though he had no idea how it *could* see without any eyes.

"*Gottenyu*, it really is you! Thank God! Do you know how worried we've all been, young man? Where have you *been* all this time? You couldn't call? It was too much trouble to pick up a phone and say, 'I'm all right, you shouldn't worry, I haven't been run over by a car?' You think maybe we didn't *care* where you were all this time?"

"Broom, he's lost his memory," Gonzago said.

Angelo stared at the broom with fascination. "I'm sorry," was all he could think to say.

"Ach! Forgive me, *bubeleh*, I don't know what's the matter with me. I knew that," Broom said. And then it sniffled, a singularly curious phenomenon, since it didn't have a nose. "It's just that I've been so worried, my bristles have been falling out. But at least you're safe now, that's what counts. How do you feel? Have you eaten anything? Want I should make you some nice soup? A quiche, maybe?"

"I could do with something to eat," said Angelo.

"*Oy*, wait, what am I talking?" Broom said with chagrin. "There's nothing in the kitchen! Nobody went for groceries! A list, he tells me. Make a list. Okay, so I make a list, and what does he do? Leaves it on the kitchen table, that *dumbkopf*. *Veys mir?*"

"It's quite all right, Broom," said Gonzago. "We'll simply step out downstairs to the cafe and have something. That is, if you would be so kind as to wait by the phone, in case any of the others call. If they do, you can tell them Modred's back and we're downstairs at Lovecraft's."

"That dive? I can imagine what kind of food they serve in a place like that, where the waitresses all look like raccoons and the waiters look like waitresses."

"Actually, it's very good food, Broom," Gonzago said. "I can vouch for that personally. Sebastian and I have many of our meals there. However, I will make sure someone goes out for groceries as soon as the others return, even if I have to do it myself. Frankly, I'm looking forward to trying some of your cooking. I hear you make excellent kreplach."

"Well, excellent, I wouldn't know," said Broom modestly, "but it'll stick to your ribs, at least."

"Then we shall obtain all the necessary ingredients for you at the first opportunity," Gonzago promised. "In the meantime, we'll be downstairs. Call down if you hear from any of the others."

Angelo buttoned up his shirt, put his jacket back on, and

accompanied Gonzago down to the cafe. "I seem to remember Broom," he said vaguely, "but I'm afraid I don't remember you. Have we met before?"

"Actually, we haven't," said Gonzago. "I teach at the university, with Sebastian."

"You teach thaumaturgy?"

"English," said Gonzago.

"You're not an adept?"

"Yes, but I am also a writer," said Gonzago as they walked down the stairs. "I fear I am a bit, shall we say, too erratic to teach thaumaturgy."

"Erratic?"

"I have, my boy, what is known as a slight drinking problem, and inebriation is not exactly conducive to instructing young minds in the finer points of magic. It is, however, an absolute requirement in grading undergraduate compositions. Here we are. After you. . . ."

They went down the steps from the sidewalk to the entrance of Lovecraft's, and Gonzago was immediately greeted by one of the staff, who seated them at a table near the back.

"The usual, Gonzo?" asked the waitress.

"Please, my dear, and a menu for my friend, here. He's feeling somewhat peckish tonight."

"Right away," she said, and brought a menu.

Angelo stared at it for a moment, then shook his head. "I don't really know what I like," he said. "It's strange. I had some linguine the other day, but they don't seem to serve that here. Perhaps you could recommend something?"

"Delighted to, my boy. They serve some of the best hamburgers in town here. You can't go wrong with that."

"All right."

"One Miskatonic Special for my friend," Gonzago told the waitress.

"Sure thing. And something to drink?"

"Black coffee, please," said Angelo.

"Right away," she said, and went to place their order.

"So, does anything seem familiar?" asked Gonzago.

"I'm not sure," Angelo replied. "Have I been here before?"

"I believe Sebastian mentioned that you have, yes," Gonzago said.

"But I've never met you here?"

"No, we have never met, but it is entirely possible that I was present during one of your visits to these premises. Present, that is to say, but not necessarily conscious."

Elvira brought coffee for Angelo and a large, double Irish whiskey for Gonzago. "So, here's to fond memories," he said, raising his glass in a toast, "and hoping you will soon recover yours."

Angelo smiled. "It's odd," he said. "I'm supposed to be somebody called Modred, and your friend Sebastian knows me by that name, as does Broom, but though it seems vaguely familiar, it doesn't really feel like my name. Maldonado called me Johnny Angel, apparently some sort of diminutive of Giovanni Angelico."

"And that name feels more familiar to you?"

"Somewhat. But it still doesn't seem quite right, somehow."

"How about the name Angelo?"

"Angelo?"

"John Angelo," Gonzago said.

Angelo frowned. "Angelo. Yes, that strikes a chord."

"It's who you are, you know," Gonzago said.

"I thought my name was Modred?"

"That, too, in a certain sense," Gonzago said. "It's actually rather complicated. You are, or perhaps, more correctly, *were* John Angelo, a detective lieutenant in the New York City Police Department."

"I was a *cop*?" said Angelo. "Then . . . what was I doing working for a man like Maldonado?"

"You were a special undercover officer with the Organized Crime Task Force," Gonzago explained.

"Christine Mathews," Angelo said suddenly.

"The district attorney," said Gonzago. "Yes, she runs the task force. Excellent. You're remembering."

Angelo shook his head. "That just came to me, suddenly. Little bits and pieces, like remembering Broom, but I can't seem to pull any of the threads together. Where does Modred fit in?''

"Ah, well, that's the complicated part," Gonzago said. "Let's see if we can pull some of these threads together, as you put it. . . .''

As they spoke, a man on the other side of the bar leaned over and spoke quickly to the woman he was with, then moved toward a pay phone and quickly dialed a number. He didn't take his eyes off Angelo and Gonzago.

"Vinnie? Franco. You'll never guess who I'm looking at right this minute. Johnny Angel. Yeah. I'm at Lovecraft's. He just came in with some old guy, looks like an adept. They got their heads together at a table in the back. Right, I figured you'd be interested. First he falls down on a job and disappears, then there's cops stakin' out his place, and now he's meetin' with some adept, just about the time we got that shipment comin' in. I told ya you had Joey all wrong. He might be cocky, but he ain't no stoolie. Angel's your man. What you wanna bet the guy he's with is a Bureau agent? No, I think they're gonna stay awhile. They ordered food. Yeah, you bet your ass I'll be here."

He hung up.

CHAPTER
NINE

MCGUIRE HUNG UP the phone and turned back to them with a grim expression. "Well, your story checks out," he said. "But if it wasn't for the fact that you have some of the top police officials in the world vouching for you, I'd think you were all crazy."

"I wouldn't blame you," Wyrdrune said. "But now, at least, you know we're telling you the truth."

"Either that or you've pulled off one hell of an international conspiracy," McGuire said wryly. "But I don't believe that. Inspector Renaud and Chief Inspector Blood impressed me as very sober and responsible individuals and they backed up your story one hundred percent. However, I think they're both dead wrong."

"Wrong?" said Kira with a frown. "What do you mean?"

"If they've convinced me of anything, it's that this thing is much too big for you people to be handling all by yourselves," McGuire said. "Trying to keep something like this quiet is insane. You simply can't sit on this kind of information."

"Can you imagine the panic it would cause if this got out?" asked Wyrdrune.

"That's like telling me I've got to suppress information

about a serial killer, because the citizens would panic,'' said McGuire. ''And that's exactly what we're talking about here, isn't it? Serial killers. Necromancy is a felony punishable by death. And if there's a necromancer on the loose in this city, the people have a right to know about it, so they can take steps to protect themselves.''

''And just how do you expect them to do that?'' Kira asked. ''It's not just a matter of not going out alone after dark, McGuire. You have no idea what you're dealing with. There's no defense against a necromancer, unless you happen to possess magic that is stronger.''

''A necromancer can accumulate power much more quickly than a thaumaturge,'' added Wyrdrune, ''and these beings are immortal. Any one of them is at least ten times more powerful than a human mage. If you went public with this, all you would succeed in doing would be to start a worldwide panic. Can you imagine the kind of climate that would create? You'd have people arming themselves and forming vigilante groups. Every adept would suddenly be suspect. Everybody with red hair would be at risk. You'd have rioting, and innocent people would be killed. That's exactly the kind of situation the Dark Ones could take advantage of. You'd be playing right into their hands.''

''I doubt that,'' said McGuire. ''In any case, this whole thing is out of my jurisdiction. It's got to be turned over to the Bureau.''

''The *Bureau*? Have you forgotten that it was a Bureau agent who staged the raid on our place in an attempt to kill us?'' Kira said. ''The Bureau represents no threat to the Dark Ones. You saw what they could do with just one Bureau agent in their power. And who knows how many others they may already have under their control?''

''All the more reason for the proper authorities to be informed of this,'' McGuire insisted. ''If these Dark Ones are as powerful as you say they are, then they represent the single greatest threat this city, the country, and even the entire world has ever faced. It's simply too much for you to deal with all by yourselves. And you haven't got the right to make that kind of decision for everybody else. I don't know how you convinced Blood and Renaud and the others to keep quiet about this, but they're way off base. The Bureau and the I.T.C., at the very least, have to be informed.''

''I was hoping we could make you understand,'' said Wyrdrune. ''I didn't want to have to compel your cooperation.''

''Is that a threat?'' McGuire asked tensely.

''Steve, listen—'' Gypsy began, but McGuire interrupted her.

''No, *you* listen, Natasha. You brought these people here. Maybe you think what they're doing is the right way to go about this, but I don't. And just because I don't agree, simply because I'm trying to do my job to protect the people of this city, they're threatening to force my cooperation through magic. Well, now how in hell does that make them any different from the Dark Ones? If they get to make those kinds of decisions, and use magic to enforce them, then who's going to protect us from *them*?''

For a moment no one spoke, and then Gypsy said, ''He's right, you know.''

Kira and Wyrdrune exchanged glances. Wyrdrune took a deep breath and exhaled heavily. ''I can't say that I don't see your point,'' he said. ''But you're putting us in a very difficult position. A part of me has to admit that your argument has a lot of merit, but another part of me, the part that is the runestone's avatar, does not agree.''

''Yeah,'' said McGuire. ''That's the inhuman part. And however well intentioned the spirits of this Council might be, they're still not human. Their motives may be good, but they still regard humans as inferiors. From what you've told me, that's been their entire history. But whatever *they* are, *you* are human, regardless of the runestones. Ask yourself what you would do if you were in my place.''

Wyrdrune gazed at him steadily for a moment, then sighed and shook his head. ''I'm not sure I'd do any different, to be perfectly honest with you. But the fact remains that we're faced with a threat that's a great deal more deadly than a human serial killer, and if news of this got out, it would have a tremendous impact on society. First, there would be the matter of convincing both the Bureau and the I.T.C. Granted, with the help of people like yourself, Mike Blood, Becky Farrell, Katayama, and Armand Renaud, that may not be so difficult, but both the Bureau and the I.T.C. think we're the ones responsible for the killings, and before anything else happens, they'd want us to turn ourselves in. There would be investigations, and testimonies to grand juries, and all sorts of bureaucratic hassles and meanwhile we'd be out of circulation. We simply can't afford to do that. Then there wouldn't be anything to stop the Dark Ones."

"Maybe there's another way," McGuire said. "If we could take one of these Dark Ones alive—"

"Forget it," Kira said. "Even if you could figure out a way to do that, there isn't a jail on the face of this earth that could hold one of them."

"What about your friend Slade?" McGuire asked. "If he's Merlin reincarnated or whatever, and he can prove that, then his word would carry a considerable amount of weight. Especially if he can manifest as one of these Old Ones, the way he did back in your penthouse."

"We need Billy," Wyrdrune said. "Besides, you know as well as I do that they wouldn't be content with just him. They'd want all of us to come in and testify. And if the Dark Ones have suborned any of the high-ranking Bureau or I.T.C. officials, which is entirely possible, they could control the situation."

"Not if the runestones can detect these acolytes, as you claim," McGuire said.

"Oh, sure," said Kira. "All we'd have to do was point at some top Bureau or I.T.C. official and say, 'He's being controlled by the Dark Ones. My runestone's glowing.' I'm sure they'd buy that right away."

"They might, if you gave them a chance," McGuire said.

"You've got a lot more faith in due process than we have, McGuire," Kira said. "I've been through it before, you know. I've got a record. I know exactly how it works. Or doesn't work."

"So then where does that leave us?" asked McGuire.

"I guess that's up to you," said Wyrdrune. "It would be nice if we could do this with your cooperation. But if not, then we'll just have to do it on our own."

"Wyrdrune, wait—" Gypsy began, but at that moment the phone rang.

McGuire glanced at them. "Mind if I get that?" And without waiting for a reply, he went into the kitchen to answer it. They heard him give a couple of short, terse answers, and then a moment later he came back in.

"That was the commissioner," he said. "I've been ordered to turn the entire case over to the Bureau. As of this moment, I'm out of it."

Wyrdrune nodded. "They got to somebody," he said.

"You're telling me they got to the commissioner?" said McGuire with disbelief.

"Not necessarily," said Wyrdrune, "although it's certainly possible. But they got to somebody who had enough clout to pull some strings and get you out of the way. Have you annoyed anybody in the Bureau lately?"

"Case," McGuire said. "The New York Bureau chief. But that doesn't mean anything. Case has jurisdiction in crimes involving magic and I've been stepping all over his toes. He just finally ran out of patience and placed a call to Washington and slapped me down."

"Maybe," Wyrdrune said. "And on the other hand, maybe not. There's one way of finding out for sure."

"You mean get you near Case and see if your runestone glows?" McGuire said.

"Exactly."

"And if it doesn't?"

"Then you called it and it's just a routine battle over turf," said Wyrdrune. "Either way, it looks as if the matter's no longer in your hands."

"I might have a few things to say about that yet," McGuire said. And suddenly he produced a gun. "You're both under arrest. You have the right to remain silent. You have the right to an attorney. If you choose to give up those rights, anything you say can be—"

The gun suddenly wrenched itself out of his hand and went flying across the room. It struck a wall and fell to the floor, behind a chair.

McGuire simply stared. Finally, he said, "That was stupid. It might have gone off on impact."

Wyrdrune merely opened his hand to reveal the pistol's magazine. He held up a round in his other hand. "And one in the chamber," he said.

"Very impressive," said McGuire.

"Child's play," said Wyrdrune. "Wait'll you see what the Dark Ones can do."

McGuire's lips tightened in a grimace. "All right," he said. "It's your play."

"I think we'll be leaving now," said Wyrdrune.

"I'm not going to keep my mouth shut about this," said McGuire.

"Do whatever you think you have to do," said Wyrdrune. "I'm tired of arguing about it. And I'm not going to impose my will on yours." He tossed the pistol magazine back to McGuire, then handed him the remaining bullet. "But before you go off half-cocked, no pun intended, at least think about what we said. You asked me what I'd do if I were in your place. Well, I'd think about it real hard. Because if you do choose to go public with this, whatever happens will be your responsibility."

They walked out and shut the door behind them.

"As strange as it all sounds, I have no doubt that it's all true," said Angelo as the waitress brought their after-dinner drinks. "It all seems to feel right, in a peculiar sort of way. If that makes any sense at all."

"I suppose it does," Gonzago said. "Did anything start coming back to you as I was speaking?"

"A few things," Angelo replied. "But it's like being in a fog. Every once in a while, there's a clear spot and I can see something, and then it closes in again."

"Give it time," Gonzago said. "It will all come back to you, I'm sure."

"That's if there *is* time," Angelo replied. "What if these Dark Ones strike again and I don't remember how to use the runestone?"

"Well, if I understand correctly," said Gonzago, "it isn't really a matter of you knowing how to use it, it works sort of on its own, the way it did in the hotel when one of the spirits manifested. I find that aspect of your story particularly fascinating. So far as I know, none of the others has ever had a similar experience."

"It's ironic," Angelo said. "Not only are these spirits of the runestone part of who I have become, but so is Modred. Perhaps that's why I was so ready to believe that I was really Johnny Angel. I'm a cop, and yet a part of me is a professional killer."

"A *former* professional killer," said Gonzago.

"That's supposed to make it better?"

"No, I suppose not," said Gonzago. "I can see where that would give rise to a certain amount of inner conflict."

"That's putting it mildly, don't you think?" said Angelo.

"Perhaps you shouldn't think about it that way," Gonzago said.

"How should I think about it?"

"Well, do you believe in reincarnation?"

"Under the circumstances, it would be kind of silly if I said no, wouldn't it?" said Angelo.

"Mmm, yes, good point. Well, if we are to assume that you have had other past lives—besides the ones we've been discussing, that is—would you feel responsible for what occurred during those lives?"

"I don't see how I could."

"Precisely. In a sense, this is more or less the same sort of thing," Gonzago said. "You are not exactly Modred, that is to say, the son of King Arthur, who lived as a mercenary and eventually became the assassin known as Morpheus. That was another life, another incarnation, as it were. There is no way you could have been responsible for that. You weren't even born yet. Nor are you exactly John Angelo, the police detective, although your memories of that particular past life, such as they are, may be the ones you identify with most. That John Angelo died. Nor are you the Old One you manifested in the Plaza Hotel. Those are all past lives, past incarnations. Except unlike most people, in your particular case, there is a stronger thread of continuity. You are the result of different life forces that have all united in one person, and that person is who you are right now, not who you were before. In a manner of speaking, you're just a newborn babe. Until a relatively short while ago, the person you are now did not even exist.''

"So then, who *am* I? Am I Modred? Or am I John Angelo?''

Gonzago shrugged. ''Well, as near as I can tell, my boy, that is entirely up to you. Since you are a newborn, more or less, you are starting off with a clean slate. It seems to me that you can be anyone you want to be.''

"How about Donald Duck?'' asked Angelo wryly. ''His life seems a lot less complicated.''

"Yes, but think of the stress levels,'' said Gonzago. ''It must be hell to be wired that tight all the time.''

Angelo smiled. ''You're all right, Gonzo. A little strange, perhaps, but I like you anyway.''

"The feeling's mutual, my boy,'' Gonzago said.

"It's all so very strange,'' said Angelo. ''I remembered Broom, and I seem to remember Wyrdrune and Kira, but I can't for the life of me remember what they look like. I remember Merlin now, but I can't remember Billy. And I seem to have an image of Makepeace as a rather large and boisterous man.''

"You see? Your memory is starting to come back to you,'' Gonzago said.

"But only in a very haphazard way,'' Angelo replied. ''It's incredibly frustrating.''

"Don't try to force it. Just let things happen at their own pace. Doubtless, the runestone is working to heal you even as we speak. It must have expended a great deal of energy simply in the act of saving your life. To some degree, its recovery must be directly related to your own.''

"So I'm the weak link, then?''

"You could look at it that way, I suppose," Gonzago said, "but on the other hand, without you, the runestone would not really be able to function."

"But they functioned without anybody else for all that time," said Angelo.

"It was a static situation," Gonzago explained. "They only had to exert their spell over one narrowly defined locality. They had no need of bodies with which to move around. Nor did they need to channel their energies through organic beings. People, in other words. That sort of thing exerts a certain amount of wear and tear."

"So in order for the spirits of the runestone to be fully recovered, I have to be fully recovered."

"Even magic has to follow the laws of energy," Gonzago said.

"So does that mean the runestone won't be up to full strength until I get my memory back?"

"I shouldn't think so," said Gonzago. "I would think it's more a matter of getting your strength up. Physically, that is. But you seem to be doing splendidly for a chap who was dead only a couple of days ago."

"I do feel a little better," Angelo admitted. "When I got here, I was dead on my feet."

"And that's how you're gonna be when you leave here," said Maldonado from behind him. "Dead."

As Angelo started to move, Maldonado opened his coat slightly to display the cocked semiautomatic. At the same time, two other men moved up behind Gonzago, holding their guns so that no one else could see them.

"Don't even think about it, Angel," Maldonado said. "If that's really your name. As for you, old man, you so much as blink or move a pinkie and we'll plug you right here."

"As I prefer to remain unplugged, I will remain perfectly still," Gonzago said.

"And keep your mouth shut, too," said Maldonado. He looked at Angelo with an evil smile. "So, looks like Joey wasn't the one with a big mouth, after all. It was you all the time, you bastard. You're a fuckin' cop."

"The old man has nothing to do with this, Vinnie," said Angelo. "Leave him out of it."

"Oh, I'm supposed to take your word for that?" said Maldonado with a sneer. "Like your meetin' a Bureau adept has nothin' to do with that shipment comin' in tomorrow? Yeah, right. You think I'm a fuckin' moron? We're all gonna take a little walk. The old man, too. Move it."

"I don't think so," Angelo said.

"What?"

"I said, I don't think so. You're planning on killing us both anyway. Why should we make it any easier on you? We're not moving."

"You want it here? You want innocent people to get hit by stray fire, huh, cop?"

"You going to kill everybody in here, Vinnie, just to make sure there aren't any witnesses? That's what, sixty, seventy people? You boys got that many bullets?"

"Sixty, seventy people makes sixty, seventy different eye-witness accounts," said Maldonado. "I ain't too worried about it. So what's it gonna be, cop? Somebody else gets hurt, ain't no never mind to me."

"I don't think you've got the nerve for it, Vinnie," said Angelo. He tensed, ready to make a move.

"Have it your way," Maldonado said.

Suddenly both Angelo and Gonzago vanished.

"What the hell . . ." said Maldonado.

"Where'd they go?" said Franco.

They glanced all around them. There was no sign of the two men.

"Would you gentlemen like a table?" asked the waitress, coming up to them.

The men kept their guns concealed. They glanced uneasily at Maldonado. "No," said Maldonado. "No, we were just lookin' for someone." He glanced at the others. "Shit, let's get the hell out of here."

They quickly moved toward the door. The waitress watched them go, then shrugged. She looked up. "You need anything, Gonzo?"

"No, thank you, dear, we're fine," Gonzago said from where he and Angelo were lying pressed up flat against the ceiling. "Just the check, if you don't mind."

"Sure thing, hon. Don't fall, now."

"Never!" Gently as feathers, they drifted back down to the floor.

"That was rather a unique solution," Angelo said, still a bit taken aback by what had just happened.

"Well, as I have a tendency to rather overindulge in spirituous consumption," said Gonzago, "some time ago I struck upon the notion of having a wee kip on the ceiling, the better to avoid people stepping on my prostrate form and possibly incurring injury. The management does not object, as it does not really interfere with business and has occasion to cause some mild amusement. I've done it in my cups so many times, I can do it in my sleep, by now. In fact, I have. It's become something of a habit. Never thought it would come in handy for being set upon by ruffians, though."

"It's a good thing they did not look up," said Angelo.

"Well, I'm sure I would have thought of something if they had," Gonzago replied. "Not exactly friends of yours, I take it?"

"They work for Tommy Leone," Angelo replied. "That was Maldonado, the one I was telling you about."

"I see. Not a very pleasant fellow, is he? They seemed to think I was an agent of the Bureau of Thaumaturgy."

"Yeah, I caught that, too," said Angelo. "I wonder why? From what Maldonado said, it apparently has something to do with this shipment coming in tomorrow. I had assumed it was drugs, but why would the B.O.T. be concerned with narcotics?"

"They would if it was Ambrosia," said Gonzago.

"Ambrosia? What's that?"

"If you had all your memory, you'd know," Gonzago said. "It's a new wrinkle in thaumagenetic engineering. A strain of magically developed hemp that comes from the Orient. You can either smoke it or ingest it. It seems to have caught on with some students at the university, which is how

I know about it. It enhances tactile and visual perceptions and has mild hallucinogenic properties. But primarily, it's an incredibly powerful aphrodisiac that turns males into rampant satyrs and females into insatiable nymphomaniacs.''

"I can see why it would be popular with college students," Angelo said.

"It's nothing to joke about, my boy," Gonzago replied. "The stuff is virulently addictive. I understand you may not get hooked the first or second time, but once it has a hold on you, it virtually takes over your life. You can turn someone into a sexual slave with that stuff, and if you're not in absolutely peak physical condition, you can literally fornicate yourself to death.''

"Who the hell would buy something like that?" said Angelo.

"Young people, who are less afraid of risk and think they'll live forever," said Gonzago. "And unscrupulous people, who seek to control and manipulate others. Thaumagenetically engineered drugs are still something relatively new, but it was, perhaps, an inevitable development. Necromancy is not the only way in which magic can be misused.''

"They'll have to be stopped," said Angelo.

"Perhaps you'd best leave that to the Bureau," said Gonzago. "At the moment, we're concerned with something much more dangerous than Ambrosia.''

"But I'm the only one who knows the shipment is coming in tomorrow," Angelo said.

"Do you know *where* it's coming in?"

Angelo sighed and shook his head. "I either don't know or else I can't remember. But Maldonado knows.''

"And Maldonado just tried to kill you," said Gonzago. "Me, too, come to think of it, but that's not really the point. Your cover has been blown. There's nothing you could possibly do now. Quite aside from which, you are not a police officer anymore.''

"No, I suppose I'm not," Angelo replied. "But on the other hand, I guess that means I don't have to worry about doing everything nice and legal, by the book.''

"I don't think I like the sound of that," Gonzago said. "I hope you're not thinking what I think you're thinking."

"What other choice do I have, Gonzo? I can't simply look the other way while they bring in a shipment of thaumagenetically engineered drugs. Besides, even if I wanted to, I don't think I have that option. Maldonado's not going to give up on me. It's not just the shipment, it's a matter of credibility for them. They have to take me down. And now they think you're involved in this, as well. We're going to have to stop them, before they stop us, permanently."

Gonzago sighed heavily. "Unfortunately, I cannot find any flaws in your argument. But those gangsters are not our only problem. The Dark Ones are not going to give up, either. And as far as I know, you are still wanted by the police. Kira, Wyrdrune, and Gypsy have gone to meet with Deputy Commissioner McGuire. With any luck, that may take care of at least that one problem, but there is still the matter of the Dark Ones."

"Gonzo?" said the waitress, coming up to their table. "There's a phone call for you."

"Thank you, dear," Gonzago said, getting up to answer it. "Maybe that's good news. Keep your fingers crossed, my boy. And don't sit with your back toward the door."

CHAPTER TEN

TWO OF THEM, thought Case, as he sat behind his desk, staring at the couple seated across from him. They looked enough alike to be brother and sister. And the way the woman was looking at him, he felt like an insect about to be dropped into a jar of alcohol. Anyone else would have mistaken her expression for desire, but Case knew better. It wasn't sexual hunger she was projecting, but a hunger of an entirely different sort. He felt an impulse rising up within him that he hadn't felt since he was a small child, an impulse of blind, unreasoning terror. He wanted to run, but there was nowhere to run to. If it wasn't for Beladon, he thought, she'd take me right here.

Vampires really did exist, he thought, but they were much more frightening than the ones depicted in the movies. These vampires, like their mythical counterparts, lived forever, only they did not sleep in coffins. They felt perfectly at home out in the daylight, and they were not afraid of garlic or crucifixes. And they did not drink human blood. They drank something far worse. They drank human souls.

"So what progress have you made?" asked Beladon, as calmly as if he were asking him about some routine report.

"I've made progress on two fronts," Case replied.

"McGuire is no longer going to be a problem. I've had him ordered off the case and everything he's got is being turned over to this office. So there won't be any more interference from the police. From now on, the Bureau calls the tune. Secondly, I've contacted our Washington headquarters and arranged to have copies of all the district attorney's Organized Crime Task Force files delivered to this office. Christine Mathews protested strenuously, of course, but there really wasn't anything that she could do." He picked up a thick file folder and handed it to Beladon. "These are all the files pertaining to John Angelo and his undercover activities."

Beladon took the file and started to peruse it.

"As it turns out," continued Case, "the D.A. didn't have a leg to stand on. Angelo discovered evidence that Tommy Leone's bunch were dealing in thaumagenetically engineered drugs. They're expecting a shipment of Ambrosia from the Orient, and that clearly gives the Bureau jurisdiction in the matter. As of now, both the police department and the D.A.'s task force are under my direct authority insofar as anything that pertains to this situation."

"And that is all you have managed to accomplish?" asked Beladon, raising his eyebrows.

Case felt a sudden chill go through him. "It's not insignificant, you know," he protested quickly. "It takes time to get these things done. You have to work through the system. I mean, after all, that's why you came to me, isn't it, to take advantage of the system? We're now in a position where it's working for us."

"But you have come no closer to locating the avatars than you were before," said Beladon.

Case's glance went from Beladon to the female and then quickly slid away. He wished she would at least say something. It was giving him the creeps, the way she kept looking at him like a hungry cat. "It's only a matter of time now," he said. "This is a big city. We've got a lot of people out there looking for them, but they could be anywhere." That sounded too lame. His mind raced to think of a stronger note to finish on. "Every cop in town has Angelo's description," he said. "And I've got every Bureau agent in this office working on this case. Now that we don't have to worry about McGuire sticking his nose in where it doesn't belong, we'll run him down, don't worry."

"I fail to see the purpose of these documents," said Beladon. "How do they help us?"

"It's a file on the investigation Angelo was working on before he took part in that raid," said Case. "Where he was staying, what he was doing from day to day, all the people he was in contact with. The police have already got his apartment staked out. If he shows up there, I'll know it right away. Otherwise, there's a good chance he may get in contact with some of those people, since that's what he was doing before."

"But you do not have any way of knowing that for certain," Beladon replied.

"No, but if he doesn't get in contact with them, they'll start looking for him, too. They've already lost several major shipments to police seizures. Those were just ordinary narcotics, but now that they've got the Ambrosia coming in, they'll be especially anxious. Angelo was working undercover as part of their operation. If he's suddenly disappeared, it won't take much for them to put two and two together. They'll figure out he was the informant and they'll put a contract out on him."

"A contract?"

"It means they will offer a substantial sum of money to anyone who kills him," Case explained. "So either way, he's a walking dead man, no pun intended."

"I see. And this man Leone is the one in charge of this operation, as you put it? The one who will offer the money for Angelo's life?"

"He's the one," said Case.

"And who is this man Maldonado?"

"His chief lieutenant. He's the one Angelo was working with on his undercover job."

Beladon pursed his lips thoughtfully and looked back down at the file. Case risked another glance at the female. Her eyes were still boring into him. He quickly looked away.

"There is a chance that these men might be useful," Beladon said. "What, exactly, is this Ambrosia they are expecting to receive?"

Relieved at what appeared to be a reprieve, Case quickly explained about the new thaumagenetically engineered drugs that had started appearing on the market recently, and he briefly described Ambrosia and its effects.

Beladon made a grimace of disgust. "And humans are anxious for this substance?" he said.

"Some humans, yes," said Case. "There's always been a large market for illegal narcotics, and the demand for this new thaumagenetic stuff is growing larger every day."

"This may be even easier than I thought," said Beladon. He glanced at his companion. "Who but humans would manufacture substances that render them weak and vulnerable? They have made much progress, but they have grown decadent. They themselves are giving us the tools with which to subjugate them."

"What are you saying?" Case asked uncertainly.

"Merely that if it does what you describe, then this Ambrosia, and the people who distribute it, could serve our purposes."

"Wait a minute," Case said. "You're not seriously thinking of taking over Leone's operation, are you?"

"And why not? If humans have an attraction for this substance that turns them into mindless, rutting animals, then why not provide it for them? It will merely make things easier for us."

Case moistened his lips. "Look, haven't you got enough to worry about with finding these three with the runestones? You don't want to go getting into the drug business. You've got no idea what that involves."

"I imagine these men Leone and Maldonado would know all that was necessary," Beladon replied. "They would simply continue distributing this Ambrosia, only they would do so under our supervision, so that they could attain the widest possible distribution in the shortest possible time."

"Jesus, you don't understand," said Case. "I can't simply

look the other way on something like this. It's my job to prevent that sort of thing. What you've asked me to do so far, well, that's one thing, and I've already taken some pretty big risks for you, but if there's a sudden flood of magically enhanced drugs in the city, I'm going to have all sorts of people coming down on me wanting to know why, from the mayor all the way up to Bureau headquarters. And the last thing any of us needs is to have our connection exposed."

"And how would that happen, unless you were to reveal that connection?" Beladon asked.

"Well, now, don't get me wrong," said Case quickly, "I'd never talk, of course, but they'd simply tie me in with Leone's mob and that would be the end of it. I wouldn't be much use to you in jail, would I?"

"You could be easily replaced," said Beladon. "It will be up to you to continue to prove your usefulness to us. Otherwise, what becomes of you does not concern me. For the moment, I am satisfied with you. You may live a little while longer."

"But you said I could have him," said the female, speaking for the first time, and Case felt as if the floor had dropped out from beneath his feet.

"Be patient, Delana," the necromancer said. "This human can still be of some use to us. I know you hunger. We shall find you someone else."

"When?" she demanded.

"Soon. Very soon. Before the day is out. Come."

With a sick feeling, Case watched them leave the office, then he leaned forward suddenly and vomited into his office trash pail.

Angelo looked awkward as Kira threw her arms around him. She sensed him stiffen and backed off. "My God, you don't remember me, do you?" she asked with a stricken expression.

"I . . . I'm not really sure," Angelo replied uncertainly. "You . . . you *seem* familiar, but . . ." His voice trailed off and he simply shook his head.

"Don't worry about it," Wyrdrune said. "It'll all come back to you before too long. The runestone will see to that. The important thing is that you're safe."

"I feel . . . a certain comfort in your presence," Angelo replied. "I can't really explain it, it simply feels right being here."

"It should, Modred, old friend," said Wyrdrune, clapping him on the shoulder. "That's the link between us. It's only going to get stronger."

"Modred," Angelo said. He shook his head. "I'm not sure if I'll ever get used to that name."

"What would you like us to call you?" Kira asked.

"John, I guess. That name seems to fit more, somehow."

"All right," said Wyrdrune. "John Angelo it is, until you tell us different."

"You have no idea how relieved we are to see you . . . John," said Kira. She smiled. "That's going to take some getting used to, I guess. How do you feel?"

"A bit confused, still, but no longer quite so weak as I felt before," he replied. "Gonzo was kind enough to get me something to eat downstairs. What's more, he saved my life, too."

"Why, what happened?" Wyrdrune asked with a concerned expression.

Briefly, Gonzago filled them in on what had happened.

"That's just what I was afraid of," Wyrdrune said. "Now we have the mob to worry about, as well. On top of that, we've got yet another complication. I'm afraid McGuire's going to be a problem." Quickly he filled the others in on what transpired during their meeting. "I should have made him forget he'd ever seen us," he said when he was finished, "but I just couldn't do it. I guess what he said got to me. If we start going around controlling people all the time, we're not much better than the Dark Ones. Every time I've done it, even when it seemed absolutely necessary, it's left a bad taste in my mouth. I didn't become a wizard so that I could use people."

"You didn't become a wizard at all, warlock," Kira said

wryly. "The runestones made you one. And maybe they've done more than that. Maybe they've been influencing our judgment too much."

"So where does that leave us with McGuire?" Billy asked.

"I honestly don't know," said Wyrdrune. "But he had a damn good point. We've been sitting on this thing for quite a while now, and I think it was only a matter of time before word of it got out somehow. Too many people know already. We really don't have the right to make this kind of decision for everybody else. Maybe it would be better if it was all out in the open. I'm tired of looking over my shoulder all the time, wondering if it's the Dark Ones, the Bureau, or the police."

Kira glanced at him curiously. It was the first time she had heard him voice any of the same concerns she'd felt. "Maybe we're all tired," she said. "None of us have had a life since this whole thing started."

"Some of us have had several lives," said Wyrdrune wryly.

"Oh, that's the other thing I meant to mention," said Gonzago suddenly. "In all the excitement, it completely slipped my mind. John, here, apparently manifested one of the Old Ones."

"He did *what*?" said Wyrdrune.

"One of the spirits of the Council," said Gonzago. "Or an entity that was a sort of group representation. Neither of you had mentioned having experienced such an effect before, so I thought it might be significant."

"You thought it *might* be significant?" said Kira. "Is there anything *else* that you forgot to tell us?"

Gonzago simply shrugged. "No, I don't think so. Unless it's that notion John has about the Ambrosia."

"*Ambrosia?*" Kira said. "Jesus, what does that evil stuff have to do with any of this?"

Gonzago glanced at Angelo. "I think perhaps you'd better tell them what you told me, my boy."

"Perhaps we'd all better sit down," said Angelo. "It seems

we've got a great deal to discuss, and I'm not even sure I understand all of it.''

"That's a good idea,'' Wyrdrune said. "Broom! Put on some coffee!''

"*Again* with the coffee?'' Broom called from the kitchen. "That's it! I'm on strike! You people have gone through an entire can in just two days. You're all going to ruin your kidneys! Aside from which, how am I supposed to make coffee without any filters? Make a list, you said. You want a list? Here, Mr. Big Shot, you've got your list. I'm not lifting another finger around here until somebody goes to the store and that's final! You can all save the world *after* you've gone shopping.''

"Right,'' said Wyrdrune, looking at the list with a grimace. He held it up. "Anybody feel like making a grocery run?''

"Donuts,'' said Kira. "We need some donuts.''

"And I am out of cigarettes,'' Jacqueline said.

"Ah, I don't suppose it would be too much trouble to stop at the liquor store and pick up a bottle or two of some Scotch while you're at it?'' said Gonzago. "Single malt, if you don't mind.''

Wyrdrune rolled his eyes, and with a weary sigh picked up a pen and started writing.

It had been almost fifteen years since McGuire had quit smoking. In all that time, he had never been seriously tempted to start again. During those first few weeks, when his withdrawal symptoms were at their height, there had been times when he had experienced strong cravings for a cigarette, such as when he was having morning coffee or an evening drink with friends, or moments when he was under stress, but his resolve had remained strong. It had been so hard to quit that it had merely strengthened his desire to stay away from the damned things, and even when new strains of thaumagenetically engineered tobacco had appeared, resulting in cigarettes that posed no health risk whatsoever, he had remained smokeless. For all those years, he had kept a pack of unfiltered, premagical, emphysema-inducing, heart-attack-risk-incurring, cancer-causing, secondhand-smoke-hazard cigarettes on his bookshelf, in plain sight, where they could serve as a symbol of his willpower and dedication. After fifteen years, those cigarettes tasted stale as hell.

They were so dry they burned like haystacks in the Kansas sun, and inhaling them was like breathing pure carbon monoxide. McGuire had chain-smoked almost the entire pack, washing them down with vodka. He had never quit drinking, so his tolerance for alcohol was fairly high. He wasn't drunk yet, but he was working on it.

He had already been on the phone, again, to Chief Inspector Michael Blood of New Scotland Yard and Inspector Armand Renaud of the Paris police. He had discussed the situation at length with Akira Katayama, of the B.O.T. in Tokyo, and with Captain Rebecca Farrell of the L.A.P.D., as well as with Ben Slater, the irascible Los Angeles reporter, who had a great deal to say about the biggest story of his entire career— the one he couldn't write. All of them had said more or less the same thing. They thought disclosure would be a serious mistake. They thought it would cause an upheaval in society the effects of which would be impossible to predict, and they thought that the negative effects would probably outweigh the positive ones. But, like Wyrdrune, they thought he had a valid point. It was one they'd all wrestled with themselves, and some of them were still quite torn about it, but in the end, they had decided to keep their knowledge to themselves. They had all seen what the Dark Ones were capable of doing, and they all thought that full disclosure would probably make little difference in the long run, that only the power of the runestones could defeat the necromancers.

However, having said that, every one of them had then gone on to say that if Wyrdrune had left the decision up to him, they would all support him in whatever it was he chose to do. And if he chose disclosure, they would back him up to the fullest extent of their abilities. Ben Slater had said it best. "Whatever you decide, McGuire, we're all in this together," the gruff reporter said. "I'm here anytime you need me, day or night. All you have to do is pick up a phone and I'll be on the next plane to New York. Just say the word."

The trouble was, McGuire wasn't really sure which way to go. At first, he'd felt strongly that keeping the existence of the Dark Ones secret was absolutely wrong. Now, after speaking with the others, he was having a few doubts. Once this thing is out of the bag, he thought, there'll be no turning back. It was a momentous decision. Why did it have to rest with him?

He needed to talk it over with somebody else, somebody who was not already in on the whole thing, somebody who would have a different perspective and whose fresh reaction he could judge, somebody whom he could trust with the secret if, at length, he decided to allow it to *remain* a secret. He picked up the phone and dialed Christine Mathews.

"Christine? Steve," he said, slurring his words slightly. "We need to talk."

"McGuire?"

"Yeah. Look, uh, we need to talk. I'm at my place. Can you come over right away?"

"Can't it wait until tomorrow, Steve?"

"No . . . no, it can't wait, Christine, I need to talk to you right now. It's really important."

"Steve, have you been drinking?"

"Yeah, a little. Oh, and when you come over, can you bring a couple packs of cigarettes?"

"You're *smoking*?"

"Yeah. How about that?"

"Are you all right? What is it, what's happened?"

"Just do me a big favor, Christine, and get over here. I don't want to discuss this on the phone. I want to see your face when I tell you about this. I really need your help on this decision."

"Is it about Angelo?"

"In a way, yeah. How long has it been since you had your mind blown?"

"My mind doesn't blow easy."

"It will when you hear this."

"Well, now I'm dying of curiosity. All right, I'll be there in about half an hour. Oh, what brand do you smoke?"

"Anything with a warning label on it."

"They haven't made those in about ten years."

"Then I don't care. Whatever."

"Okay, I'm on my way."

He hung up and poured himself a fresh drink. Then he grimaced, poured it out, and went to make a fresh pot of coffee, instead. Twenty minutes later, he had smoked up the last of his outdated cigarettes. He felt dizzy and he had a headache. The buzzer sounded from the lobby.

"That was fast," he said to himself. But when he pressed the intercom button, it wasn't Christine Mathews.

"McGuire, it's Case. We need to talk."

"Case?"

"Look, I know this is irregular, but I'm in deep, deep trouble and I really need your help. I know we've had our problems, but I didn't know who else to turn to. Can I come up, please?"

"You got any cigarettes?"

"*Cigarettes*? Yeah, why?"

"Come on up." He buzzed him in. What the hell, he thought, the D.A. and New York Bureau chief. If he was going to tell anybody about this, he couldn't have picked a better place to start. A few moments later there was a knock at the door. He opened it to admit a haggard-looking Case.

"Jeez, you look like hell," he said.

"Frankly, you don't look much better," Case said. "You been drinking?"

"Some. But I've got a fresh pot of coffee on."

"Well, I could sure as hell use a drink."

"Help yourself. Bottle's on the table. I'll get you a glass."

"Thanks," said Case, sitting down at the table.

"So, what's the problem?" asked McGuire.

"You'd better sit down for this. I'm about to drop a real bombshell on you."

"That right? Well, I'll see your bombshell and raise you

one nuke," McGuire said, setting a glass down in front of him. He sat down at the table with him. "Okay. Go ahead."

Case poured himself a drink, tossed back about half of it in one gulp, then took a deep breath. "To tell you the truth, I'm not really sure where to start."

"The beginning's usually a good place."

"Yeah, well, what would you say if I told you that I'm guilty on several major felony counts, including aiding and abetting a necromancer?"

"Did you say a *necromancer*?"

"Yeah," said Case, taking another drink. He took out a pack of cigarettes and pushed it toward McGuire. "And what's more, that ain't the worst of it. This isn't any ordinary necromancer."

"Don't tell me, let me guess," McGuire said. "This one's not human."

Case almost dropped his drink. "Holy shit. You *know*?"

"Looks like we've both got the same bombshell. Christine Mathews is going to be over here in about five or ten minutes. I was going to drop it on her, but it's nice to have some corroboration."

"Jesus Christ," said Case. "I can't believe it. How long have you known?"

"About your involvement?" He shook his head. "I didn't. You just told me. But I found out about the Dark Ones earlier today."

"The Dark Ones? Is that what they call themselves?"

"Well, I don't know what they call themselves," McGuire said, "but that's how they were identified to me."

"My God," said Case. "You've actually spoken to them, haven't you? The avatars, the ones with the runestones."

McGuire nodded. "Yes, they came to see me and they laid it all out for me. It's one hell of a story."

"You probably know more than I do, then," said Case.

"Well, I'll go over the whole thing as soon as Christine gets here. Meanwhile, why don't you tell me your end of it. You're on the hook, aren't you?"

"Yeah," said Case heavily. He refilled his glass. "Big time."

"But you're not under a spell of compulsion," said McGuire as he lit up a cigarette, "otherwise you wouldn't be here. So what did he do, bribe you? Promise you something? Use blackmail?"

"All of the above," Case replied. "They gave me just a hint of what they were capable of doing, and it was enough to scare the crap out of me. You haven't met them, you don't know. They're capable of causing pain you just would not believe. And they told me—"

"Wait a minute," said McGuire. "You said *they*? There's more than one?"

"There's at least two of them," said Case, "a male and a female. I thought it was only one, at first. He was bad enough. His name is Beladon, but I just met the female today, and she makes Count Dracula look like a mosquito. Her name's Delana, or something like that, and I was as close to her as I am to you right now, and let me tell you, I was so goddamn scared I tossed my cookies." Case gulped down his drink and reached for the bottle.

"Take it easy on that stuff," McGuire said.

"Screw that," said Case, filling up his glass again. "I've got so much adrenaline pumping through me right now, I don't think I could get drunk if I wanted to. And believe me, I want to." He took another gulp. "I'm telling you, McGuire, these people are fucking terrifying. They're not people. I don't know what the hell they are."

"I think I've got some idea," said McGuire. "I'm not going to judge you, Case. I don't think you had much choice."

Case sighed heavily. "I appreciate that," he said. "It doesn't make me feel a whole lot better about what I did, but it's decent of you to say that."

"I mean it," said McGuire. "I don't know that I wouldn't have done the same thing in your place. We all like to think we know ourselves, but we're only human. And they're not. What did they make you do for them?"

Case grimaced. "Jump through hoops, is what they made me do. I gave Beladon everything he wanted. I gave him all the information I had; I had Bureau headquarters get me the D.A.'s file on Angelo and I turned that over; I pulled strings and got you to back off, I just totally caved in."

"There's not much point to self-recrimination," said McGuire. "At least you're doing the right thing now. What finally made you come to me?"

"I'd like to think it was my sense of duty finally waking the hell up, but the truth is it was fear. The minute they don't need me anymore . . ." He shook his head. "You should have seen the way that bitch was looking at me. Now I know what a mouse feels like when it's staring at a cobra. I'm scared out of my wits, McGuire. I'm just a miserable, fucking coward."

"But you didn't run," McGuire said. "You could have."

Case stared at him and licked his lips nervously. "Yeah. I guess I could have, at that."

"But the point is that you didn't," said McGuire. "And you're probably not so important to them that they'd waste time trying to find you. No offense."

Case nodded. "Yeah. Maybe I'm stupid. Maybe I should be looking for some deep, dark hole to crawl into."

"And maybe you're not quite the coward you think you are," McGuire said. "Sometimes heroes are just cowards who were too scared to run."

Case gave a small snort. "Where'd you get that?"

"I just made it up. But I'm sure somebody important said it first. The question is, what are we going to do about it?"

"Damned if I know," Case said miserably. "How the hell do you fight necromancers who can't be killed?"

"Is that what they told you?"

"Well, they're immortal, aren't they?"

"The way it was explained to me, they live practically forever because their cells are capable of almost infinite regeneration. But they do age, apparently, although at an incredibly slow rate, and they *can* be killed."

"How?"

"A well-placed bullet right between the eyes should do the trick, if I understand correctly. Or any immediately fatal wound."

"You're kidding me. You mean I could have simply *shot* the bastards?"

"Well, that's easier said than done," McGuire said. "You're dealing with necromancers, after all. They're much more powerful than any human adept. And these necromancers aren't even human. They've been at it for a long, long time. You'd have to take them completely by surprise, and your aim had better be damn good."

"I never was much good with a gun," said Case. "Not much call for it in my line of work."

"Mine, either," said McGuire, "but I still remember how to shoot. The problem is, we're in a real legal gray area here. We're officers of law, not judges and juries. How do we justify what amounts to murder?"

"Are you serious? How else are we supposed to stop them? These people aren't even human."

"Prove it," said McGuire. "They appear biologically similar to us, right? Well, unless an autopsy can tell the difference, you kill them and you're liable to wind up facing charges."

"Right. Find a jury anywhere that would convict me, under the circumstances."

"That's just the point," McGuire said. "We have to explain the circumstances and make it convincing. I think there's an excellent chance we can pull it off, because we're not the only people who know about this and the others are all willing to testify. But we can't simply take the law into our hands. We both have to go to our superiors with this."

"Terrific," said Case. "And what am I supposed to do in the meantime?"

"Meanwhile, you're going to have to hang tough. Our best chances still lie with the runestones," said McGuire. "Angelo is now one of the avatars, as you know. The other two are a young adept named Wyrdrune and a young woman named Kira. They've also got some help and, as near as I can tell, almost unlimited resources. However, they're still wanted on international warrants. Before we do anything else, we've got to get those warrants lifted, and we've got to get them the full backing of the authorities.''

"That's going to take time," said Case. "And it may not be easy.''

"We don't have any other choice. Is there any chance you can play along with the necromancers in the meantime?''

Case moistened his lips nervously and shook his head. "I don't know. They haven't read my mind. Leastwise, I don't think they have. They function on intimidation, and they're damned good at it, too. They probably don't think I'd have the nerve to cross them.'' He sighed heavily. "But, man, the very last thing I want to do is have to face them again.''

"Well, this is where you start earning your big paycheck,'' said McGuire.

Case closed his eyes for a moment and compressed his lips into a tight grimace. "Right. What the hell, I've got nothing to lose except my soul.''

"The avatars are probably going to be in touch with me soon," McGuire said. "I'll tell them what we've decided. It would also help if I could give them some idea of what the Dark Ones are up to. Have they confided anything in you?''

"Not a lot," said Case, "but wait'll you hear what they have told me. They saw that file Mathews had on Angelo's operation, and they've decided to go into the drug business.''

"What?''

"Tommy Leone's started dealing in Ambrosia," Case said. "He's supposed to have a big shipment coming in sometime soon. Beladon has decided it serves his purposes to make humans weak with thaumagenetic drugs, so he's going to take over Leone's operation and increase distribution.''

"Good God," McGuire said. "That's all we need. Immortal necromancers taking over organized crime. As if things weren't bad enough already.'' He bit his lower lip. "But at least it gives us something to work with. If they're going to target Leone's operation, then we'll know where to watch for them.''

The buzzer sounded.

''That's Christine,'' McGuire said, getting up from the table. ''Now we'll get some idea of just how hard this thing is gonna be to sell.''

CHAPTER
ELEVEN

CALADOR HAD BEEN chafing for the opportunity to do something and now that it had finally arrived, it wasn't at all what he'd expected. He had been well on his way to establishing his domain in the remote mountains of the country the humans called Afghanistan when Beladon had found him. He already had Delana with him then, and Calador chose not to test Beladon's power because he did not think he could prevail against the two of them together. With or without Delana, Beladon was strong. He had been strong in the days before the war, and he was strong now, though the centuries of confinement had weakened them all. Calador had not been certain he would have been a match for him.

If there had only been more time. From the moment he escaped the pit where they were all confined, he had searched for a place where he could begin to establish his domain, an isolated place that could still provide sufficient human resources to increase his power. He had known that it would not take long before the others started to compete among themselves for dominance, and he wanted to be ready when the time came to determine the matter of supremacy. But Beladon had not given him that opportunity. Yet, the opportunity had not been lost, thought Calador. It had merely been postponed.

He detested this country where Beladon had brought them. Its flatness and lack of natural majesty was a poor substitute for the raw and savage beauty of the mountains he had left behind. The human tribes who lived there had been simple creatures, fierce and primitive, easily brought under his control. They had regarded him as an earthly incarnation of a god, just as they had in the old days, and there was a comforting familiarity in their behavior. They seemed not much different from the humans he had known before, a bit more intelligent perhaps, but that was only to be expected as the species had evolved. Still, they seemed a far cry from what Beladon claimed the humans had become.

On the other hand, he was forced to admit that these humans had made more progress than he had given them credit for. They had truly accomplished a great deal. Still, they were merely humans. What amazed him was that some of them had been able to learn magic. Beladon had said that it was because surviving Old Ones had mingled with their population after the Great War, and they had interbred. The very thought filled Calador with disgust. It was like mating with beasts, for they were little more than that, despite all their advancements. Calador could scarcely believe that Beladon perceived them as a threat. To an immortal who was weak, perhaps, a sufficient number of them might represent a threat. However, they were no match for a necromancer at the peak of his abilities.

In the absence of the immortals, there had been little to check the growth of their population, and the planet was now teeming with them. However, all that meant was that there would be no shortage of the life force resource for a long, long time to come. This new idea Beladon had put forth, using this Ambrosia substance to make them docile and ensure their continued reproduction, seemed absolutely pointless. He was beginning to sound like one of the members of the Council, who had always thought more of the humans than they had deserved.

The time was not yet right to risk pitting his powers against Beladon. He needed to be certain of success. Delana was the key. She was a prime young female, a far better mate for him than for Beladon. And as unattractive as this country was, despoiled by the massive constructions of the humans, it was rich in the life force resource. Beladon was much too slow to take advantage of it. He was too cautious, too concerned about the threat posed by the avatars who bore the runestones that had held them in a living death for all these years. Calador would not make the same mistake. The way to deal with the spirits of the Council was through strength.

"You are unusually quiet tonight," Delana said.

She was sitting beside him in the crude conveyance the humans called a "car." It was one of those belonging to the estate where they were staying. Its thaumaturgic batteries had just been freshly charged and they had driven it to the area known as the South Shore of Long Island, to a community known as Long Beach. It now sat parked across the street from the iron gates of Tommy Leone's home.

"I was merely thinking," Calador replied. "Does it not strike you as rather wasteful, this errand we are on?" He stressed the word "errand," lacing it with sarcasm to underscore the way that Beladon was treating them. It was time to begin planting the seeds of dissatisfaction in her mind.

"Wasteful?" she said. "In what way?"

"Traveling in this crude vehicle, for instance," Calador replied, "when we could easily teleport. This takes so much more time."

"But it also conserves our energies," Delana said. "Beladon explained that, did he not?"

"Oh, yes, he explained," Calador said scornfully. "Since we came here, he has done precious little save explain things."

Delana gave him a curious look. "I had thought that you were merely impatient. But you do not agree with his methods?"

"For all his explanations, I fail to understand them," Calador replied. "We are immortals, Delana. We are the Dark

Ones. We once ruled all that we surveyed. Yet look at us now. We hide. We masquerade as humans, cutting our hair and wearing these foolish garments. We play at intrigue with these inferior creatures, treating them as opponents worthy of respect instead of the chattel that they are. Is this what we have come to?''

''Beladon has explained what happened to the others, who were careless and too quick to act. He—''

''Beladon has explained,'' Calador repeated scornfully. ''Can you not think for yourself? What do we really *know* of how the others fell? Perhaps they failed because they were weak. Perhaps they failed because they lacked resolve. Perhaps they failed not because they moved too quickly, but because they were not quick enough. It is strength that ensures victory. When was the last time you felt the power of fresh life force flowing through you?''

She moistened her lips. ''It has been a long time.''

''And with each day that passes, your hunger ever increases,'' Calador replied, ''as does mine. Yet Beladon counsels discipline and patience. Soon, he tells us. Soon we may feed the hunger. But when? Is it truly the runestones that he fears, or does he fear that *we* may grow too strong?''

''Beladon denies himself, as well,'' she said.

''We have only his word for that,'' Calador countered. ''How do we know what he does while he is absent? Can you say for sure he has not fed?''

He saw the uncertainty in her eyes and smiled inwardly. He knew that appealing to her hunger, the hunger he himself knew only all too well, would bring immediate results.

''You need not answer,'' he said. ''Your loyalty is admirable, but I often wonder if it has not been misplaced.''

''Beladon is strong,'' she said, though there was doubt in her voice. ''He knows much more about this new world we have awakened in than either of us does. He has taken time to study it, and to formulate his plans. We can profit from his knowledge.''

''Perhaps,'' said Calador, ''but at what cost? I do not fault Beladon for his ambition. Indeed, I commend him for it.

However, it is his ambition and not mine. In the old days, Beladon was among the strongest of us, but do you recall how he maintained that strength? By subjugating others to his will. By controlling a greater number of acolytes, and maintaining greater access to the life force resource. And by making certain that no one could accumulate more power than he had at his command. It is no different now. He seeks to do exactly the same thing."

"He said he wants to unify the others—"

"Yes, of course. Under his control. He will respect their decision, he claims. But who will question his right to supremacy when he has become the strongest? You know as well as I what will become of anyone who dares to challenge him once he has assumed the mantle of supremacy."

"And yet you dare to question his methods and his aims," she said. "Are you not afraid that I will pass on your remarks to him?"

"I am not one to live with fear," said Calador. "You are free to do as you desire. Beladon trusts you, because he has selected you to be his consort. At least, for now. And that is why he has sent us on this petty errand for him. It is merely a small test, both of your loyalty and of my obedience. Once we have carried it out, he shall praise us in paternal tones and reward us by allowing us to feed the hunger, but not too much. He means only to whet our appetites and make us anxious to please him, so that we may feed again. And that, Delana, is how he shall control us, by remaining stronger and making us come to feel dependent on him."

"He has said nothing to me of such things," she said.

"Why should he? He already owns you."

"No one owns me!" she said angrily.

"Perhaps not," said Calador. "But you have given your allegiance to him, have you not?"

"I have merely joined my strength to his, the better to destroy the runestones, so that all of us may live free of their threat and prosper in our power."

"I see," said Calador. "And just what is it we are doing here tonight that will further that cause?"

She remained silent.

Calador nodded. "Yes, you cannot answer. I do not see how this serves that purpose, either. The only purpose this shall serve is to gain Beladon more human acolytes, for it is his bidding they shall do, not ours."

"You seek to test his power," she said.

"I seek only to assert my own," Calador replied. "If you wish to subordinate your strength to his, your will to his, then that is your decision. But I think it is a waste for you to cheat yourself of your own destiny."

"Which you see as being linked to yours, perhaps?" she asked archly.

"I will not deny that I sense your power and am drawn to it," said Calador smoothly. "But I have no desire to subjugate your will to mine. That would diminish you, and it would diminish me. What need is there for us to compete among ourselves? There are so many humans now, this world is choked with them. Why waste our energies against each other when we could both grow strong together? Think what we could accomplish."

"Those are almost the very words that Beladon had used when he first found me," she said.

"Indeed? Well, then you must judge his words against his actions, just as you may judge mine. Have you both grown strong together? Have you satisfied your hunger? Or have you been told to wait until the time is right? And who is to say when that shall be? You? Or Beladon? Has he told you when that time will be? Or has he just said, 'Soon'?"

"I do grow weary of that word," she admitted.

"I do not say, 'Soon, Delana.' I say . . . *now*. We have been sitting here and watching humans arriving at this dwelling all evening long. Shall we wait until they all depart, and then bring back this man Leone to await Beladon's pleasure? Or shall we take advantage of this opportunity and then decide how best to employ the strength that we shall gain? I am willing to be charitable. Let Beladon have the human named Leone, if that is all he wants. Why should we not take the others for ourselves?"

Delana stared hungrily at the house across the street. "Why not, indeed?" she said.

Calador smiled. It had gone even better than he had anticipated. Beladon had underestimated him, and he had denied Delana for too long. He did not even suspect it, but he had already lost his grip on her. And once she had absorbed fresh, invigorating life force, he would not regain it. Together, the two of them left the car and started walking toward the house.

Wyrdrune hung up the phone in the kitchen, took a deep breath, and let it out slowly. Then he went back to the others in the living room. "Well, that was certainly interesting. Not exactly what I'd planned on."

"Don't worry, you did the right thing," Makepeace said. "Let the police handle these gangsters. Drug enforcement cannot be our concern."

"It isn't just the drugs," said Wyrdrune. "There's still a hit out on John. Not much we can do about that now, though. Not without taking the law into our own hands, and McGuire was very emphatic about our staying out of it."

"How did he sound?" asked Angelo.

"He asked about you," Wyrdrune said. "He's concerned. He's going to lift that A.P.B. on you, but he's going to have to do some fancy explaining. And there's been an interesting new development. Case, the New York Bureau chief, was with him when I called. And so was the D.A."

"So then he's gone ahead and brought in the Bureau," Gypsy said.

"Actually, it's the other way around," said Wyrdrune. "Are you ready for this? Case has been working with the Dark Ones."

"*What?*" said Kira.

"Apparently, there are two of them, and they never bothered actually placing him under a spell," said Wyrdrune. "They used terror and intimidation. They felt that he would be more useful to them if he was able to function freely, and it seems he has been. He's kept them informed of all the details of the investigation and he's given them the D.A.'s task force files, as well.'' He glanced at Angelo. ''It was too much for Case. He's scared. They just finally pushed him to a point where he got too scared to be intimidated. They now know all the details of the case you were working on, and they've decided to make use of that information.''

''How?'' asked Angelo.

''They're planning to take over Leone's operation,'' Wyrdrune said.

''You mean distribute the Ambrosia?''

''Knowing them, they'll probably take over everything he's into and make use of his people. As for the Ambrosia, they may just give it away,'' said Wyrdrune. ''After all, why bother using magic to enslave people when you can get them hooked, instead? They're learning to do things the modern way.''

''Damn,'' said Kira. ''But that means we know what their next move's going to be. If they're going to go after Tommy Leone—''

''I'm way ahead of you,'' said Wyrdrune. ''Unfortunately, so is McGuire. He's already gotten in touch with the police in Long Beach and arranged for round-the-clock surveillance on Leone and his people. They're going to coordinate with the N.Y.P.D., the Bureau, the D.A.'s task force, and the D.E.A. And he wants us to stay out of it.''

''That's crazy,'' Kira said. ''Did you tell him he doesn't stand a chance? What the hell does he think he's going to do, *arrest* them?''

''He seems to understand what he's doing,'' Wyrdrune said. ''Or at least, he thinks he does. He said he's not going to take any chances. He'll have Case with him, and if the Dark Ones show up, they'll simply open up on them with all the firepower they've got. If they do that, it just might do the trick.''

''*If* they do that,'' Billy said.

''And *might* just isn't good enough,'' Kira added. ''McGuire just doesn't learn. They tried the same sort of thing on us back at the penthouse, and we got away, didn't we? Unless they have the advantage of complete surprise, it'll never work. They're all liable to get killed. And the Dark Ones will be that much stronger. We've got to be there and you know it.''

"That's what I figured you'd say," Wyrdrune replied. "The only trouble is, all we know is that Leone lives somewhere in Long Beach. I already tried information and he isn't listed. Just where are we supposed to go?"

"He's got an estate just off Ocean Boulevard," Angelo said suddenly. He blinked several times. "I've been there before. I'm pretty sure I remember where it is."

"All right!" said Kira. "We're in business!"

"Not yet we're not," said Wyrdrune. "He's starting to recall things, but there's still too much he doesn't remember. We can't afford to take any chances. We need to know if he can form the Living Triangle."

"Well, there's only one way to find out," said Kira. She took off her glove and held her hand up, palm facing out. The sapphire runestone began to glow.

Wyrdrune removed his headband, revealing the glowing emerald set into his forehead. Angelo swallowed hard and started to open up his shirt. "I'm not sure I know what to do," he said. But even as he spoke, the ruby in his chest, over his heart, started to grow bright.

"The runestones know," said Wyrdrune. Then, turning to the others, he added, "Shield your eyes."

"The hell with that," said Gypsy. "I'm not about to miss this."

The emerald in Wyrdune's forehead suddenly flared with a blinding green light and a beam of pure thaumaturgic force lanced out from it like a laser and struck the sapphire stone in Kira's palm. The gem seemed to absorb the beam of force and reflect it, adding its own energy to it as a second beam shot out from it and struck the ruby in Angelo's chest. Angelo gasped involuntarily, and then a third beam shot out from his own runestone and struck the emerald in Wyrdrune's forehead, completing the triangle. It took no more than an instant, but in that instant, the entire room was bathed in searing light that flickered from blue to red to green, growing brighter and brighter until it washed out everything in the room.

Gypsy cried out, covering her eyes.

Slowly, the incandescently glowing triangle of light started to revolve. Wyrdrune, Kira, and Angelo were no longer visible. They were somewhere inside the whirling maelstrom as it spun faster and faster, raising a wind inside the room as it formed into a pyramid, spun faster still, and elongated into a cone that suddenly seemed to suck up inside itself with a whistling, howling noise . . . and then it was gone.

The others sat, dazed, as papers blew about the room and fluttered rustling to the floor and silence returned to the apartment.

"My God," Gypsy said with awe.

"My sentiments exactly," said Gonzago.

There was a loud pounding on the ceiling and they all jumped, startled, except for Makepeace. "All right, Mrs. Pietruskiewicz!" he called out, loudly, toward the ceiling. "We'll try to keep it down."

Broom came shuffling in from the kitchen, took one look at the room, and raised its arms up to its head, or at least where its head would have been if it had a head. "*Oy!* I just cleaned up in here! What *is* it with you people? You're all *meshuggeneh*! I've *had* it! You can just clean this up all by yourselves, thank you very much. I quit!"

Tommy Leone sat leaning back in the leather office chair behind the desk in his den, his feet encased in brand-new running shoes and resting on the table, crossed at the ankles. He wore brown velour athletic sweats that had never seen a jogging track or the inside of a gym, something to which his large and overweight frame attested. The zipper on his top was pulled halfway down, revealing a hairy chest, an ornate golden crucifix on an intricately linked chain, and a medallion of the Virgin.

"I want that son of a bitch *dead*, you understand me?" he

said. "I want his head in a fuckin' box, delivered to that bitch D.A.!"

"We're working on it real hard, Tommy," Maldonado said. "Word's out on the street. We've got ten grand on Angel's head. He won't be able to hide for long."

"You're real generous with my money, Vinnie," said Leone wryly. "That dough'll come outta your cut. You brought him in. He was your responsibility. What's more, you had him and you blew the hit."

"He had an adept with him that helped him get away," said Maldonado.

"I don't wanna hear no excuses. I just want the job done, period. If we lose this shipment on account of this, your next address is gonna be the East River, got me?"

"Don't worry, I'll take care of it," Maldonado assured him. "He may know when the shipment's coming in, but he doesn't know *where*. I'm not that stupid."

"Stupid enough to think I could've been the stoolie, when it was your man Angel all along," said Joey Battaglia with a sneer.

"You shut your mouth, punk," Maldonado said, fixing him with a glare. "You got no room to talk. It's a funny thing how your whore and Angel disappeared together, ain't it?"

"If Blue took off, it's because Angel warned her you were after her," said Joey. "She didn't know anything, and even if she did, she knew well enough to keep her trap shut. You can't put this off on me, Vinnie. You screwed up."

"I've had about all I'm gonna take outta you," said Maldonado, stepping toward him, but Franco got between them.

"Leave it alone, Vinnie," he said. "The kid's right. You blew it. If you'd simply whacked him instead of running your damn mouth, we wouldn't be worrying about Angel now."

"He wants a piece of me, let him come ahead," said Joey defiantly.

"Enough!" Leone shouted. "I've had it with this bullshit. You guys want to wave your dicks around, do it *after* the job's done. Once the shipment's in and Angel's feeding fish,

I don't give a rat's ass what the hell you do. But right now, both of you shut the fuck up."

"Sure thing, Mr. Leone," Joey said. "You're the boss."

Maldonado made a little circle with thumb and forefinger and brought it up to his lips, making little sucking noises.

"Can it, Vinnie," said Leone. "Jesus, you're acting like a couple of fuckin' twelve-year-olds. Now I want to know what's being done about—"

A sudden burst of fire from a machine pistol interrupted him, and then, just as abruptly, it was cut off.

"What the hell was that?"

"It sounded like it came from down by the gate," said Franco, moving toward the door and reaching inside his jacket for his piece.

"The rest of you, go see what it is," Leone said quickly.

The others moved to follow Franco, but as Franco reached the door, it suddenly slammed shut. Franco grabbed the doorknob and twisted it, but the door refused to open.

"What the hell?" he said.

"Open the goddamn door!" Leone said.

"I'm tryin', but it's stuck or something," Franco said.

"Here, let me," said Joey, reaching for the doorknob.

"I am afraid that no one will be leaving," Calador said.

The others spun around to see Calador standing behind the wet bar, pouring a drink. Delana was seated at the bar, facing them, her long legs crossed attractively.

"Who the hell are you?" said Joey. "How did you get in here?"

"They're adepts, you fucking moron," Maldonado said.

"How perceptive of you," said Calador sarcastically. He handed the drink to Delana and came out from behind the bar. "But we are much more than mere adepts. Which of you is named Leone?"

"That'll be me," said Tommy, getting to his feet behind his desk. "And whoever the hell you are, you'd damn well better have a warrant."

"A warrant?" Calador asked casually. "A warrant for what?"

"You got a paper with a judge's signature, I want to see it," said Leone. "Otherwise, you can get the hell out of here right now."

"Such insolence will not be tolerated," Calador said. "On your knees and beg forgiveness."

"*What?*" Leone said with disbelief.

"I said, on your knees, you fat slug." Calador's eyes flared with bright blue light and Leone screamed, clutching at his head as he collapsed to his knees. "I am master here."

"*Fuck* you!" Joey Battaglia shouted, shoving Maldonado aside as he raised his semiautomatic and pumped eight 10-mm hollowpoint bullets into the necromancer as fast as he could pull the trigger. The first four struck him squarely in the chest, and as he jerked back, the next two hit him in the throat and mouth. The seventh and eight rounds went right through his skull, sending fragments of bone and brain tissue out in a spray against the wall.

"*No!*" shouted Delana, and with eyes blazing blue fire, she threw out her arm, fingers extended, toward Battaglia. The bolt of thaumaturgic force she hurled struck Joey in the chest and burned a hole through his torso big enough to throw a basketball through.

"*You fuckin' bitch!*" Franco cried out, and he fired his gun at her point-blank. The others followed suit, but they had lost the advantage of surprise and, with it, any hope of survival. They all kept firing until their magazines were empty, but none of the bullets reached her. They were all incinerated in midair as they got to within a foot of her, and it looked as if she were surrounded by a star burst of miniature fireworks. And then there were no bullets left.

Like an enraged bull, Maldonado bellowed and charged her, but her eyes flared as she swept her arm out in a back-handed motion and the big man went flying across the room to crash into the opposite wall, though she had never even touched him. The others panicked and attacked the door, but it refused to open. Heat began to build up rapidly inside the room until the temperature was like that inside a blast furnace. The paneling started to crack and peel away from the wall.

The glass windows exploded and the drapes burst into flame. The men clawed at their throats, vainly trying to breathe in the unbearable heat that seemed to suck the air right out of their lungs. They collapsed to the floor, their skin turning red and blistering, splitting open like the baked earth of a desert in a scorching drought. It all happened in an instant as the room was turned into an inferno of searing heat and then the screaming started as Delana took their souls.

She felt the vibrant force of their life energy flowing through her and she gasped with rapture as she took it in, feeling the strength welling up within her and making every fiber of her body sing. She drew it in the way a man dying of thirst would gulp down cold, refreshing water and she wanted more. It had been so long, so very long, and she was so very hungry.

She turned her attention to Leone, who was cowering back against the wall, eyes rolling in his blackened, cracked, and blistered face with stark terror.

"No," he whimpered, "please, God, no! *Don't*! I'll do anything you want! *Please*! *Don't*! I'll do anything, I swear, *anything*!"

"Then die," she said, bending over and seizing him by the throat. Her eyes flashed as twin beams of force streamed out of them, burning through Leone's pupils and deep into his brain. He screamed hoarsely as she drained him and threw his lifeless body down onto the floor.

There were shouts and hammering on the other side of the door, and then automatic rifle fire stitched through it as the men outside attempted to shoot off the lock. With a snarl, Delana threw her arm out and hurled a bolt of force right through the door. It was as if the heavy, solid-core door had been struck by a bazooka. It blew apart in splinters of wood and flame, and there were screams as the men on the other side were caught in the thaumaturgic blast. Delana came striding through the eddying smoke of the burning door frame, held out her arms, and took in the life force of the survivors.

More men appeared at the far end of the hall and when they saw her, her skin glistening with sweat, her red hair wild, and her eyes blazing with unearthly light, they opened fire. The bullets never reached her. She threw her arm out toward them, fingers splayed, and it was as if she had fired a flamethrower. The wallpaper bubbled and burst into flame as blue fire streamed down the hall toward them, enveloping them, and as they screamed in agony, dropped their guns, and beat helplessly at their flaming hair and clothing, she took them, as well.

She walked down the burning corridor and came into the large living room of the estate. At the far end of the room, Tommy Leone's wife stood on the stairs in her robe and nightgown, her small daughter behind her, clutching at her hem. She saw the smoke pouring into the living room from the corridor and cried out her husband's name. Delana came out of the smoke like a wraith, moving toward her.

The swirling vortex appeared over the front lawn of the estate and descended to the ground. When it dissipated, Wyrdrune, Kira, and Angelo stood there, staring at the smoking house. The firemen who were not busy bringing out the bodies gaped at them and backed away.

"We're too late," said Angelo. "They've already been here."

Their runestones were still glowing as they picked up the residue of necromancer magic. In the distance, there was the sound of rapidly approaching sirens.

"Something went wrong," said Wyrdrune as he stared at the fire-blackened house. "They came here to possess Leone, not kill him."

"It looks as if they killed just about everybody," Kira said.

"I've got to go in there," Wyrdrune said. He started walking toward the house.

"Wyrdrune, wait!" Kira called after him. When he kept going, she hurried after him and Angelo followed. Behind them, a convoy of police vehicles came screeching to a stop out in the street. Several cars continued on through the gates and up the driveway.

"Hey, buddy, you can't go in there!" one of the firemen

shouted as he came out of the house, dragging a length of heavy hose. They continued on past him. The fireman glanced toward his companions out on the lawn. "Why the hell didn't you stop them?"

"You want to stop them, be my guest," one of the others said, and walked back toward his fire truck.

They went through the relatively undamaged living room and down the corridor, following the signs of destruction toward Leone's den. Several firemen saw them and started to order them out, but fell silent at the sight of the brightly glowing gem in Wyrdrune's forehead. They came into the den, where several slickered firemen were in the act of removing the last of the bodies.

"Leave them alone," said Wyrdrune.

The men turned toward the sound of his voice. "What the . . . who the hell are you?" one of them said. "What do you think you're doing? Get these people the hell out . . ." And then his voice trailed off as he stared at the three intruders.

"Leave," said Wyrdrune softly.

Without a word, the men left what they were doing and walked out of the room. Wyrdrune moved directly to Calador's body and stood over it, looking down. His runestone flickered. Kira and Angelo came up behind him.

"Yeah, something went wrong, all right," said Kira.

"You had to do it, didn't you?" McGuire said from behind them. As they turned, he came into the room, followed by Case and several other officers. The odor of smoke and char was heavy in the air. The uniformed officers had their weapons drawn. "Put 'em away," McGuire said to them.

"You think *we* did this?" Wyrdrune asked.

"What else am I supposed to think?" McGuire said tightly.

"You *know* these people?" a police captain who stood with him asked.

"Yes, I know them," said McGuire. "But they're not the ones I thought we'd find here."

"You mind telling me what the hell this is all about?" the captain asked McGuire.

"It's about him," said Wyrdrune, glancing down at Calador's body.

Case moved forward quickly and looked down at the blackened body, then frowned. "He's not the one," he said.

"What are you talking about?" said Kira. "He's one of them. There isn't any doubt, believe me."

"I'm telling you, this isn't him," said Case.

"Are you *sure*?" Wyrdrune said.

"The body's been burned and the face is unrecognizable," said Case, "but I'm telling you, this isn't him. Beladon was a big guy, about six feet six. This one can't be more than five-ten or eleven, tops. What's more, he didn't die from magic. He's been shot several times with powerful, large-caliber slugs. The entire top of his head's been blown away. See for yourself."

"That means there were more than two of them," said Wyrdrune grimly. "There were at least three."

"Would somebody mind telling me what's going on here?" the Long Beach police captain asked irritably. "What are we talking about? You told me this was going to be a major drug bust."

"It's a lot more than that, Captain," Case said. "This entire house is positively vibrating with thaumaturgic trace emanations. We're dealing with necromancy here. That makes it the Bureau's jurisdiction."

"Hell," the captain said. "All right, I'm outta here. You people need anything, you know how to reach me."

"Captain," Case said, "needless to say, we want to keep the necromancy angle quiet, at least for now."

"It's your show, Agent Case," said the captain. "This is one headache I don't need. C'mon, boys."

"What the hell happened here?" McGuire asked when they had gone.

"I'm not sure," said Wyrdrune. "We only got here minutes before you did."

"I thought I told you people to stay out of it."

"Jesus Christ, McGuire, take a look around you," Kira

said. "This is what you would've been going up against. These men all had guns. A fat lot of good that did them."

"It did somebody some good," said Case, looking down at Calador's body. "The fire's damaged the room severely, as has the water from the firemen's hoses, but there's a lot more heat damage than damage from the flames, and the bodies haven't been completely burned. This wasn't arson. At least, not in the conventional sense. This was thaumaturgic force, but on a level of magnitude I've never seen before."

"One of Leone's men must've caught this one by surprise and dropped him," Wyrdrune said. "And then all hell broke loose."

"We'll have to question the firemen," said Case. "They got here pretty quick. Maybe somebody saw something."

"Sir," said a uniformed policemen, coming to the door. "You might want to see this." He handed Case a file folder.

Case opened it and said, "Shit."

"What is it?" asked McGuire.

"D.A. Mathews's task force file on Leone and his operation," Case replied. He glanced up at Angelo. "I guess this was mostly your work. Names, addresses, it's all here." He looked back at the cop. "Where did you find this?"

"In a vehicle parked across the street," the cop said. "The doors were just left open and the key was still in the ignition. We're running a make on the plates now."

"It was undoubtedly stolen," said McGuire. "Wonder why they didn't use it to get away."

"No need," said Wyrdrune. "They probably used it to get here to conserve their energies, but they absorbed enough life force here to teleport clear across the country without breaking a sweat."

"So you're telling me they could be anywhere?" McGuire said.

"No, they're still here," said Case. He glanced up at Angelo and the others. "There's still something here they want."

CHAPTER
TWELVE

THEY STOOD OUTSIDE on the lawn of the Leone estate, watching as the fire department wrapped up its operations and the trucks pulled off. Curious onlookers had gathered just outside the gates and the police out in the street were busy keeping them at bay. The night was lit up with the flashing of revolving lights on the squad cars.

"Leone was a known organized crime figure," McGuire said. "For the time being, we'll use the story of a gangland hit over a drug deal gone bad and an arson in an attempt to cover it up. I'll work up the fine points later. Meanwhile, we're all going to have to talk. This thing is getting way out of control."

"It's never been under control to begin with," Wyrdrune said.

"I'm going to have to do a lot of fast talking over the next couple of days," McGuire said, "and I'll have Case to back me up. We've got Christine Mathews in our corner, and both Blood and Renaud should be arriving soon. I've got a call in to Katayama, but I'm going to need you three to help me sell this to the higher ups."

"You still don't understand, do you?" Kira said. "There just isn't enough time for all that. The Dark Ones are still out there somewhere. You saw what they did here tonight. They could easily do the same thing all over the city.''

"She's right," said Wyrdrune. "They've got to be stopped, and we're the best chance you've got. We simply don't have time for investigative committees or grand juries or whatever. If that's what you want to do, you're on your own.''

"Now you listen here, Karpinski," McGuire began, but he was cut off.

"The name is Wyrdrune. Mel Karpinski was another lifetime. In many ways, he doesn't really exist anymore.''

"Look, I don't care who the hell you think you are or what—''

"Sir, we've got the rundown on those plates," one of the officers said, approaching McGuire. "The car is registered to Ryan Keith, in Oyster Bay. And it hasn't been reported stolen.''

"Ryan Keith, the actor?" said McGuire.

"I think so, sir. There are a number of expensive vehicles registered to that address.''

"You didn't call him, did you?" Wyrdrune said quickly.

"Uh . . . no, sir. Mr. Keith hasn't been contacted yet.''

"Make sure he isn't," Wyrdrune said.

"Wait a minute," said McGuire. "What do you think you're—''

"McGuire, listen to me," Wyrdrune said. "We may have gotten lucky. If the car hasn't been reported stolen, they may be using Keith's place as their headquarters. They'll realize they made a mistake leaving it behind. If we move fast, we just may—''

"*Hold* it," said McGuire. "Nobody's moving anywhere. Before anyone goes off half-cocked, we're going to have to coordinate with the police in that area first and make sure—''

"Screw that," said Wyrdrune. "What's Keith's address?''

"I said *hold* it!" McGuire repeated.

Wyrdrune gazed directly into the young officer's eyes. "What is Keith's address?" he asked in a firm and level tone.

The officer's eyes glazed over slightly and he gave it to him.

"Let's go," said Wyrdrune.

"You're not going anywhere," McGuire said, reaching for him, but the emerald runestone in Wyrdrune's forehead flashed and McGuire jerked his hand back, startled, as the beam of force lanced out toward Kira's upraised palm. It seemed to bounce off her sapphire runestone, change color, and strike the ruby in Angelo's chest. McGuire, Case, and the others shielded their eyes from the blinding glare as it increased, growing so bright it blotted out everything else around it. The triangle started to revolve. It spun around faster and faster, raising a strong wind and driving the others back as it extended out into a glowing pyramid and then formed a cone like the funnel cloud of a tornado, howling and crackling with thaumaturgic discharges. And then it sucked up into itself and, with a sharp, cracking sound, simply disappeared.

"Holy shit," McGuire said softly.

"Yeah. Argue with that," said Case.

"How long does it take to get to Oyster Bay from here?"

"If we go all out, an hour, maybe, if the traffic's light on the parkway."

"Damn it," said McGuire. "Can you use a spell to teleport us?"

Case looked at him uneasily. "I can, but it'll take a lot out of me. And it'll be risky. I've never been out there before. I could wind up dropping us into the bay, or worse."

"I'll take my chances," said McGuire. "Do it."

Case sighed. "All right. Give me about a minute to focus and get ready."

"Go ahead," McGuire said. Then, turning to the young officer, he said, "Get on the horn to the police up there, local and county, and tell them to get all their available units out to Ryan Keith's place right away."

"Uh . . . what should I tell them, sir?"

"Hell, tell them it's a B.O.T. operation. Chief Agent Case of the New York office and Deputy Commissioner McGuire of N.Y.P.D. require all available assistance for a major felony magic crime arrest. And tell 'em we expect heavy resistance and to load for bear. Got it?"

"Yes, sir."

"Well, what are you waiting for? *Move!*"

Beladon knew something had gone wrong when he saw Delana come back alone. And even if it wasn't for Calador's conspicuous absence, he still would have known from her appearance and the vibrance of power he sensed surging through her as she came into the living room.

"I see you have fed your hunger," he said, calmly facing her from across the room as she came closer. "Where is Calador?"

"Dead," she said.

Beladon nodded slightly. "Somehow, I am not surprised," he said. "Disappointed, yes, but not really surprised. Was it you who killed him?"

"No," she said, stopping a short distance away from him, her eyes burning. "It was one of the humans. One of Leone's men who took Calador by surprise and treachery. He is dead, as well. They are all dead. Calador is revenged."

"Calador was a fool," said Beladon simply. "He took his superiority too much for granted. Even an inferior opponent can triumph if one is careless. As you, too, have been careless. I wanted Leone and his people alive."

"Did you truly expect me to let them live after what they did?" she asked. "Should Calador's death have gone unpunished?"

"Calador got no less than he deserved," Beladon replied, sitting down in an armchair and crossing his legs casually. Delana remained standing.

"And a threat to your supremacy has been eliminated," she said.

Beladon shook his head slightly and sighed. "How little you understand me, Delana," he said. "I had thought that you would know me better by now. Calador's death diminishes us all. There are not so many of us left, you know. All those who died trying to escape the Eternal Circle of the pit, the ones the avatars had hunted down and killed . . . how many of us does that leave? Perhaps a dozen, more or less. A mere handful of survivors, all scattered, hiding in their sanctuaries, hoarding and gathering their power, fearing that the others may grow stronger first. When I think of what we could accomplish were we all united . . ." He sighed wearily. "I had thought you understood."

"I understand only that Calador was right," she said. "He may have underestimated the humans, for which he paid the price, but he had not underestimated you."

"And what about yourself?" asked Beladon, raising his eyebrows.

"I know what you desired," she said. "You wanted me for your consort, and Calador for your retainer. You wanted acolytes so that you could increase your own power while you kept us weak, so that we could not challenge you. Well, I am no longer weak, Beladon."

"No, I can see that," he replied. "You are most compelling in your newfound strength. Vibrant and exciting. It is what I had always wanted for you."

"And is that why you had denied me for so long?" she countered scornfully. "Was it merely to whet your appetite? Or mine?"

"Neither," he replied. "I had explained it all to you before. Must I explain it all again?"

"I know your explanations all too well," she said. "Calador was not the only one who wearied of them. The humans have evolved. They are stronger now, and smarter, and our feeding will only alert them to our presence in their midst. We must bide our time and make our plans and prepare to deal with the avatars while we seek out the others. . . . No, Beladon, you are wrong and Calador was right. I see that clearly now. The way to deal with the avatars is through strength, strength such as I feel coursing through me now. Calador's mistake was in believing that the humans would frighten easily, but they have forgotten us. Too much time has passed, and our names no longer make them tremble.

Tonight, I have given them but a small reminder, and it was only the beginning."

"Yes, now that you have tasted life force once again, and now that you have once more felt the power, you are hungry for more," said Beladon. "That has always been our only weakness, Delana, the price of necromancy. The more power we expend, the more the hunger grows."

"That is as it should be," she said.

"That is how we were defeated," he replied. "We cannot let the hunger drive us. We must master it, Delana. We must have discipline, else our own greed will destroy it. There is no stronger weapon that the avatars and, yes, even the humans can use against us."

"The humans!" she said with disgust. "They exist only to provide our sustenance and serve our needs. I made short work of them tonight. I brushed them away like flies and drank their essence. Once they have seen what we can do, once they have been reminded who we are, they shall all cower at our feet!"

"You underestimate them," Beladon said softly.

"And you have grown soft and weak."

"Is that what you truly believe?"

"I am not afraid to put it to the test," she said.

"So. It has come to this," he said with resignation.

"You still believe that you are stronger?" she said.

"Perhaps," Beladon replied. "And perhaps not. But whoever has the greater strength, our strength is greater still together. There is no need for us to put it to the test, Delana."

"If we do not, then we shall always wonder who is stronger," she said, "and sooner or later, one of us will be tempted to find out. I shall no longer subjugate my will to yours, Beladon, and I am not so foolish as to think that you would cease in your attempts to dominate me. Our aims are not the same, nor are our methods I can no longer accept yours, and you refuse to accept mine. I see no other way."

"What if I were to tell you I am content to let you go your way? It is a large world, Delana. Surely there is a corner of it you can stake out as your own."

"And wait until you have grown strong enough to come and seek me out again? I think not. Besides, a mere corner would not be enough. I want it all."

"That is your hunger speaking, not your better judgment," said Beladon. "You are still intoxicated from all the life force you have absorbed so greedily. This is not the time for us to settle this. Wait until—"

"I am done waiting! This matter shall be settled *now*!"

Beladon sighed. "Very well, if you insist."

The shotgun blast echoed through the house and Delana's chest exploded. Her eyes bulged as she was thrown forward to the floor. She fell on her side and slowly rolled onto her back as Beladon stood over her, hand outstretched and glowing. With blood bubbling forth between her lips, she tried to raise her head. Ryan Keith stood there stiffly, eyes vacant, holding the still smoking shotgun.

"I told you," Beladon said softly as he absorbed her life force and took all her newly gained strength for his own, "it is not wise to underestimate the humans."

Then he heard a loud report from outside, almost like a clap of thunder, and the sudden noise of howling wind. He looked up sharply.

"The car," he said. He looked down at Delana. "Foolish. Very foolish." He raised his hand and clenched it into a fist, then extended his index finger. The tip of it began to glow.

Moments later, the front door blew off its hinges and a whirling vortex sparkling with thaumaturgic discharges swirled into the house. For an instant it hovered in the large foyer, then moved into the living room. Spinning round and round, it formed into a glowing pyramid as it slowed down, and then the pyramid became a triangle of light that spun in midair, slower and slower, settling to the floor, until it winked out and they stood there, surrounding a wind-disheveled Ryan Keith, who stood in the center of the living room, holding an empty shotgun in his hands.

He stared at them wide-eyed, looking as if he were in shock. "I . . . I don't understand," he said. "What happened? Who are you people?" And then he saw the body on the blood-soaked carpet. He looked down at the shotgun in his hands and dropped it. "Oh, my God. I . . . I must have killed her." He gazed up at them helplessly and swallowed hard. "I . . . I don't even know who she is! I don't know what happened! I don't remember anything, I swear to God! *You've got to believe me!*"

"We believe you, Mr. Keith," said Angelo, coming forward, taking his arm and guiding him over to the sofa. "It will be all right, I promise. I'm sure help is on the way."

Kira and Wyrdrune stood looking down at Delana's lifeless body. "Well, that's two down," she said. "If they keep this up, they'll be doing our job for us."

"I wouldn't count on it," Wyrdrune said. He pointed at the opposite wall. There was a message scorched into it in large, flame-blackened letters. It said, "Another time, another place."

"Shit," Kira swore. "He's gone. We're too late again."

"Well, I guess you can't win them all," said Wyrdrune.

"I wouldn't exactly call this a loss," she said, looking down at the female necromancer's body. "That makes two less Dark Ones to worry about."

"Only in a manner of speaking," Wyrdrune said. "This one has been drained. He took all her power. And she had herself one hell of a feed tonight."

Kira glanced over at Keith, who was sitting on the couch, being comforted by Angelo. "I wonder why he let him live," she said.

"Who knows? Perhaps as a reward for taking this one down," said Wyrdrune, looking at Delana's body, "although he clearly doesn't remember doing it. He was obviously manipulated."

"A necromancer with compassion?" Kira said dubiously.

"No, I doubt that," Wyrdrune replied. "Maybe the only reason he left Keith alive was to show us that he wasn't greedy." He grimaced and shook his head. "We blew it. This one's going to be bad news."

"Are any of them *good* news?" Kira said wryly.

"Yeah," said Wyrdrune. He pointed at the floor. "This one. And the one back at Leone's."

"Amen to that."

"Well, at least we got Modred back," he said.

Kira glanced toward Angelo. "I'm not so sure about that. He seems like somebody else, altogether. Modred may be in there somewhere, but I just can't see him."

"He still hasn't got it all together," Wyrdrune said. "Give him some time. All things considered, he's doing very well. Especially for somebody who died."

There were two loud thumps above them, as if something fell onto the roof. They both looked up quickly, then through the high cathedral ceiling they heard a muffled shout.

"Jesus H. Christ!"

Kira smirked. "McGuire," she said.

"He's persistent as all hell, I'll give him that," said Wyrdrune, shaking his head.

"Case, get us the hell down from here!"

"Now what?" said Keith, staring up toward the ceiling with alarm. "What in God's name is going on here?" He brought his hands up to his head. "Now I'm hearing voices! I must be losing my mind!"

"Take it easy," Angelo said. "I heard them, too. There's someone on the roof." He looked up at the others. "Are they going to need help getting down?"

"Probably," said Wyrdrune. "Case had to teleport them both clear across the island. He's probably a little woozy."

"I'll go look for a ladder," Angelo said, getting up.

"No," said Wyrdrune. "Leave them up there for a while."

Angelo frowned. "What for?"

"Let McGuire stew a bit. It'll do him good."

"Can somebody please tell me what's happening?" asked Keith pathetically. "Am I going crazy?"

"No, Mr. Keith," said Kira. "You're not going crazy. You've just been through a terrible ordeal, but it'll be all right. There are a few things you're not going to remember, but you're probably better off that way."

"Did I . . . murder that young woman?" he asked fearfully.

"No, it was more like self-defense," said Wyrdrune.

"Self-defense?" Keith shook his head helplessly. "I must be in shock or something. I just can't remember anything."

"This young woman murdered a lot of people, Mr. Keith," said Wyrdrune. "You shot down a vicious serial killer and saved a lot of lives. Remember that."

"I did?"

There was the sound of sirens in the distance, rapidly approaching.

"The police are going to be here soon," Wyrdrune said to the distraught man. "When they get here, you just tell them the two people on the roof can explain everything."

"You're leaving?"

"Yes, we have to go. You'll be all right now, I promise."

Keith shook his head, as if he didn't really believe him. "Who *are* you people?"

"Well, let's just say we're fans. I've seen your movies."

"Oh," said Keith, looking disoriented. "Did you want an autograph?"

Wyrdrune smiled. "Some other time."

EPILOGUE

THEY ALL SAT together at a long table in the back room of Lovecraft's Cafe. It was well after closing time, but through a special arrangement with the management, they had rented the place to have a private meeting. The serving staff had all gone home, but refreshments had been set out for them and there was fresh coffee. It was the first time they had all ever been together. Seated at the table were Wyrdrune, Kira, Billy, Angelo, Makepeace, Gypsy, Gonzo, Jacqueline, and the recent arrivals: Chief Inspector Michael Blood of Scotland Yard, Inspector Armand Renaud of the Paris police, Agent Akiro Katayama of the I.T.C., Captain Rebecca Farrell of the Los Angeles Police Department, and Ben Slater, of the *L.A. Times*.

"I think it came off quite well, indeed," Blood said. "Much better than I had anticipated, frankly. They all seemed very much impressed."

"Well, I don't know if they were impressed, but I sure as hell was," Slater said, taking a swig from a bottle of imported beer. "It's the first time I've ever been in the same room with the director of the F.B.I., the attorney general, the director of the U.S. Bureau of Thaumaturgy, the head of the Washington office of the I.T.C., and the director of the National Security

Agency, not to mention assorted aides and V.I.P.s. And when I met the rest of you guys, I started wondering what the hell I was doing there.''

"I thought you injected a refreshing note of candor into the proceedings,'' Katayama said with a smile. "I especially enjoyed it when you called them all . . . please, what was it again?''

"A bunch of paper-pushing, thick-headed, senile, bureaucratic assholes,'' Rebecca Farrell said with a wry grimace. "Ben always did have a way with winning people over.''

"Yeah, well, they pissed me the hell off,'' Slater grumbled. "They just weren't listening.''

"I think you managed to get their attention,'' Blood said with a smile. "However, I thought the 'senile' part was pushing it a bit. The attorney general is scarcely over forty.''

"We've got her to thank for pulling it all together,'' Billy said. "We owe a debt of gratitude to Christine Mathews for calling up her old law school buddy and setting it all up.''

"Rather like the 'old girl network,' to coin a phrase,'' said Blood. "However, I think it was your testimony that really turned the trick. When you proved that you were Merlin reincarnated, as it were, the entire hearing took a different turn.''

"I imagine it did,'' said Wyrdrune. "Shame we had to miss it.''

"Yes, they were most anxious to meet the three of you,'' said Renaud. "However, when we explained the situation about Beladon still being at liberty, I think they understood.''

"Any luck in that area?'' Blood asked.

"Unfortunately, no,'' said Wyrdrune. "He seems to have disappeared. We've been combing the city; we've been out driving all over Long Island; we've been watching the papers and the TV news for stories of any murders that might indicate his presence . . . nothing.''

"He's either lying low or else he's left the area,'' said Kira. "We'll keep trying, though.''

"Yeah, well, it seems like we've made a complete mess of it this time,'' said Wyrdrune sourly. "We were just plain lucky that things fell apart for them. We didn't have a thing to do with it. We blew it.''

"Oh, I don't know,'' McGuire said as he approached them from the entrance to the bar. "Tommy Leone never got his hands on that Ambrosia, and he won't be getting his hands on anything else, ever again. We found some papers in his safe that'll help Christine put away some people we've been after for a long, long time; and thanks in some measure to me and my influence with the district attorney of this fine city, from now on, you're going to have the authorities working with you instead of against you. I think you had something to do with all of that. And you found your friend again. Am I too late to join the party?''

"How did you know where to find us?'' Kira asked.

"I'm a cop, remember? I had Chief Inspector Blood here tailed.''

"You're joking,'' Blood said with astonishment.

"Nope. As to how I got in here . . .'' He held up a key. "You'd be surprised what the threat of a health inspection can accomplish.''

"The chief inspector of New Scotland Yard tailed like a common criminal,'' Renaud said with a chuckle. "And you never even knew it.''

"I wouldn't laugh too hard if I were you, Renaud,'' McGuire said. "I had a tail on you, as well.''

The grin slipped from Renaud's face.

"You had *all* of us followed?'' Katayama said.

"No, just you three,'' said McGuire. "I visit L.A. on occasion, and I don't want to get arrested for jaywalking or running a stop sign.'' He grinned at Farrell. "As for Slater, I know better than to try tailing a veteran reporter. They know all the tricks in the book, including the dirty ones.''

"Yeah, we made up most of them,'' said Slater gruffly.

"Have a seat, McGuire,'' Wyrdrune said.

"I can't believe you didn't invite me to this shindig,'' said McGuire. "After all I've done for you, too.''

"Well, we couldn't have you consorting with known felons, Deputy Commissioner,'' said Kira. "Besides, we thought you might still be a little miffed about being left up on the roof."

"Yes, I was going to talk to you about that," said McGuire with a grimace. "We managed to keep what happened at the Keith house pretty much under wraps, but by now every cop in New York and Long Island knows I got stuck up on the roof of some damned actor's home. Nobody knows what really happened, but you wouldn't believe some of the stories going around." He glanced at Angelo. "Hello, John. How's the memory coming?"

"I've been working with Jacqueline and Sebastian," Angelo said, "and Gypsy has been a great help, too, but there are still large gaps."

"Well, hang in there," said McGuire. "I'm sure you'll recover. All it takes is time. You've got that now. Officially, you were wounded in the line of duty and had a near-death experience. The hospital adept will back me up on that one. As of yesterday, you're on disability retirement. And there's a commendation in it for you. You were a hell of a good cop. The department's going to miss you."

"A police department commendation," Angelo said. "Rather ironic, when you consider that a part of me was once a professional killer."

"Yeah, well . . . we won't talk about that," said McGuire, a bit uneasily.

"Speaking of recovering, how is Ryan Keith?" asked Wyrdrune.

"He'll be okay," McGuire replied. "That serial killer story you gave him was a good one."

"It was pretty much the truth," said Wyrdrune.

"I embellished on it some," McGuire said. "I tied it in with some of the killings you've been suspected of, the ones the other necromancers did, and told him and the other people in the house that they were heavily drugged. Being an actor, he even wound up filling in some details of his own. That guy's got some imagination. Believe it or not, he's even working up a screenplay about the whole thing as a vehicle for himself."

"You're kidding," Kira said.

"Scout's honor," said McGuire, holding up three fingers. "He's already got his agent working on the option."

"How's Case?" asked Wyrdrune. "I'm surprised he didn't come with you."

"He's not doing too well, I'm afraid," said McGuire somberly. "He feels a lot of guilt about what's happened. The fact that no one's pressing any charges only makes it worse, so he's punishing himself. I just spoke to him this afternoon. He's going to submit his resignation to the Bureau."

"It was hardly his fault," said Wyrdrune. "He had no choice. What was he supposed to do? If he refused to cooperate, they would only have possessed him and made him do what they wanted anyway."

"I guess he doesn't see it that way," said McGuire. "It's not easy, confronting your own fear. We all think we're tougher than we really are."

"Not me," said Slater, emptying his beer bottle. "I'm a confirmed coward." He raised his voice. "Hey, Broom, is there any more beer?"

Broom came in carrying a tray with several bottles on it. "No, there isn't any beer. This is a bar, you *bulvon*. What do you think they sell here, blintzes?"

"Thanks, sweetheart," said Slater, grabbing Broom as it set the tray down on the table. "Give us a kiss. Where the hell's your mouth, anyway?"

"*Feh*! Get your hands off me, you big ape!"

"You know, I think the two of you belong together," Wyrdrune said. "What do say, Ben? You want to provide a good home for a slightly used familiar?"

"Bite your tongue!" said Broom, pointing a rubbery finger at him. "Honestly, I don't know why I put up with all of this abuse. You cook, you clean, you scrub, you rub your bristles to the nub and this is the thanks you get! *Hmmmpf*!"

"That reminds me," said Gypsy as Broom retreated to the kitchen. "I need to send my mother a birthday card."

"Much as I dislike to bring up a rather unpleasant subject," said Gonzago, "has anyone considered the possibility of Beladon taking his revenge on Agent Case? He did betray him, after all.''

"But Beladon doesn't know that," said McGuire. "If he tries to contact him again, Case will let us know immediately. I think he's hoping that'll happen, so he'll have an opportunity to redeem himself, but I don't think there's really any chance of that. Beladon's long gone."

"I'm afraid you're right," said Wyrdrune. "He'll hole up somewhere, probably very far away, and work on his next move. And he'll undoubtedly try to find some of the others. He's smart. He doesn't let the hunger drive him. He'll come at us again, but only when he's ready, and only on his own terms.''

"Well, next time he might not find it so easy," said McGuire. "We know about them now. And next time, we'll be ready."

Case sat alone at his desk in his darkened apartment, illuminated only by a desk lamp. There was a bottle of whiskey on the desk beside him, and a glass. He had given up on the glass, and drank straight from the bottle. It was almost empty. His hair was disheveled and he hadn't shaved in several days. He hadn't bathed, either. He was beginning to notice his own stink. He thought that seemed appropriate. He jumped when the voice spoke from the darkness.

"What a pathetic sight. I've seen corpses that looked better.''

Case almost dropped his bottle. "*You!*" he said.

Beladon stepped forward into the light. "You seem surprised to see me. Did you think I would leave without saying good-bye to my faithful servant?''

Case hurled the bottle at him. It missed by a wide margin and shattered against the wall.

"Ah, the courage of the grape," said Beladon. "Or is it the malt? I do believe you're drunk."

Case got up from his chair, unsteadily, leaning on his desk. "Screw you, you bastard."

"You are a deplorable sight," the necromancer said. "I

fear that you will be of little use to me in this pitiful state.''

"I'm through being of use to you," Case slurred, staggering from behind the desk.

"Are you?"

"That's right," said Case. "I told 'em about you, you son of a bitch. I told 'em everything."

"Did you, indeed?" said Beladon, raising his eyebrows. "How very unfortunate for you."

"That's right, I told 'em," Case said, moving closer. "So what're you gonna *do* about it?"

"Ah, I think I begin to understand," said Beladon. "You are suffering from the emotion you humans call guilt. You are filled with remorse for what you have done and now you seek to provoke me, so that I will take your life and end your misery. Well, your life force is a paltry thing, not even worth the small amount of energy required to take it."

"You go to *hell*!" said Case, and swung at him. His blow connected and Beladon staggered back. He brought his hand up to his face with an astonished expression and it came away wet with blood.

"Why, Agent Case," he said in a tone of surprise. "I do believe you broke my nose."

"C'mon!" said Case, swaying drunkenly. "C'mon and *finish* it!"

"No," said Beladon, staring at him hard. "That would be giving you exactly what you want. I have a better fate in mind for you."

Case felt a sudden chill in his head as if icy tendrils were starting to wrap themselves around his mind.

"You will serve me all the rest of your days," said Beladon, "and in the most degrading ways imaginable. You shall have no will of your own, but you shall remain aware, with perfect clarity, of every single loathsome thing you do."

"*No!*" Case trembled with the effort to shake off the invasion of his mind, but the icy presence insinuating itself into possession of him was relentless. He felt himself starting to slip away.

With his last ounce of willpower, he focused his energies on the whiskey glass still on his desk. It jiggled slightly, then slid across the desk and leapt into his outstretched hand. He grabbed it and closed his fist around it, hard. As it shattered, cutting him, he squeezed its jagged edges and the pain momentarily snapped him out of it. With a hoarse scream of triumph, he bolted for the window and hurled himself through it, smashing through the glass. For an instant Beladon was stunned into immobility, then he rushed to the broken window.

It was thirty stories down, and as Case fell, the necromancer heard him laughing.

By the year 2000, 2 out of 3 Americans could be illiterate.

It's true.

Today, 75 million adults… about one American in three, can't read adequately. And by the year 2000, U.S. News & World Report envisions an America with a literacy rate of only 30%.

Before that America comes to be, you can stop it… by joining the fight against illiteracy today.

Call the Coalition for Literacy at toll-free **1-800-228-8813** and volunteer.

Volunteer Against Illiteracy. The only degree you need is a degree of caring.

Ad Council Coalition for Literacy

Warner Books is proud to be an active supporter of the Coalition for Literacy.